ZACK

St. Martin's Paperbacks Titles by
Cheyenne McCray

Romantic Suspense

Moving Target
Chosen Prey

Urban Paranormal Romance

Dark Magic
Shadow Magic
Wicked Magic
Seduced by Magic
Forbidden Magic

Anthology

No Rest for the Witches

ZACK

Armed and Dangerous

Cheyenne McCray

ST. MARTIN'S GRIFFIN

NEW YORK

ZACK. Copyright © 2008 by Cheyenne McCray, LLC. All rights reserved. Printed in the United States of America. For information, address St. Martin's Press, 175 Fifth Avenue, New York, N.Y. 10010.

www.stmartins.com

Library of Congress Cataloging-in-Publication Data

McCray, Cheyenne.
   Zack: armed and dangerous / Cheyenne McCray. — 1st ed.
      p. cm.
   ISBN-13: 978-0-312-38671-9
   ISBN-10: 0-312-38671-0
   1. Women ranchers—Fiction.   2. Government investigators—Fiction.
3. Arizona—Fiction.   I. Title.
   PS3613.C38634 Z25 2008
   813'.6—dc22   2008025087

10   9   8   7   6   5   4   3   2

To everyone at St. Martin's Press.
Thank you for believing in me.

Acknowledgments

Much appreciation goes to the folks in Sulfur Springs Valley in Cochise County, where I grew up, way down in southeastern Arizona.

To the ICE (Immigration and Customs Enforcement) Office of Public Affairs for the extremely helpful information they provided, some of which is included in the Author's Note.

To Allan Sperling, retired ICE special agent. Thank you for all of your help relating to some of your personal experience, and for giving me a clue.

To Anna Windsor, who holds my hand when I need it, and Tee O'Fallon, who kicks my ass to get things right. To Cassie Ryan, for being so supportive and making me laugh.

To Tracey West, my lifesaver. Thank you more than I can say for helping me keep a grip on my sanity.

To my agent, Nancy Yost, who worked to make things happen in the best way possible.

To my editor, Monique Patterson, from psycho-chick.

As always, I used a great deal of creative license.

Any mistakes or errors are mine and mine alone.

Author's Note

At this time, according to the Immigration and Customs Enforcement Office of Public Affairs, southern Arizona is the number one corridor for the smuggling of persons, and probably close to that for narcotics, especially marijuana.

Within Arizona, the west desert—between Nogales and Yuma—would be the number one corridor, with Cochise County the next highest area. In 2006, more than seven hundred thousand pounds of marijuana were seized along the Arizona border.

ICE will investigate any crime with a nexus to the border, to include the virtual border, as the day of more and more computer-based crimes is upon us. ICE has some of the broadest investigative jurisdiction and authority of any law enforcement agency.

ICE investigations include traditional customs fraud (such as the over- or undervaluation of goods/merchandise), child pornography, cross-border money laundering, and more.

Any violation of the Immigration and Nationality Act (INA) falls within ICE jurisdiction. This extends beyond human smuggling/trafficking to include persons who overstay visas, gangs, and any other criminal activity where there is an international nexus.

According to ICE, the list is very extensive. The list would include cattle rustling, if there is a nexus to the border.

To My Readers

Zack: Armed and Dangerous takes place in Sulfur Springs Valley in Cochise County, where I grew up. My parents' ranch is twenty-five miles from the Mexican border.

Zack has its foundations in a novel I wrote several years ago for a small e-publisher. If you read that short novel, you will find this endeavor far different. Longer and richer with more action, adventure, and mystery.

Along the lines of change, *much* has changed within the government since I originally wrote that novel referred to earlier. Under the Department of Homeland Security, agencies and departments have been reorganized and restructured. I hope I have accurately reflected some of those changes in this novel.

May you enjoy Zack Hunter and Sky MacKenna. And as I've been told many times:

You'll never look at cheesecake the same way again.

ZACK

Chapter 1

While Skylar MacKenna inhaled the familiar smells of dust, livestock, and testosterone, she couldn't help but enjoy watching the men work. The flex of muscle, lean bodies in tight Wrangler jeans, leather chaps, tanned forearms . . . it was enough to leave any woman panting.

Skylar shifted in her saddle as she watched her ranch hands count the cattle they'd rounded up over the weekend. Empress, Skylar's Quarter Horse, pawed at the ground beneath them as the sorrel mare tossed her head and whickered.

The sight of the hard, muscled bodies should have moved Skylar, but . . . no man had since *him*.

She didn't want to think about him. But sometimes memories of Zack Hunter came to her hard, fast, and unbidden.

The busy hum of deep male voices and bawling cattle filled the otherwise still air. Saddle leather creaked as Skylar leaned down and rubbed the side of Empress's neck.

Skylar frowned and straightened in her saddle. Damnit, why couldn't she let those memories go? It was such ancient history.

As she pushed up the brim of her straw Resistol western hat, Skylar's gaze followed Luke Rider, her new foreman, as he rode his dun, the Quarter Horse's powerful haunches bunching as she flowed smoothly between Luke's thighs. Now there was one fine-looking male—a bad boy with luscious chestnut brown hair, wicked blue eyes, and a body that was made for sweaty sheets and long nights.

In the past month since Skylar had hired him, Luke had definitely given her the impression that he was more than interested in breaking her no-dating-employees rule. And considering how gorgeous he was, even she called herself a fool for not taking him up on his unspoken invitation. But she just wasn't interested. Besides, why complicate a perfectly good business relationship?

And then there was Wade Larson, who owned Coyote Pass Ranch, the spread neighboring hers. For years the man had made it clear he wanted her. She'd dated him a few times recently, and Wade was a handsome man, but she never felt that sizzle with him like she'd had with Zack. So despite Wade's continued persistence, she had broken it off and intended to keep it that way.

Damnit. She was over that idiot, Zack Hunter. Ten years was too long to allow that man to come into her mind and trample all over her heart and soul.

Sweat trickled between her breasts and she unfastened another snap on her western shirt, hoping a light wind would kick up and cool her skin. As she shifted again, the small Smith & Wesson in the holster on her waistband felt comforting. She was a crack shot—her father had taught her to shoot from the time she could hold a firearm.

Arizona was a "right to carry" state and for years she'd had a concealed-weapon permit. She kept the S&W on her most of the time in case she ran across a rattlesnake—but also because it made her feel safer as a woman who lived alone in a valley on the Mexican border. The Flying M Ranch rested at the foot of the Chiricahua Mountains that were like a railroad for drug and illegal immigrant smuggling from Mexico into the United States.

September sunshine heated her face, the sky an achingly clear blue. Not even a breeze stirred the mesquite bushes or tumbleweeds on her ranch.

September. A strange sensation came over her as her thoughts turned unwillingly to another September—almost exactly ten years ago, when she'd met the dark and dangerous Zack Hunter.

Skylar closed her eyes. Apparently there was no stopping it.

Her hand automatically moved to her throat and she finally allowed herself to remember. Memories came to her, sharp and vivid. The sound of his deep voice calling her Sky, rather than Skylar like everyone else did. His sinful grin, his muscled chest and athletic build. And the feel of him sliding inside her—

"Skylar?"

She snapped her eyes open, a rush of heat flushing up her face to the brim of her hat as she looked into Luke's intense blue gaze. Her foreman was sitting astride his dun, and his face was coated with dirt and sweat. It just made him look even sexier.

With his forefinger he pushed up the brim of his Stetson, his handsome face creased into a frown. "You all right, boss?"

Skylar pulled her shirt away from her chest, trying to cool off, and pretended not to notice how his gaze drifted to her cleavage. "Where do we stand with the count?"

Luke's jaw tightened and his features hardened. "We're down over fifty head."

"Fifty?" Skylar clutched Empress's reins, unable to believe

what Luke had just said. "How the hell did they steal so many without us being on to them?"

Luke's gaze had a predatory gleam before he tugged his mare's reins and turned back toward the corral. "I don't know," he said over his shoulder, "but I aim to find out."

Skylar looked off toward the mountain range two miles away at the foot of her property. What the hell was going on? It was like the mountain was opening up and swallowing her cattle whole.

With a groan of frustration, Skylar guided Empress across the rangeland to the barn. For a moment Skylar considered going on one of her usual long rides to clear her head, but it was already getting late in the afternoon.

The livelihood of her ranch depended on her livestock. She raised the best Angus in the valley and she was working to develop a profitable breeding program. Satan, her prized yearling who had a pedigree a mile long, was her hope for building a championship breeding program that would put the ranch far into the green.

If her herd continued to diminish, her ranch would gradually be destroyed before she had a chance to make it as profitable as she was working toward. She wouldn't have the cash to pay for more championship breeding stock. Eventually she wouldn't have enough income to pay her ranch hands.

No way was she going to let that happen. One way or another she would see to it the bastards were stopped—the bastards who were stealing her ranch's future.

It was a road he hadn't traveled for almost ten years, Zack Hunter realized as his black government-issued Ford Explorer hit a pothole, jarring his teeth along with his memories.

Sunshine glinted off the windshield, endless acres of grass and barbwire fence scrolling by as he guided the SUV down the dirt road to the MacKenna Ranch. One of the largest ranches in the county, the Flying M was over a half-hour drive from Douglas, a dingy town along the Mexico border in southeastern Arizona.

September. It had been September when he'd first met Skylar MacKenna.

Zack's SUV shimmied along the dirt road, but he barely noticed as his thoughts turned to Sky—her smile that had held all the innocence of youth and all the promise of a woman.

He had loved looking into her seductive eyes that were an unusual color of green, the same shade as her August birthstone. Her copper hair had felt so soft and silky every time he slipped his fingers through it—he loved when she left her hair down.

How often had he circled the tantalizing mole above her left breast with his tongue? And God, those legs. He could almost feel her long legs clamped around his hips and hear her sensual cries as he buried himself inside her.

Damn. He'd grown hard just thinking about her.

Zack's jaw tensed as he thought about the girl—the woman— he'd walked away from all those years ago, six months after they'd met. She'd been nineteen, starting her first year of college, and he'd been twenty-three, a deputy with the county sheriff's department.

Sky had been the only woman to see past his hard exterior to his very soul.

He shifted his grip on the steering wheel, the scenery a blur as it passed by. How he'd wanted to cherish her, protect her from what evil there was in the world.

His thoughts crowded him as he remembered Sky's teary face

the night he'd been arrested. Her promises when she'd come to visit him that everything would be all right.

But her eyes had been filled with horror and he'd been certain that it was because of what he'd done.

Even though charges had never been pressed and he'd been able to return to his job with the county sheriff's office, Zack had thought he wasn't good enough for her.

Sky had been so young, so vibrant. But she was also a straight arrow, no toe over the line, not under any circumstances. A man who skirted the law, no matter what his reasons, well, that wouldn't work for Sky.

Still, she'd acted like he'd nearly crushed her heart, leaving her like he did.

At the time he thought he'd done the right thing when he'd told her good-bye. That she'd been too young.

And his demons too dark to slay.

Zack squinted in the bright sunlight as he glanced through his windshield up at the cloudless blue expanse before returning his gaze to the dusty road. The case that had him heading to the ranch was almost an excuse to see Sky—almost.

Ever since the day he'd left her, he'd never been able to get her out of his mind, and he wasn't sure he ever could.

He *knew* he never would.

As he'd faced each and every one of his demons over the last ten years, he'd come to the realization that he wasn't the same person he'd been then. The same young man who'd been so immersed in rage that he'd thought he'd never find his way out.

Except with Sky. She had made him feel different. Happy for the first time in his life, and not like the angry person he'd been deep down inside.

But one violent night had changed everything.

Zack ground his teeth.

One night. One night with a fucking bastard whom Zack had almost killed.

Sky's image filled his mind. What if she wasn't at the ranch? What if she was married now, with a couple of rugrats and living off in a city in some other state?

The mere thought of Sky with another man had Zack gripping the steering wheel so tight he was bound to snap it.

When he had made the decision to transfer to Douglas to be closer to his ailing mother, he had hoped Sky would still be here. That they could pick up where they'd left off.

Hell, more than hoped.

He didn't know if Sky was still around, but he intended to find out.

Zack slowed the SUV as he crossed over a cattle guard that rattled and thrummed under the wheels of the Explorer. Herds of sleek Black Angus lined each side of the road, lifting their heads to watch him pass by and then returning to graze.

Apparently the rains had been good this summer, as the grass was still green in patches and plentiful. He noted the well-kept barbwire fences, stock tanks, and windmill. Ray MacKenna always did keep his place in fine shape, and he certainly had the money to do it.

Zack didn't expect his gut to clench the way it did when he drove up to the sprawling ranch house. A vivid memory of Sky came to him. Of her running from the front porch to greet him, her smile brilliant, then throwing her arms around his neck and treating him to her soft lips. Her husky voice telling him she missed him, and her firm body pressed tight to his.

With a groan, he brought the SUV to a halt in front of the MacKenna Ranch house, dust swirling around his vehicle in a beige cloud. He took in the changes of the last ten years. The oak trees and weeping willows were taller and the porch that ran the length of the house was practically overflowing with houseplants—a woman's touch.

His heart rate kicked up a beat. Could Sky still be here?

Or had Ray gone and remarried? After Nina MacKenna's death, everyone was sure Ray would never tie the knot again.

Zack's gaze passed beyond the house, extensive barn, corrals, and ranch buildings to the tawny Chiricahua Mountains rising behind. The old tire swing still hung from the lower branch of the oak in front of the barn. He remembered pushing Sky in that tire, spinning it around, and claiming a kiss when he caught her to him.

Zack climbed out of the Ford Explorer, crammed his black Stetson on his head, and slammed the door a little too hard. Shoving the memories to the back of his mind, he headed up the steps, then through the maze of plants on the porch. Wind chimes hanging from the porch's beams made a haunting sound as the slightest hint of a breeze stirred. Almost ghostly.

But the only ghosts around were the memories of Sky. He knocked. No answer. Ray must be off working on horseback or in his truck.

Was Sky around?

Zack was turning from the door when he heard a shriek.

Sky.

Hair prickled at the base of his neck.

He automatically drew his 9mm P226 SIG Sauer from the holster on his hip. The scream had come from the barn. Zack made sure everything was clear and hurried to the barn, his boots making no sound as he crossed the hard-packed earth.

Everything was quiet. Too quiet.

Pausing beside the open barn door, he listened, his heart beating a rapid rhythm.

"You sonofa—," a woman said, and then came a thump and another cry.

He rounded the doorway in a crouch, his weapon raised. Sky MacKenna was sprawled on the barn floor with her back against a hay bale, her blouse gaping open. She was glaring into a horse stall.

Zack clenched his jaw. He'd kill the man who'd dared to shove her down like that.

"Come out with your hands up," Zack said in a deadly tone, his eyes focused on the stall. He remained crouched and prepared for the slightest movement. "Don't make me wait."

He heard a click and glanced at Sky to see she had a handgun trained on him. The moment she saw his face she slowly lowered the small Smith & Wesson, a stunned expression on her features.

Zack kept his SIG in his hands, the barrel still in position as he glanced from her to the stall.

"Go ahead. Arrest the bastard." Sky waved toward the stall with her free hand while she stuffed the handgun into the holster at her side. "Cuff him while you're at it. Once you've frisked the sonofabitch, that is. I'll get a kick out of seeing you try."

Zack eased closer to the open stall and peered over the wooden side rail to find a good-sized black bull yearling straining against a rope tie. The corner of Zack's mouth twitched.

"I'm gonna have to take you in, son," he said with mock seriousness to the fire-eyed yearling. "For disturbing the peace and knocking around a beautiful woman."

The moment the last two words were out of Zack's mouth, it seemed like the entire ranch went silent. He turned to look at Sky and he could see reality sinking in, her lips forming a frown as she narrowed her eyes.

Now, she knew. After all these years and that awful good-bye, Zack had returned to Douglas.

Chapter 2

Hurt, pride, and anger flashed across Sky's face, and then worse—
indifference.

Zack holstered his gun, then extended his hand in an offer to
help Sky to her feet. She moved her fingers to her neck, like she
couldn't decide if she should ignore his hand or accept it.

He'd forgotten that nervous habit of hers. How she'd rub the
base of her throat when she was feeling self-conscious or uneasy,
leaving the fair skin red. And how he'd loved to kiss that soft
skin whenever she did that.

As if she could hear his thoughts, she moved her fingers away
from her throat. With a little tilt of her chin, she reached up and
clasped his hand.

That touch, that simple touch, brought back every bit of
yearning he'd ever had for her, and even when she was standing,
he couldn't let go. She was tall, only four inches shorter than his
six feet two. The perfect height for kissing. He had always loved
that she matched him. As if she had been made just for him.

And God, she still smelled the same—of the wind after a

summer storm, and orange blossoms, the scent that always drove him wild. Memories flowed through him—of how she had explored every part of his body with her inquisitive fingers, her sexy mouth, her sweet tongue.

"Sky." Zack's voice was husky with longing.

"It's Skylar." She jerked her hand from his and dusted off the seat of her jeans with her palms, never taking her eyes from his.

Zack's gaze dropped to the rise and fall of her chest, and his throat went dry. Sky's open pale blue western shirt exposed the swell of her breasts and taut nipples beneath a peach satin bra. Satin that he knew could be no softer than the satin of her breasts. Breasts that he wanted to caress. Nipples he wanted to taste, right there in the barn.

"You might want to fix that." He allowed his fingers to touch the edges of the open vee of her shirt before letting his arm drop to his side again.

Pink touched Sky's cheeks as she glanced down and then brought her hand to her gaping shirt. He noticed her fingers trembled as she fumbled with each snap.

He took the opportunity to study her long legs in snug jeans, her copper hair escaping the single braid that fell across her shoulder as she bent over. When she finished, she lifted her head and her green eyes met his.

"It's been a long time," Zack said in a low rumble.

Frowning, Sky took a step forward, and to his surprise she reached out and touched the scar that creased his left cheek. Instead of flinching from the memory of how he got that mark, he felt like a tamed beast.

"It never went away," she said softly.

Zack stood mesmerized by her beauty. Her touch that was almost as innocent as she had been when his face had been slashed.

Her finger trailed the scar that went from his ear almost to his mouth. She paused, her gaze riveted on his lips, and he damn near stopped breathing.

Sky jerked her hand away like she'd come to her senses and she took a step back, her cheeks going pink again. "So. What are you doing here?"

I came back for you.

Likely Sky wouldn't be too keen on him telling her he'd come back for her ten years after he left. Instead, he said, "Is your dad around?"

A glimmer of laughter came back into her eyes. "If he was, he'd likely run you off with his old Remington."

"I was afraid of that." Zack's mouth turned up in a slight grin, and then his tone went serious. "I've missed you."

She cocked her head and studied him for a moment. "Did you have anything in particular to say to my dad, or is it something you can tell me?"

Zack fished his wallet out of the back pocket of his Wranglers, drew out his business card, and handed it to her.

Sky took it from him, her fingertips lightly brushing his, and glanced at the card with the ICE logo. "So, you're now a federal agent with Immigration and Customs Enforcement."

"I transferred to Douglas last week," he said as he slid his wallet into his back pocket. "I'm out introducing myself to ranchers in the area. The mountains behind your ranch are being used to smuggle narcotics from Mexico."

"What's new? That's been going on for years." Sky gave a little shrug. "Enough drugs and illegals come through that range to keep every law enforcement officer in the Southwest busy."

Zack frowned. True, it was common knowledge, but it still bothered him that Sky seemed so unconcerned that danger passed her back door daily. "If you see anything suspicious, give me a call."

Now if that wasn't lame *and* corny, he didn't know what the hell was.

Sky fixed a smile on her face as she shoved the card into the front pocket of her jeans. "Great, Special Agent Hunter."

He shook his head. "It's Zack to you, Sky."

"Skylar, not Sky." She folded her arms beneath her breasts. "So that's why you came back? To rid the Southwest of drug smugglers and illegal aliens."

"Something like that." He hooked his thumbs in his belt loops.

A horse whickered and the red roan poked his head over a stall door in the half of the huge barn that housed her Quarter Horses. Sky moved toward the roan. "How's my boy?" she murmured as she rubbed the stallion's nose.

She stood in a shaft of sunlight and Zack's breath caught in his throat. Dust motes swirled in the air around Sky, and her hair shone like burnished copper.

"How's your brother doing?" she asked, her attention on the horse.

Zack swallowed, wishing Sky was stroking him instead of the damn horse. "Cabe's a detective with the Bisbee Police Department. What's your sister up to?"

"Trinity got a wild hair after she graduated from college and she's been in Europe ever since." Sky rubbed the horse behind his ears. "Sometime before Christmas she'll be coming home. First visit in four years."

Zack gave a low whistle. "That's a long time to be gone from home."

"You should know, Zack." Sky patted the horse's neck and turned back to him. "So you went to the Federal Law Enforcement Training Center like you wanted."

"Yeah." Zack tensed as he saw a flicker of pain in her eyes. "After I graduated from FLETC I went into Customs, long before it was rolled into Immigration and Customs Enforcement." He moved closer, wanting to be near her. "How about you? What've you been up to all this time?"

Sky flicked a piece of straw off the top of the stall. "Other than trying to figure out who swiped fifty head of cattle, not a whole hell of a lot."

"Rustlers." Zack shook his head. "I know about the thefts, but didn't know you were hit."

"Yeah." An expression of frustration and anger glinted in her eyes. "It started week before last." She looked like she was gritting her teeth. "Bastards."

A frown creased her features again as she added, "How did you hear about it?"

"Work." Zack jerked his head in the direction of the Mexican border. "Been some concern the situation might involve thieves coming across the line."

"Isn't that a little far-fetched?" Sky gestured toward the bull in the stall. "Can't imagine herds being shuttled into Mexico without anyone noticing."

"Just the same, ICE is now involved," Zack said. "How'd it start?"

"First we noticed our herd was down a few head." Sky made a sound of irritation. "Then a dozen or so heifers just up and disappeared. Last night at least freaking fifty head were taken. Looks like the bastards are getting cockier."

His mouth tightened. "Or more stupid."

"Even though we've got cattle insurance," Sky said, "this sucks big-time. There's no way to replace the quality of the herd I've cultivated over the past several years."

With a sigh that made her frustration clear, she leaned back and braced her arms on the stall behind her. The motion caused her breasts to jut out and her blouse to gape, showing that satin bra and her generous cleavage.

Zack swallowed. "When'll your dad be back?"

"He was here a week ago, so he's not likely to visit for at least a couple of months. We expect him and his new wife for Thanksgiving or Christmas, not sure which."

We. Shock rippled through Zack as it occurred to him that Sky truly could be married, living at the ranch with her husband. No ring on her finger, but that didn't mean anything. She could keep it off while she was working. Zack had thought he was prepared for the possibility, but right now he couldn't imagine any man being with her. The thought made him want to kill the bastard, whoever he was.

Zack had been her first lover, and he should have been her only lover.

No, goddamnit. He'd given up that right the moment he walked away.

His scar ached from the memories that still haunted him and he rubbed what had been a deep knife cut. "Ray retired?"

"Couple of years ago." Sky nodded as she spoke, crossing her arms over her chest again, as if protecting herself from Zack.

It almost killed him to even think she could be married. "So, you and your, ah, husband run the ranch?"

She lifted one slim brow and one corner of her mouth rose. "I run it myself."

Even as heat burned in Zack's gut he had to ask. "What does your husband do?"

"Not a darn thing," she said, her expression still amused.

Fuck. Goddamn. Shit. She is *married.* And apparently to a lazy sonofabitch.

Zack would kill the bastard. Sky deserved better than that. "So where is he?"

She cocked her head to the side. "Nowhere."

Zack narrowed his gaze. "What—"

Her laughter cut across his words. "I'm not married."

Relief surged through him, hot and satisfying. "You never married?" His tone dropped.

The fiery glint came back in her eyes, rivaling the devil of a yearling a few stalls down. "Well, I wasn't pining after you, if that's what you're asking."

His muscles tensed like tightly strung barbed wire as he reminded himself she'd said "we." Hell, she could have a boyfriend. A fiancé.

Whoever he was, he was a dead man.

This time Zack's voice came out in a growl. "Who'd you mean by 'we'?"

She shrugged. "Me and my Border Collie, Blue."

Zack didn't know whether that meant she was a free woman

or not, but he didn't care. He was back and in these few moments with Sky he'd made up his mind. He intended to make her his. Again.

When Sky spoke next, her voice was low. "What about you? Did you ever marry?"

"Who'd marry this ugly mug?"

She cut him a sharp glance. "If you're fishing for a compliment, you've come to the wrong woman."

"Then I'll give you one." Zack moved a step closer. "Sweetheart, how'd you grow to be more gorgeous than you were a decade ago?" He barely held himself back from touching her. "You were the most beautiful thing I'd ever seen that first time I laid eyes on you at the rodeo, when I watched you win the barrel racing competition." He sucked in his breath at the memory. "And now look at you."

Sky closed her eyes. "I'd forgotten how you always knew the most charming words."

Before Zack realized what he was saying, he started to ask, "Sky—" He stopped himself from telling her what it was he really wanted. "You think we can be friends again?"

Christ. Could he be any more lame?

"Friends?" She opened her eyes and moved her fingers to her throat. After a moment's hesitation, she gave him a shrug and a little smile. "Why not? We're almost ten years older and we've both grown up. A lot."

Her eyes roamed over him as she spoke the last words, and he wanted her more than ever before. And that was saying something.

When her gaze met his again, he knew she'd noticed his desire. "Yes," she said, her voice low and husky. "We're both all grown-up."

In the next instant, she dodged around him and headed to the stall with the yearling that looked like he must be the spawn of the Devil. "You little imp," she said in a low croon as she laid her hand on the upper railing of the stall. "What am I going to do with you?"

The bull glared, his head lowered and looking as if he'd like to take her out, and Sky smiled at him. "If you don't settle down, you're going to end up at the slaughterhouse rather than becoming lord of the manor with all the pretty ladies." She shook her head. "I sunk way too much money into you, buddy, for you to turn into T-bones and hamburger."

"What's his name?" Zack said.

"Satan." Sky glanced over her shoulder at Zack. "I thought about naming him Zack, but that's what I named the old jackass out back." She said it with a straight face, but he saw the wicked spark in her eyes.

He grinned. He'd forgotten her teasing sense of humor and her ability to make him laugh. She turned to the bull, and Zack walked up behind her so that just inches separated them. He drank in the scent of her that mingled with the smells of horse, hay, sweet oats, and barn dust.

"Sky." He noticed the slight shiver that ran through her at the sound of his voice.

"I keep telling you, it's Skylar." She spun around and her eyes widened when she saw how close he was. She tried to step away, but her back was against the side of the stall.

"You've always been Sky to me," he said softly.

She raised her chin, and he noticed a streak of dirt across her cheek. "It's Skylar to you now, just like everyone else."

Almost without thought, Zack reached up to wipe the smudge

away, needing to feel the softness of her skin beneath his fingertips. Her lips parted and her eyes widened as he gently smoothed
the dirt from her cheek. Slowly he trailed his thumb down her
soft skin to her full lips. Needing to touch her. Needing to wipe
away the memories of their good-bye.

He felt lost in the sensation of being near Sky again, her presence seeping into his blood like wildfire. "It's been much too
long."

Sky's lips trembled beneath his thumb. "Zack—"

He didn't give her a chance to say anything or to refuse what
he wanted. Needed.

He caught her face in his palms, slipping his fingers into her
hair, and brought his mouth down on hers.

She gasped and he took advantage of her parted lips and
slipped his tongue into her mouth. He growled as he took
from her and she made a slight sound of refusal. She braced her
palms on his chest and tried to push him away, but he only
kissed her harder, putting every bit of ten years of loss into
that kiss.

In only moments she made soft little moans and gripped his
shirt in her fists as she pressed her body to his. She kissed him
back and she and Zack both demanded and took what they
wanted, but gave at the same time.

She felt so good in his arms. Soft, sweet, and so perfect that
he wanted to keep her against him forever. He wanted to be inside her, feeling her take him deep as they got lost in each other.

Zack released a low, hungry groan as he rubbed his aching
erection against her belly.

Sky jerked away. Out of his arms.

Her eyes were wide and a little wild as she brought her fingers to her mouth. She shoved past him and headed out the barn door, almost at a run.

He followed, catching up to her in a few strides. She stopped by the driver's side door of his black SUV. She had her back to him, her hands now clenched into fists to either side of her.

Zack suddenly felt like the world's biggest ass. "Sky—"

"Time to hit the road, Zack." She slowly turned around as the breeze blew a strand of copper hair across her face and she pushed it behind one ear. She had composed her expression, but her lips were red and swollen from his kiss and her eyes gave her away—he'd rattled her. More than rattled her.

"Go," she said.

He couldn't make himself leave, but he forced himself to stand where he was and not kiss her again.

Damnit, but he needed to be near her a little longer. There was so much he wanted to ask her now that he'd seen her again. So much he wanted to know about her.

So much time to make up for before he claimed her for good.

Before he could get out another word, the ring of horse hooves against stone caught Zack's attention. He turned to see a man on a Quarter Horse approaching them.

"Luke." The sound of relief was obvious in Sky's voice as the man dismounted.

In seconds, Zack sized up the man Sky called Luke. From years of law enforcement training, Zack instantly cataloged the man's height, hair and eye color, posture, mannerisms, and the hard, intense look in his gaze.

Zack's body went rigid. Did this man have some kind of claim on Sky? If he did, Zack planned on clearing the ground with him. Not that the man looked like he'd be easy to take down. But the way Zack was feeling right now, he could use a good fight.

"Everything all right, Skylar?" the man asked, his eyes fixed on Zack.

"Of course." Sky's smile seemed forced. "Luke, this is Zack Hunter, an old," she moved her gaze to Zack, "*friend* of mine. He's with Immigration and Customs Enforcement now." She gestured to the man. "Zack, this is Luke Rider, my foreman."

As Sky mentioned ICE, Zack could swear he saw something flicker in Rider's eyes. Maybe Zack imagined it. Maybe not.

Rider held out his hand and Zack shook it. The man had a strong grip. A little too strong, like he was warning Zack. They gave each other one-word greetings. "Rider," Zack said with a nod, and the man returned it with a nod of his own as he came back with, "Hunter."

"Well." Sky glanced toward the house when they'd released hands. "I've got to check on Blue," she said before she returned her gaze to Zack.

Zack glanced in the direction of the house, then back to Sky. "What's wrong with him?"

With a confused frown, Sky shook her head. "Last night he got sick eating raw meat, but I'm not sure where he got it."

"Vet thinks it could have been tainted beef that Blue got into," Rider said as his mare stomped one hoof, "but I'm not so sure about that."

Narrowing his eyes, Zack said, "You think it was intentional?"

"We think it might have been the rustlers trying to get Skylar's dog out of the way." Luke's gaze was still assessing. "Find it a bit strange, though, that they didn't give enough to kill him."

"Bastards." Sky had a pained expression. "I did lose a lot of cattle last night, but from our eastern range. Why would they need to poison Blue?"

"Hell if I know," Rider said, "but we're damned sure going to find out." He held on to his mare's halter. "What's ICE's involvement?"

"We received intel that beef has been crossing into Mexico," Zack said. "That makes it an international customs matter."

Rider frowned for a moment. "Got any theories?"

"Working on it." Zack turned his attention to Sky and took a step closer to her. So did Rider, as if he was protecting her. Zack barely bit back a snarl. Instead he ignored Rider and said to Sky, "You live alone?"

She nodded. "Have been for the past few years, since Trinity's been in Europe."

"I don't like any of this a damn bit." Zack focused on Sky. "You need to watch out for yourself."

Rider gripped his mare's bridle as the horse nudged his arm with her nose. "Been telling Skylar the same thing."

"I've been doing just fine. Me and Smith." She looked from Rider to Zack as she reached up to pat the S&W in its holster on one side of her jeans. "I'd better see how Blue's doing."

"You be careful." Zack tipped the brim of his Stetson, then grabbed the door handle of his SUV. "Later, Sky."

"Skylar." She smiled too brightly. "See you around, Special Agent Hunter." And with that, she strode toward the house without looking back once.

As she jogged up the steps and crossed the porch, Zack watched her fluid movements. He had a side view, and couldn't help enjoying it. The way her breasts bounced and her tight backside swayed. She opened the front door and then closed it behind her.

When she disappeared behind the closed door, Zack turned his attention back to Sky's foreman.

Rider took the mare's reins and swung up into his saddle so that he was looking down at Zack. "The men and I keep a pretty good eye on Skylar," Rider said in a tone obviously meant to warn Zack.

For a moment he just looked at Rider. "If any man hurts Sky," Zack said in a low, controlled voice, "in *any* way, I'll tear the sonofabitch to pieces."

Without waiting for a reply from Rider, Zack jerked his door open, tossed his Stetson onto his passenger seat, and climbed into his Ford Explorer.

He didn't like how Rider stayed on his horse and watched him drive off, as if protecting Sky from Zack.

Once again, Zack found himself clenching his hands around the steering wheel before he forced himself to relax. He tamped down his anger, something he'd learned to control over the last ten years.

Maybe Rider *was* just watching out for Sky.

That damn sure better be all.

Zack's thoughts turned back to the kiss in the barn and heat rushed through his body straight to his groin.

No matter what Sky might think, Zack intended to make her his woman again—this time for keeps.

Chapter 3

Zack Hunter. His name rippled through Skylar in silvery waves as she leaned against the closed door, her eyes shut, his image filling her mind, her lips still tingling from his kiss.

She'd wanted to run her fingers through his sinfully black hair, touch the hard planes of his face, kiss the fine lines at the corners of his gray eyes, and run her tongue along the cleft in his chin.

And Lord, how she wanted to explore his muscular physique, smooth her hands over his broad chest, squeeze his large biceps, and meld her body against his lean hips and powerful thighs.

She waited until she heard his SUV start. After the sound of the engine had completely faded, she scrubbed her sweating palms on her jean-clad legs and opened her eyes.

When he'd come barreling into the barn, it was as if her thoughts about him that morning had summoned him to her—like some demon lover come back to torment her.

Zack. Here. Now.

The moment she processed who he was, all she'd been able to

do was stare at him. So many thoughts had flashed through her mind. In that instant, she had wanted to yell at him for breaking her heart into a thousand pieces. And then she wanted to throw her arms around him and let him hold her like he used to.

How could she feel like that after the way he'd left her?

Skylar hugged herself and thought about what she'd lost. What *they'd* lost, no matter what he'd thought at the time.

For six months they'd been virtually inseparable. Even though he'd never told her, she'd been sure he was in love with her. It showed so clearly in the way he talked with her, held her, made love to her. Like she was the most exquisite gem on earth.

Damn. Skylar's eyes suddenly ached and a tear threatened to roll down her cheek. She *was not* going to let him do this to her again.

She slid down the door until she was sitting on the hard tile, wrapped her arms around her knees, and pressed her face against her legs. Images of the past came to her, and her heart felt like Zack had taken it away from her all over again.

A handsome deputy sheriff and a wide-eyed first-year Cochise College student . . .

That hot, sweaty September rodeo . . .

Even after all these months and years, Skylar could still taste the sawdust and salt on her tongue.

I took the trophy in women's barrel racing.

And Zack took my heart. I was standing with my friends as they congratulated me, and I had that feeling. Somebody there. Somebody watching . . . me.

Skylar clenched her hands to keep herself grounded as she wrapped her arms around her knees tighter. She couldn't help but remember how she'd turned slightly and had seen *him.* She had caught her breath at the sight of his gray eyes looking at her so intensely, like he'd already claimed her.

A whirling sensation had stirred in her belly, as if she were still on her mare and barrel racing. Heat had flushed Skylar's cheeks as his gaze slowly traveled over her. Her body had responded, her nipples tightening beneath her western shirt, and that place between her thighs had tingled. Her lips parted as if she could already feel the pressure of his mouth on hers, his hands caressing her body.

The corner of his mouth had curved slightly, an arrogant expression on his face that told her he knew exactly how he was affecting her.

A flash of anger had had her straightening her spine and turning away from the cocky jerk.

Trying to bring herself to the present, Skylar sighed and raised her head and looked around her living room. In one corner were hers and her sister Trinity's trophies from numerous rodeos they'd competed in from the time they were very young until they each went on to pursue their college degrees.

Still Skylar couldn't get the memories out of her mind. It was as if the trophies called forth more images. Especially the trophy she'd won that night. As her gaze rested on it, she swallowed.

"Congratulations, Sky MacKenna."

That was the first thing Zack ever said to her—in a voice so deep it had caused shivers to roll down her spine. Sky couldn't forget those words, how he'd sounded, or the way his warm breath tickled her ear as he leaned close.

Of course, she'd turned around so fast she'd almost smacked right into him.

Then he touched her.

Just to steady her shoulders, but she held on to that stupid trophy like she was warding him off. As if she ever could. So tall, so virile. Her senses and hormones melted at the exact same moment.

What chance did I have against that tall drink of perfect man?

None.

Not then, and not now.

Skylar gave up and let herself slip completely back in time, to that perfect, steaming moment when her life changed forever.

"How do you know my name?" she'd asked in a shaky voice. "And it's Skylar, not Sky."

"They announced it over the loudspeakers." The look in his eyes had a hint of amusement in them. "And you're too pretty to be a Skylar. You're definitely like the sky on a clear day. Beautiful."

She hadn't been able to think of anything to say. All she could do was stand there, her face burning, clinging to her only lifeline, the gold-plated trophy.

"Save a dance for me tonight, Sky," he'd murmured, his gray eyes clearly confident that she wouldn't deny him.

And God help her, she couldn't say no.

She'd given a nod. "I-I've got to go."

The smile he'd given her was devastatingly sensual. "I'll see you tonight."

She'd nodded again before she turned from him and pushed her way through her group of friends and the rodeo crowd.

Her thoughts had whirled. She hadn't known what had just happened. If she had known what the future would hold, she would have run hard and she would have run fast.

Right?

Skylar raised her face from bent knees and banged the back of her head hard against the door. She looked up at the off-white-painted ceiling. A spider had decided to make itself at home in one corner. She'd have to get the broom and take care of it—

Why was she thinking about spiders?

Anything to stop thinking of him.

Zack Hunter.

But as Skylar stared up at the ceiling she couldn't bring herself to regret the time she'd had with Zack. It had only been six months, but it had been the most precious six months of her life.

No, she couldn't regret a moment with him.

She banged the back of her head against the door again. Trying to think about something else couldn't get Zack's face out of her mind.

"Goddamnit, Zack," she said in a hoarse whisper. "Why did you have to come here? Why did you have to kiss me?"

The room remained eerily quiet in response.

A hard knock on the door startled the silence as the vibrations traveled through her.

Zack?

Another hard knock. She pushed herself away from the door, got to her feet, and faced it. Her hands shook. The brass was cool against her palm as she opened the door, then let out a breath of relief when she saw it was Luke.

Or was it disappointment because it wasn't Zack?

Not going there.

Luke pushed up the brim of his Stetson as he stood on her porch and appraised her. "Everything okay, Skylar?"

She did her best to smile and not look rattled. "Sure. Fine."

He frowned and the look in his eyes told her he didn't believe her one darn bit. "Mind if I come in?" He took off his hat as she backed away so that he could step through.

"This Zack Hunter," he said after she shut the door. "I got the feeling you weren't too happy to see him."

The way she'd all but run Zack off her ranch, no wonder Luke was concerned. "He's an old boyfriend." She shrugged as if Zack appearing out of the blue was nothing. "It's been ten years since I saw him last and he was stopping by to say hi."

As Luke studied her like he was deciding whether to let it lie or press her, Skylar couldn't help but compare him to Zack. Yeah, Luke was hot, but in her mind no man had ever measured up to Zack. She had often wondered if perhaps her memories had become distorted, and that he wasn't half the man she remembered him to be. But after today, she knew the truth.

He was twice the man she remembered.

Crap.

God, seeing Zack was sending her imagination into overdrive.

"Let me know if you need anything." Luke interrupted her thoughts as he hit his Stetson against his leg. "I mean it."

"I think one of the best decisions I've made was hiring you." Skylar had no problem smiling at his genuine concern. Luke never made her feel like she couldn't take care of herself because she was a woman. He simply watched her back as he would for any man. She patted the cell phone in its holster at the waistband of her jeans. "I'll call you first thing if something comes up."

"I expect you to." He had two phones holstered on his belt. One was a phone she'd provided—she gave each one of her men a cell phone to make sure she could reach them at any time when they were on duty or in case there was an emergency. The other phone on Luke's belt was no doubt for personal use.

"Promise." She laid her hand on his forearm as he grasped the door handle, and he paused. "Thanks for caring."

Luke opened the door and she let her hand drop away. "Just watch your ass, Skylar."

She nodded and he walked through the door and shut it behind him.

Almost mechanically, Skylar drew the Smith & Wesson from the holster at her side. She slid it into a hidden drawer beneath an end table next to the couch. Her thoughts immediately turned from Luke's concern to Zack and she rubbed her temples.

She'd had almost a decade to ready herself for the possibility she'd see Zack again. But nothing had prepared her for today. He'd filled out in a hard, masculine way that made him sexier than ever. Even that scar he'd gotten from the fight with his stepfather made Zack's features more rugged and heartbreaking.

"Get a grip, Sky," she muttered, and then stomped her boot on the tile, the sound echoing through her empty living room. *Damnit!* She hadn't thought of herself as anything but Skylar since Zack had left her all those years ago. Only Zack had ever called her Sky. "*Not Sky. Skylar, Skylar, Skylar,* Skylar."

A combination of anger, frustration, and sadness raged through her like a dust storm. How dare he? How dare he come back and do this to her again?

She stopped by an end table beside the rich leather couch and traced her fingers over one of her dad's bronze Remington sculptures. She looked down at the extremely valuable sculpture named *Outlaw.*

Outlaw. The way Zack had stolen her heart, he was just as much of an outlaw.

Skylar snatched her hand away from the sculpture, feeling as if it had burned her. The heat of her anger increased and she curled her fingers into her palm. Did everything have to remind her of him?

She pinched the bridge of her nose. The memory of his good-bye was as vivid as the images from the day they'd met.

Her heart had ached for him as she'd gone to him at the sheriff's department. This time he wasn't leaving the jailhouse as a sheriff's deputy.

This time he'd been arrested for almost killing a man.

His stepfather.

The bastard who'd married and physically abused Zack's mother hadn't pressed charges. Instead he'd fled the state taking all of Zack's mother's cash with him.

When Skylar had met Zack outside the county jail just outside of Bisbee, Zack had looked so angry that she'd taken an involuntary step away from him. Hurt, then more anger had flashed in his eyes.

"Don't shut me out!"

Skylar squeezed her eyes closed at the memory of her own plea. How hard it had been to talk. How her breath left her like someone had punched her right in the gut.

She had asked him to stay.

Begged him to talk to her.

And he'd walked right past her and ignored her as she called to him. One tear after another had rolled down her cheeks as she watched him climb into his truck and drive away.

Maybe it was then she knew she had lost him. She just would never have admitted it to herself.

Everything had changed.

Everything.

Bastard. Skylar brought her fingers from her face and opened her eyes as she clenched her fists, willing the memories to leave her alone. "Go away!" she shouted out loud to the huge living room.

But the memories wouldn't stop.

He hadn't returned her calls for two days. Two days that she'd cried her heart out.

When he finally stopped by the ranch she had run out into the driveway, flung her arms around his neck, and pressed herself against his hard body. She still remembered how wonderful he had smelled. Masculine. Spicy.

"I love you," she'd whispered. "I love you so much."

Zack pulled her arms from around his neck, took her by the shoulders, and set her apart from him.

Instantly she'd felt the loss, a chill overcoming her body so violently her skin prickled.

Every word he uttered in the next moment had hit Skylar like a hammer blow.

"I'm not ready for a commitment," Zack had said in a hard voice. "We're both too young." Ice had flooded her veins as he continued, "It's best to break it off before things get serious."

"Best?" she'd whispered, but he kept talking.

"I'm leaving for the Federal Law Enforcement Training Center in Georgia. At FLETC I'll train to be a federal agent." His eyes had softened for the briefest of moments before he added, "I'm not good enough for you, Sky."

And like that, it was over. Zack had turned and walked away from her and her love.

Skylar had stood in the driveway like a frozen statue, unable to move, unable to speak.

He hadn't looked back. He had climbed into his truck and driven off, leaving only a dust cloud in his wake.

And she'd never seen him again.

Until today.

"Goddamn you, Zack Hunter." Skylar wanted to scream it at the top of her lungs, but it came out hoarse and filled with pain. "I should hate you," she added. Her voice lowered to a whisper as she repeated, "I should hate you."

Chapter 4

Zack's SUV's tires rattled over the cattle guard again as he left the Flying M, his thoughts wholly on Sky. How Sky had tasted, how her nipples had hardened against his chest, the feel of her silky hair between his fingers, and her soft lips beneath his.

With a hell of a lot of effort, Zack fought down the lust that had filled him since seeing her. He forced his thoughts from the beauty and fire of Sky to the irritation of having to meet an old rival. Not an enemy, but almost as bad.

Zack, his mother, and his brother, Cabe, had moved from Flagstaff to Douglas when Cabe got out of juvie. Zack had been a freshman in high school and almost immediately he and Larson had clashed.

Their rivalry had started when Casey Gonzales chose to go to the Freshman Winter Dance with Zack instead of Wade, and continued through their senior year when Zack had been selected captain of the Douglas Bulldogs football team. He and Wade had damn near come to blows a few times, and it was a wonder they never had.

After high school, Wade Larson had traveled the state and national rodeo circuits. After a broken pelvic bone, several broken ribs, and a crushed knee, Larson had been forced to quit bull riding.

Even though Larson's ranch bordered the MacKennas', like Zack, Larson hadn't been around the younger Sky MacKenna because Sky had been four years behind them in school. Larson probably had seen Sky on the junior rodeo circuit when he was competing, but she had been a hell of a lot younger than him—still a teenager.

Through her gossipy friends' grapevine, Zack's mother had let on that Larson had shown interest in Sky a month before Zack had met her. Apparently she hadn't been interested in Larson.

Zack shook his head. After their run-ins during high school, Zack getting the girl again had been one more blow to Larson in their none-too-friendly history.

Since Coyote Pass Ranch bordered the Flying M, Zack didn't have far to drive. Just as he was about to pull onto the road that would take him to Larson's place, he spotted two men, a truck, and an Appaloosa gelding alongside the southern fence of the ranch. Taking care not to stir up too much dust, Zack slowed and pulled off the side of the dirt road and parked behind the truck.

After he climbed out of his SUV he slapped on his Stetson and strode across the road to where one of the men was working on the fence. A late-afternoon wind picked up, stirring the grass and causing dust to swirl on the road. It was the tail end of summer and still plenty warm, and would be for at least another month yet.

One of the men was on the other side of the fence, facing Zack, but the man had his head down. Zack didn't recognize the other man.

"Larson," Zack said when the man repairing the fence looked up and Zack realized the man was the owner of Coyote Pass Ranch.

"Hunter." Wade Larson stood, pulled off his leather work gloves, and stuffed them into the back pocket of his jeans along with a pair of red-handled wire cutters. Larson had his Remington handgun in a holster at his hip, the holster secured with a strap around his thigh, in a way a lot of Arizona modern cowboys still wore their unconcealed weapons.

Larson was close to Zack's height, but wiry and athletic. By the way the man was eyeing him, and by the way his mustache curved down into a serious frown, Zack had the impression that Larson was none too pleased to see him, either.

Zack extended his hand to the man he didn't recognize, "Zack Hunter."

"Gary Woods." The big man took Zack's hand and shook it. "Sheriff's deputy."

"No doubt we'll be running into each other," Zack said. "I'm with Immigration and Customs Enforcement."

Woods gave a nod and a polite smile. "Nice to meet you, Agent Hunter, and I'm sure we'll be talking soon. In the meantime, I've got to head out. It's about time to get back on the job."

Zack returned Woods's nod before the man walked across the dirt road, climbed into his truck, and drove off.

Zack turned to Larson. "Sounds like rustlers are picking off cattle left and right."

Larson spit into the dirt at his feet, then glanced down the road toward the MacKenna Ranch and back to Zack. "What the hell are you doing in these parts?"

Zack studied Larson. The man had ignored Zack's statement outright.

"I'm working." He pulled out his card and handed it over the fence to Larson. "Stationed in Douglas now."

Zack studied the lines of Larson's frown as the man took the card, glanced at it, and slid it into the pocket of his work shirt.

"ICE. Yeah." Larson nodded. "So, tell me, Hunter. What ICE business took you out to the Flyin' M?"

Zack held back a sudden burst of anger as he pushed up the brim of his Stetson and eyed Larson squarely. The moment Larson had glanced from Zack toward the MacKenna Ranch and back, Zack figured out the lay of the land. Larson obviously had a thing for Sky again. Zack cursed under his breath. Did every man within a five-mile radius want Sky MacKenna?

Can you blame them? a voice inside asked.

Shut the hell up, Zack growled in his thoughts.

Damn. One kiss, and twenty minutes later Zack wanted to take on every man who even looked at Sky.

Was his past coming back to take hold of him again? Christ, but he'd been sure he had his anger fully under control.

Still, he clenched his teeth before he said, "I'm working this area. You have my number if you need anything."

Larson grabbed the top strand of the barbwire fence, his hands between the barbs, his smell of sweat mixing with dry grass and dust. The rancher's shirt was soaked at the armpits and around the collar, and a dark ring stained the crown of his hat. He flexed his fingers and narrowed his green eyes. "You had your chance with Skylar MacKenna and you blew it. Don't think you can come back and start where you left off."

Zack glanced down at his dusty boots. A muscle in his face twitched. That familiar pulse of darkness coursed through him like he hadn't felt for years. Dark anger he'd grown up with as a child with a sonofabitch for a father. Zack, his brother, Cabe, and their mother had known nothing but abuse until the bastard was killed when the boys were teenagers.

Once Zack and Cabe were grown, their mother had married a man she'd met in Douglas. He'd seemed like a good guy—until Zack caught him kicking and slugging Molly.

That darkness Zack had grown up with exploded and he beat the shit out of his stepfather, putting him into the hospital.

Things were different now. Over the past years Zack had proven to himself he could keep it in check, and damned if he was going to let Larson bring it out of him.

Looking from his boots to the rancher, Zack kept his tone even, his expression blank. "Like I said, I'm working the area."

"Uh-huh." Larson spit into the dirt again and then fixed his gaze on Zack. "Is that all you need?" The rancher gestured toward the fence. "Damn rustlers cut through and I've gotta fix it before more of my cattle get through."

"That about does it." *Other than wanting to kick your ass.*

Zack pulled the brim of his Stetson down and walked back to his Ford Explorer.

As Zack strode away, Larson called after him, "You just remember what I said about Skylar MacKenna, you hear?"

Forcing himself not to acknowledge Larson's parting shot, Zack climbed into his SUV and headed on out.

After meeting with Sky, Larson, and a few other ranchers, Zack returned to the Douglas ICE HQ.

He sat at his desk in front of his laptop computer, surfing the Net for recent articles relating to México.

A tremor in Mexico City, corrupt government exploits—nothing new there—famous Mexican artist dead from unknown causes.

Zack studied the next headline and he came to a halt.

MAD COW EPIDEMIC HITS SOUTHERN MEXICO.

He leaned back in his chair. *Sonofabitch.* Someone involved in the case should have seen that one coming a mile away.

Zack had that feeling in his gut he always got when he was on to something. He'd bet untainted beef was going for top dollar.

He did a little more research on the Internet on commodities. Sure enough, the price of beef in Mexico had skyrocketed.

He rolled his chair back, got up, and headed to his supervisor's office.

When he reached Denning's office, Zack shook his head as he watched the man tear into a junior special agent. Zack had met the young agent, Eric Torres, this morning.

How the hell Arnold Denning had landed the position of group supervisor Zack had no idea. The man had the management and social skills of a javelina. No, the wild pig was probably better in that department than Denning was.

Denning stood next to his desk, bracing both hands on his hips. The smell of chewing tobacco lingered in Denning's office along with his sweat and stale coffee. He paused in the middle of his rant long enough to spit a wad of tobacco into the waste can.

"Now get on the hell out of here," Denning said to Torres.

Torres gave a short nod and left the room, his face nearly expressionless. Yet by his stiff posture and the spark in his dark eyes Zack could tell Torres was pissed. The junior agent had backbone, no doubt about it.

"You should have some goddamned leads," Denning said to

Zack before he could get in a word. One side of Denning's mouth bulged from the tobacco. Made him look like a friggin' squirrel.

Zack didn't bother to point out that this was his second day at this ICE station and first day on the case. Denning was a dipshit.

"What the hell *did* you find out, Hunter?" Denning said.

"Got a better idea of which ranchers are losing the most cattle." Zack eyed Denning head-on as he started with the facts. "The ranches being hit the hardest are closest to the Chiricahua Mountains."

"Tell me something that everybody and his dog don't know," Denning said in his thick country accent as he waved a bony hand in an irritated gesture. "If you did your homework you'd know the range is used for smuggling narcotics, arms, and undocumented aliens."

Zack didn't bother to respond to that—he had more than done his homework by researching the area and the smuggling problems before he arrived in Douglas. He knew the details of the issues backward and forward.

With Denning up his ass from the first day, though, the investigation was going to be a bitch.

"There's one thing that wasn't in the reports," Zack said as he watched Denning's expression. "I believe there's a connection between the rustling and the epidemic of mad cow disease that's wiped out a good portion of southern Mexico's herds. Beef is going for top dollar in the places hit hardest."

Denning narrowed his eyes. Zack could tell the man was trying to find something to get on Zack's ass about. "Did you find anything to back this up?"

"It's just a theory right now," Zack said. "Once I build a case, we'll cut this cattle-smuggling ring off at the roots." He kept his tone even as he watched Denning.

"You damned sure better," Denning said before spitting more tobacco into his waste can.

Zack left Denning's office without bothering to give more than a nod, like the junior agent had.

Just my luck I'd end up with an asshole group supervisor like Denning. Any moron knew it took time to build a case, and Denning expected it overnight. Investigation, tracking, finding a snitch or two, surveillance, and catching the bastards in the act.

That little bit of info Zack had gleaned online from the newspaper article—he was sure it was one piece of a good-sized puzzle.

Zack stopped by the assisted-living center to check in on his mother, Molly, and spent some time with her.

After Zack's stepfather had beaten Molly that final time, she'd never been quite right. It was as if something snapped inside her after dealing with years of beatings from her first husband and then her second.

At the time Zack left for FLETC, Molly seemed fine. Zack's older brother, Cabe, had said he'd check in on her frequently.

Over the years she'd deteriorated mentally and her health had taken a nosedive. Even though she was only sixty-one, she looked and acted more like she was in her seventies. Her hands and head trembled like she had Parkinson's disease, but the doctors said her condition was due to repeated blows to the head.

Molly hadn't married until she was in her late twenties. Each time, their father had beaten her for getting knocked up, claiming she'd screwed around on him.

Not that Carter Hunter needed an excuse to pound on Molly.

That was just a way of life for them all until Cabe and Zack were old enough to start fighting back.

Yet even after all these years Zack could still hear the echo of his father's constant refrain, *"You'll never make it. You'll never be anything. You're a worthless piece of shit."*

As Zack left Molly at the assisted-living center, she smiled and blew him a kiss like she had when he was a boy. "Night, Zacky," she said, and Zack forced a smile and told his mother good night.

In the early days of her deterioration, he had to fight not to pound walls every time he saw how disabled she was. It felt like a personal failure. In his head, Zack knew a teenage kid didn't have a real prayer when it came to protecting a parent, but in his heart . . .

Yeah, well, that was a little different.

Now, Zack just hated how frail she was in every way, and wished her life could have been different.

Zack headed to his temporary home—an apartment not too far from the county fairgrounds. He shut the apartment door behind him, tossed his hat onto the coffee table, and went into the bedroom.

Once he reached his bedroom, he shucked off his boots, shirt, and jeans. It only took him a few moments to change into a pair of shorts, a T-shirt with the sleeves cut off, and workout shoes. He strode into the extra bedroom where he'd set up a small gym and tugged on a pair of fingerless weight-lifting gloves as he headed toward the barbell set.

Zack warmed up, then lay back on his workout bench, figuring some good bench presses ought to bring some relief to the tension in his muscles from the day. He gripped the barbell and raised it before bringing it to just above his upper chest. He started pumping the barbell over and over and over with more reps in each set than he normally did, and he barely rested between sets.

The protective, jealous urges he'd felt with Sky since he'd seen her again—*shit*. He increased the pace of his reps as the memory of those feelings rushed over him. Was he wrong for Sky? Just maybe he had done the right thing by leaving ten years ago.

The barbell clattered as he racked it before climbing off the bench and adding more weight. He lay back down on the bench. Zack gave a loud grunt as he raised the barbell. Brought it to his chest again. Raised it. Lowered it. Again. Again. Again. The longer he pumped iron, the more satisfying the strain in his muscles.

But hell, today was his first time seeing Sky after all these years, and the need to stake his claim on her was so strong he didn't think anything would ease his feelings until he had her.

What *did* he want from Sky?

A lifetime.

"Get a grip, Hunter," he growled as he racked the barbell, got up, and added even more weight.

At this point, he had so much weight on the damn thing, safety dictated he should have a spotter. He didn't care. The more weight, the better the burn.

He continued working out for at least another hour before he quit. He tossed his weight-lifting gloves on the bench and made his way to the kitchen, sweat soaking his hair and clothes. The workout had eased his tension and his anger. Ever since he'd started pumping weights when he was at FLETC, he put in a

good workout most weeknights, especially at the end of a stress-
ful day.

Zack splashed cold water on his face from the kitchen faucet.
Without bothering to dry his face on a towel, Zack braced his
hands on either side of the sink and stared at the stainless steel
without really seeing it.

*"No, Ellis, no!" Molly screamed as Ellis slammed his fist into her
face, causing her head to snap back and hit the brick wall. He followed
his punch by ramming his boot into her gut as he twisted her arm and
snapped it.*

*Zack had only seconds to process the scene as he walked in the front
door of his mother and stepfather's home.*

*Zack didn't stop to think. Didn't let anything get in the way of his
total and complete rage.*

*"You fucking bastard!" Zack grabbed the man's shoulder, and jerked
him around. "You're fucking dead."*

*Zack gripped the man's shoulder as he slammed his fist into Ellis
Kerrigan's face. With the first punch he felt Ellis's nose break beneath
his fist. The second punch broke the bastard's jaw.*

Ellis crashed into a glass vase, shattering it.

*The rage filling Zack was a living, breathing thing. A monster he
couldn't control. A monster he didn't want to control.*

Ellis grabbed a shard of the glass vase and slashed Zack's face with it.

*Zack barely felt the sting, or felt blood pouring down his cheek. In
the distance Zack heard Ellis's screams of pain as he rammed the man up
against the brick wall, cracking his skull. Like Ellis had jammed his
boot into Molly's abdomen, Zack kicked Ellis in the gut with all his
power.*

*Ribs cracked from Zack's kick. Molly shouted and cried and Zack
realized she was begging him to stop.*

Molly cradled her broken arm to her chest, blood on her lips, and Zack realized she was spitting up blood. "Stop, Zack!"

But he couldn't.

He couldn't rein in the monster.

The next thing he knew, men grabbed his arms and tried to hold him back from killing his stepfather. Zack was blinded with rage and it took three men to restrain him, including the one who had his arm locked around Zack's throat.

As paramedics rushed into Molly and Ellis's home, Zack knew one thing.

Ellis would never touch his mother again.

Chapter 5

Zack raised the barbell up from his chest as he ground his teeth and racked it. It was the day following his encounter with Sky. The day had dragged despite Zack coming up with a lead—a possible snitch who could end up as a good source of information for the rustling case.

He pushed himself up from the weight bench and mopped his face with a hand towel. His muscles had that satisfactory burn from a good workout.

The entire day Sky had been present in Zack's thoughts as he'd thought about seeing her again. He'd had half a mind to head straight to her ranch when he got off work. Instead, he'd returned to his apartment to think things over as he worked out long and hard in his weight room. He needed a plan to get her to trust him, and get her back in his arms.

He couldn't keep going to her ranch without an invitation and begging her to let him into her life again. Although that's what he'd do if that was what it took—show up on her doorstep every damned day.

The ring of the cell phone coming from Zack's bedroom caught his attention. He rubbed his face and neck again with the towel as he went into the room and picked up the phone.

"Unknown" came up on the display with no phone number, but that wasn't unusual in Zack's line of work.

"Hunter," Zack said as he answered the call.

"Sonofabitch," his brother, Cabe, said in his deep rumble. "You moved back to Douglas."

Using the workout towel, Zack rubbed the back of his head with his free hand. It was good to hear his brother's voice. "You talked to Mom, I take it."

"She's pretty damn happy to have her baby 'Zacky' back."

"Fuck you."

Cabe gave a low laugh. "Welcome home, little bro."

Zack shook his head. "I didn't get a chance to call you. Wasn't sure I'd get the opening and the next thing I knew I was on the road."

"Figured as much," Cabe said.

Zack rubbed his face with the towel again. "So what the hell's going on with you?"

"Keeping the streets of Dodge clean." Bisbee, where Cabe was a detective, was a town a good twenty miles or so from Douglas.

Zack leaned his hip against the counter as he asked about Cabe's wife. "How's Kerrie?"

"Gone." Cabe's tone went flat. "As in out of the picture. Screwed another cop right in the station."

"Shit." Zack rubbed his temples. "Sorry to hear that."

"Obviously I'm better off with her out of my life." Cabe's voice sounded gruff, angry, but Zack sensed the undertones of pain his brother had been dealing with.

Cabe had been through hell and back since their childhood with their father—and then the *accident,* when Cabe and their father had been on a hunting trip. The old bastard had deserved it, but Cabe was the one who'd paid. At thirteen, Cabe had begun spending a few years in juvie for involuntary manslaughter. Since he'd been tried as a minor in Arizona, the records had been sealed when Cabe turned eighteen.

Cabe never talked about the incident, and Zack wasn't inclined to open up old wounds.

"Ran into Wade Larson yesterday." Zack figured he'd better change the subject.

"Still as big an asshole," Cabe said. "I've met up with him a few times and can't say I like the man any more now than I did in high school."

"Heard anything about the cattle rustling that's been going on in this area?"

"Just that a few ranchers have lost a good number of cattle." Cabe paused. "From what I've been told, Skylar MacKenna has been hit the hardest."

Zack pinched his nose with his thumb and forefinger. "Stopped by to see her yesterday."

"Yeah?" Cabe's voice lowered. "I've seen her here and there. That girl grew up into one beautiful woman."

"Tell me about it." The image of her flushed features and swollen lips after he'd kissed her flashed through Zack's mind. He cleared his throat and dropped his hand from his face. "If you hear anything about the rustling, give me a call or drop-kick me an e-mail."

"You've got it."

After he'd ended the call with Cabe, Zack left the cell phone on the counter while he looked in the bare cabinets, then stared into the empty fridge. He slammed the door shut and picked up the phone, dialed information, got the number for Pizza Hut, and ordered. A couple of pizzas, an order of buffalo wings, and bread sticks. That ought to get him through dinner and breakfast.

Zack went to the sink and splashed cold water over his face. No clean dish towels or paper towels, so he used his workout towel to dry his hands.

The sparsely furnished apartment smelled of fresh paint and mothballs, and wasn't even close to feeling like a home. He was renting until he found a place he wanted to buy, maybe a piece of land where he could build a new house. Most of his stuff was still in storage, and the apartment had about as much appeal as a jail cell.

Yeah, he had to figure out some way to get close to Sky again, to get her to let him back in her life. With a frustrated sigh, he went to the sliding glass doors and peered through the blinds.

The apartments had been built close to the fairgrounds where rodeo events were held several times a year. The Cochise County Fair took up four days every September, and it was that time of year again. In the darkness he could see the glittering lights of the midway and Ferris wheel, as well as floodlights illuminating the rodeo grounds.

That time of year. The same time of year he'd met Sky ten years ago. And this Friday would be the rodeo dance.

Zack smiled as he remembered watching Sky barrel race on her black Quarter Horse. With superb skill, she moved at breakneck speed. The way she rose slightly off the saddle and leaned forward as she and her horse ran the cloverleaf pattern around the barrels showed their pure athleticism.

Zack had had a glimpse of her beauty beneath her western hat as she took the first-place trophy. Everything about her had called to him, and he'd had to meet her.

When Zack had gone across the rodeo grounds, he'd stopped and hitched his shoulder against a chute and watched Sky with her friends. She had a slight flush to her cheeks and her green eyes sparkled as people congratulated her. She'd taken off her hat, and her long red braid hung down her back.

He watched her for a long moment before she looked over her shoulder at him. She stole his breath as their eyes met. She brought her free hand to her throat in a nervous movement before she clutched her trophy to her, as if warding him off, and she quickly turned away.

At that moment, he knew he had to make her his.

Mine.

Zack stared across his apartment at the cell phone still sitting on his kitchen counter and made up his mind. What was the worst that could happen? Sky could hang up, which would put him right back where he was anyway.

Alone and fantasizing about having the woman in his arms and in his bed.

Many times. Many ways.

Zack grabbed the cell and walked into the living room. He kicked a box of clothing out of the way and shoved aside a stack of newspapers. He sat on the couch and started pressing the numbers to call Sky. Funny how he still remembered the MacKennas' phone number as if he'd called Sky yesterday. Unless she'd changed the number.

The phone rang a couple of times, and then Sky's sensual voice said, "MacKenna's."

Damn, but just hearing her made him hard. "Hey, sweetheart."

A pause. "Zack. I—I didn't expect it to be you."

His gut tightened. Who did she expect?

Of course she wasn't expecting you to call, you dumbshit.

He took a deep breath and tried to keep his voice calm. "Did you think it might be Wade Larson?"

"Wade? Why would you say that?"

"I saw him after I stopped by your place." Zack clenched the phone so hard his knuckles ached. "He made it clear you two are together."

Sky's voice was filled with disbelief as she said, "He *what?*"

A little of the tenseness in his body eased from Zack's muscles. At least Sky didn't think of herself as Larson's woman, even if she might be dating the man.

"He saw me coming from your place and gave me some advice. Told me in so many words to stay away from you."

"Well, that's taking neighborliness a little far," Sky muttered. "Is that what you called about?"

Jesus, Hunter, you sound like a jealous fuckhead. Okay you are a jealous fuckhead—get over it. And get on with it.

Zack cleared his throat. "I wanted to ask you something."

A long pause, then Sky said, "What?"

How hard could it be? He swallowed, feeling like he should have had a few beers before calling her. "Ah, I was wondering if you'd like to go with me this Friday to the rodeo dance at the fairgrounds."

Silence. Too long. She finally said, "Are you asking me on a date?"

She wasn't going to make this easy. "Yeah, I guess I am."

A longer silence. "Why are you doing this?"

"It'd be a start toward being friends."

What the hell am I saying?

"Friends," she repeated, her tone flat, even a little hard. "That's all you want?"

Zack rubbed his hand over his jaw as he pictured her beautiful face. "It's a beginning," he said.

He heard a thump as if Sky had hit something beside her phone, hard. "A beginning to what?"

This sure wasn't going the way he'd wanted. *What did you expect, Hunter?* "Will you go with me or not?"

Sky sighed and he imagined her fingers at her throat, the soft skin turning pink. "Tell you what," she said. "I'll be there, and I'll save a dance for you."

"One dance?" Zack leaned back against the couch and stared at the ceiling. If that was all she'd give him, he'd take it. For now. "All right."

"See you Friday, then," she said softly. God, but her voice was sexy. "So long, Zack."

"Later." Zack ended the call and tossed the phone onto the couch.

Shit. He'd gotten as far as getting her to agree to go. Now he just had to get her to spend more time with him, more than one dance.

How the hell was he going to handle seeing any other man dance with her?

Keep her too busy dancing with him to want to dance with another man.

He got to his feet and headed to the bathroom to wash off the day's grime and sweat from working out.

Once he was beneath the hot spray, Zack couldn't help but remember the times he and Sky had showered together. When he'd washed her hair, soaped her breasts, rinsed her off, and explored her naked body with his tongue and light nips of his teeth. And while under the spray he'd knelt and licked her folds until she cried out from the strength of her orgasm.

Moist steam clouded the bathroom as Zack soaped his own body, imagining it was Sky's hands washing him, stroking him. As he rinsed off, he took his cock in hand, wrapping his fingers around his erection. Warm water pelted his back and rolled down his spine as he closed his eyes and he worked himself from base to tip and back.

He wanted to see her again. Spend time with her. Hear her voice for hours, and watch her smile. He wanted to know everything about this Sky, now, in the present—and fall in love with her all over again.

Then he wanted to make love to her for hours. Days.

Yeah, he could feel himself sinking into her. Her head thrown back, her hair a wild tangle of copper across his pillow, and she would be crying his name, shouting at him to go harder. Faster.

Zack's body corded as he came in a rush and he barely bit back a shout. He continued milking his cock, the semen squirting onto the glass shower door until he was empty.

When he had spilled every drop, he placed both hands on either side of the shower door and let the shower spray pelt his relaxed muscles.

Damn, but Friday couldn't come fast enough.

Sky might think she was only giving him one dance, but Zack would be claiming her, and to hell with everything else.

Chapter 6

Sky finished applying her mascara, then studied her reflection.

Sky. It had only taken a couple of days with Zack having returned to start thinking of herself as Sky again.

Crap.

And in a little under an hour she would be at the rodeo dance in Zack's arms.

She shivered and leaned against the sink. She must have been insane to agree to spend even one *minute* more with Zack, let alone agree to a dance. She would be pressed up against his big, hard body. Those thick, corded arms would be wrapped around her, holding her close. All it had ever taken was one touch from that man to destroy her, to lay her bare and strip her of all her defenses. She felt like she had barely survived that kiss he had laid on her.

Sky's heart began to pound and she touched her throat. She raised her eyes to look at herself in the mirror.

"I can't," she told herself in a whisper. "I can't do this."

Oh yes, you can. Or are you going to let him see that he has you running scared? . . . He'll only chase you, you know.

Sky felt light-headed. Zack on the hunt was even worse. Besides, she wasn't a runner and she'd be damned if she let some man cause her to be one. Even if that man was Zack Hunter.

She took a deep breath as she stood up straight, turned, walked into her bedroom, and looked at herself in the floor-to-ceiling mirrors of her closet door.

Yesterday Sky's capricious best friend, Rylie, had gone shopping with her in Tucson and they'd had a great time. It had been good not to think about real life—failed relationships, missing cattle, and the ranch's dwindling resources.

And they'd found the perfect outfit for the dance tonight. The ivory halter dress was gorgeous and made Sky feel slightly dangerous and very naughty. Sheer netting rose from just above her breasts to the neckline that encircled her throat like a choker. The dress completely bared her shoulders and back, all the way down to the top of her ass. She enjoyed the feel of the material, silky, and luscious against her skin.

She usually kept her makeup light and natural so that it hardly looked like she was wearing any. But tonight she'd gone all out—her cheekbones appeared higher, her eyes wider, and her lips more full and sensual.

She'd pulled back her hair and swept it up with a pearl comb, copper ringlets spilling out the top in a controlled mess. She smiled at the fact it gave her that just-got-out-of-bed look that she knew would drive Zack crazy.

Whoa, slow down, girl. This dress was *not* about Zack.

Sky turned and viewed herself from another angle, then shook her head. Who was she trying to fool? This dress was *all* about Zack Hunter and showing him just what he had walked away from.

She pulled on the matching bolero jacket, then slid her feet into a pair of ivory sandals with three-inch heels. Her toenails were painted with dynamite red polish to match her fingernails. The new garters and thong underwear felt positively delicious beneath the dress. Too bad Zack wasn't actually going to see what she had on underneath.

No, it wasn't too bad at all. She was just going to give him a taste of what he'd been missing all these years.

She took another deep breath and grabbed the purse she'd bought to go with the outfit.

After tossing her lipstick into her purse, out of habit she thought about slipping her S&W out of its hiding place. No. She'd be away from the ranch, and the very real threats weren't likely to follow her there.

She said good-bye to Blue and strode out the door into the gathering darkness, taking care not to stumble down the stairs in her sandals. The pinching around her toes was a good indication she should've settled for something a little more sensible, but she'd loved the way the sandals looked with the dress.

And at this moment, she felt anything but sensible.

A crashing sound jerked Sky's attention to the barn, causing her heart to jump.

Satan bawled and she heard more crashing like the bull was butting his stall.

Were those footsteps pounding the ground away from the barn?

Heart racing, Sky unfastened the purse and withdrew her cell phone, wishing she did have her Smith & Wesson with her after all. The purse slipped from her hands and dropped by her feet. Vaguely she was aware of the contents tumbling out, thumping and clattering across the porch.

With her gaze still fixed on the barn, she punched the speed dial number for her foreman and brought the cell phone to her ear.

The line rang once. "Rider." He sounded slightly out of breath.

"Luke." Her heart still thundered as she stared at the long rust red building. "I think someone's breaking into the barn."

"I'm close," Luke said. "Where are you?"

"The front porch."

"Get back in the house," he said in such an authoritative tone it surprised her. "Lock the door."

Sky wasn't exactly dressed to head out to the barn, but she wasn't going inside her house. She could handle herself just fine if someone came up on her.

The yearling's loud bawl bellowed from the barn, followed by another crash. "Something's spooked Satan," she said.

"I'm already here."

The line cut off and Sky startled for a second when she saw the shadow of a man with a gun, his back up against the side of the barn. Her shoulders sagged with relief when she realized it was Luke. How'd he get there so fast?

Even though it was night, she made out the forms of two more of her ranch hands hurrying toward the barn, each armed with a rifle.

With his handgun held in both hands, Luke motioned with his head for Sky to get into the house.

He didn't wait for her to obey as he slipped into the barn.

Sky moved behind the countless potted vines and flowers on her porch and peered through the plants.

Darkness. Quiet.

Another crash. She jumped.

Her pulse rate spiked.

Lights flooded the barn and Sky blinked away the spots in front of her eyes.

She realized she was holding her breath and slowly let it out as she kept her gaze fixed on the now lit-up barn.

"Clear." Luke's voice cut through the night. "No one's in the barn."

"Nothing on the east side," came Hector Ramirez's voice.

"West clear, too." That was Joe.

To Sky's surprise, two of her other ranch hands shouted from the south and east pastures that they hadn't found anything. She startled when a fifth man called out, "Yard clear," from the back of the house.

Damn, Luke more than had it together. It was obvious he'd drilled the men for something like this.

A couple of moments later Luke jogged up to the porch and Sky stepped out from behind the plants.

"Someone was definitely in the barn." Luke's furious expression underscored his words. "Satan's stall was wide open and you know there's no way he could have bashed the damned door from where he's tethered."

Sky's stomach dropped as Luke continued, a hard, angry edge to his voice. "I saw shoe prints that tell me it wasn't anyone here. Our men wear boots and the prints are too big to be your shoes, Skylar, when you're not wearing your boots. Sonofabitch was probably wearing sneakers to make a faster getaway once he had Satan."

Her body prickled with heat. "So stealing the rest of my cattle isn't good enough. They want my prize bull, too."

"Shit, Skylar." Luke's jaw tightened as he gave her a long, hard look. "Why didn't you get back into the house like I told you? This could have been dangerous."

Sky narrowed her brows. "Who's the boss here?"

A flash of anger on his features almost caused her to take a small step back. "Damnit," he said, "I know you can handle yourself, but you're not exactly dressed to kick ass right now."

His expression shifted as his gaze trailed over her skimpy outfit and her cheeks warmed. "But you *are* dressed to kill," he added in his deep drawl. "Hunter's a dead man."

Even as her face grew warm, she started to tell Luke where he could put that assumption, but she couldn't think of a single retort. Luke crouched and grabbed her purse that she'd dropped by her feet and picked up the items that had fallen out, before he handed the purse back to her.

Sky stuffed her cell phone into the purse and fastened it as Luke stood from his crouch. "I'm going to the dance at the fairgrounds," she said.

"I can see that." He slipped his handgun beneath his overshirt in the holster at his side. "Save one for me. I'll head there after the sheriff's department takes a look around."

It wasn't until that moment that she noticed his spicy cologne, his clean-shaven jaw, his white western dress shirt that hugged his broad chest, and his snug blue jeans.

"Uh, yeah." Sky let him help her down the steps in her too-high heels and to her Range Rover.

When she shut the door she buzzed down the window. From the intense look on Luke's face, he apparently still had something to say.

He placed his hands on the window frame. "Skylar, this rustling situation could be heading into dangerous territory. You watch your ass, you understand me?"

There was something different to him—a hard edge like he'd been through this kind of thing before and he knew how to deal with it.

Or was he warning her in a different way altogether?

Sky mentally shook her head. Lord, now she was suspecting her foreman of being involved in the rustling. Luke? That was crazy.

"The hands and I will take another look at the barn scene and examine Satan." Luke glanced at the barn, then returned his gaze to her. "Wanted to make sure you were still okay once we cleared everything. So watch it, understand? I don't want you going anywhere alone."

"I'm fine and I'm not going to hide around my own ranch." Hell if she would give in.

He gave her an expression of frustration as he stepped away from the Rover.

She glanced into her rear- and side-view mirrors, backed out of the driveway, and headed toward the fairgrounds.

The entire way she drove down the dusty rural road to the highway, anger rolled through her. Goddamn those rustlers. It wasn't enough that they were stealing her cattle, but now they were after the bull she'd sunk so much money into.

When she closed in on the county fairgrounds, Sky managed to calm herself down enough to focus on tonight.

And Zack.

Damn him.

He'd always been so dark and dangerous to her, and was too freaking hot for his own good. And that kiss—

Sky bit the inside of her cheek. Tonight was about letting Zack know what he'd been missing. Not letting him sample what he couldn't have again. What he *wouldn't* have again.

Chapter 7

Sky arrived at the fairgrounds and parked the Rover in the dirt lot. When she climbed out, night air chilled her skin as her dress hiked up her legs. She pulled the material back down, locked the SUV, and headed toward the dance hall. Her ankles wobbled as she traveled over the uneven ground and she just hoped she wouldn't sprawl in an ungraceful heap.

Multicolored lights of the carnival midway illuminated the night. Sounds of laughter and the blare of the country-western band filled the air as she approached the dance hall.

Smells of popcorn and corn dogs brought back memories of the last time she'd been to the county fair and dance ten years ago with Zack. For the first couple of years after he'd left, she hadn't wanted any reminders of him, so she hadn't gone to the annual event. And somehow she'd never felt inclined to go again.

Her steps slowed as she got closer and closer to the dance hall, and then she stopped walking and stared at the front entrance, clutching her purse in both hands.

Maybe she couldn't do this after all. If she allowed herself to get too close to Zack, she might start to lose her heart again, and that was completely out of the question. Once was enough for this lifetime.

Chickenshit.

She whirled to head back to her Rover, and smacked into a solid wall of hard male flesh. Hands caught her upper arms to steady her, and Sky found herself looking up into Zack's eyes.

Too late.

Too late to make her escape.

The most dangerous sensations coursed through Sky the moment she found herself nearly in his arms. The warmth of his too-close body radiated through her, sending whirlwinds of desire spinning in her belly.

Devastatingly handsome, all in black from his western dress shirt to his Wranglers, he emanated pure male power and danger—danger to her resolve . . . to her heart.

Zack's broad shoulders blocked some of the light from the midway as he stood close. Way too close. His sinewy forearms flexed as he steadied her, his large hands firm around her upper arms.

The brim of his Stetson shadowed his gray eyes, but she could see a silvery glint in their gray depths as he took her in slowly from head to toe. The look in his eyes told her he was barely holding himself back from scooping her up, sweeping her away . . . and taking her.

No, she thought, clenching her thighs together. She wouldn't let that happen. Not tonight. Not ever.

"Sweetheart," he murmured, the heat of his hands blazing through her jacket. "You look good enough to eat."

"Zack." Sky heard the huskiness in her own voice, and fought to regain her composure. She put her hands against his muscled chest and pushed away from his grasp, her palms now burning from the feel of him.

"Where were you going?" He let his fingers slide down her arms as she stepped back, and she shivered from the sensual feel of his touch through her jacket sleeves. "You didn't change your mind, did you?"

"Of course not." Sky lifted her chin and did her best to give him a flirty smile.

"You want to dance out here under the stars, or go in?" His deep voice was so vibrant, so sexual, that she all but wanted to melt into his arms.

There was no running away now.

"Inside." Sky took a step away from Zack and he let his hands fall to his sides. She started toward the entrance feeling the heat of his gaze on her, and the heat of another kind flaming deep inside.

All she could think of was how hot he made her feel in every way.

As they entered the dance hall, he remained silent, only nodding to people Sky greeted as they passed by until they found the place to leave her purse where someone watched everyone's belongings. When she slipped off her jacket and revealed the sleeveless, backless dress beneath, she heard his sharp intake of breath. She couldn't help smiling to herself.

After she put the jacket with her purse, she turned to see Zack staring at her intensely. The look in his eyes—could she get any hotter? He set his Stetson next to her jacket but never took his gaze from hers.

"Are you ready for that dance?" she asked, hoping her voice

sounded steady. Casual. Not like, *I want your hands all over my body right this minute.*

"If it's only one dance, I get to choose the song." He smiled and moved close. "And I want it to be a nice slow one."

The purr of a cell phone rose up between them, just as Zack reached for Sky's hand.

She took a step back. "Gonna answer your hip?"

"Hold on a sec." Zack gave her a sheepish smile as he yanked the slim phone from his belt. He pushed a button and pressed the phone to his ear. "Hunter."

Sky watched Zack's eyes narrow as he listened to whoever was on the other end. To be honest she was thankful for the interruption—her body kept threatening to take over her common sense.

"All right," Zack finally said. "Keep me informed."

He punched the phone off and slipped it onto his belt, his eyes focused on Sky. "Now where were we?"

"Would ya like to dance, Skylar?" a man's voice broke in.

She glanced up, surprised to see Gary Woods, the good-looking sheriff's deputy. "Sure, Gary," she said, trying not to sound relieved. He usually seemed too shy to ask anyone to dance, but right now he was her own personal savior.

Gary gave a nod to Zack, who scowled and folded his arms as Sky moved with the deputy onto the crowded floor. With effort, she managed to keep her attention on her dance partner as they two-stepped to a fast tune.

But every now and then she'd catch a glimpse of Zack's expression. The look in his eyes said she had gotten a reprieve, but she hadn't escaped him. Not by a long shot. Sky swallowed and turned her focus almost desperately toward Gary.

A blue-eyed blond cowboy, Gary was the big silent type who never had a whole lot to say. However, she'd heard he had a little problem with gambling, heading up to the casinos on the reservations whenever he had some time off. One thing Sky didn't find attractive in a man was any kind of addiction, whether it was drugs, gambling, or tobacco.

But she danced with him for another song, laughing and flirting with the man the entire time—just to distract herself from Zack's dominating presence. She wasn't very successful, since she could feel his gaze like a weight on her. And she knew he wasn't happy.

Sky cleared her throat as she looked up at Gary. "Any more information pop up about those rustlers?"

"Sorry, Skylar." Gary shrugged. "Unfortunately, we're nowhere near finding the bastards."

She gave a frustrated sigh. "I feel like I'm banging my head against a wall."

"You and me both," he said with a half smile.

The next thing she knew, Luke cut in and she found herself in the arms of her foreman. She looked up at him and he gave her a sexy grin. "Hunter looks ready to pull me apart."

Sky shook her head. "The history between Zack and me is so ancient there's a foot-high layer of dust on top of it."

At that, Luke laughed. Sky caught Zack's eye as Luke turned her on the floor and she bit the inside of her cheek. Zack's scowl was positively thunderous. Where did he get off looking so possessively at her?

"Did you find anything?" Sky asked Luke as she glanced up at him.

Luke's expression changed, his smile fading. "Nothing more than what I told you earlier."

"That sucks."

"No kidding."

Tingles prickled Sky's arms as the song ended and Luke escorted her across the dance floor to Zack.

She'd barely had a chance to thank Luke for the dance when Zack took her by the elbow and propelled her from the edge of the other people dancing.

"This isn't part of the deal," she said when they reached a corner where they were somewhat alone and the music wasn't as loud.

Sheer possessiveness rolled off him. "We have a lot of catching up to do." He leaned one shoulder against the wall, boxing her into the corner, the look in his eyes showing only too clearly how worked up he was.

"What about your job? Your calls? You seem to be in demand." Sky tried to sound annoyed.

"I turned my phone off for now." Zack gave her a dark, sexy look that made her shiver. "Unavailable." He leaned close and murmured in her ear, "To anyone but you."

Sky swallowed as her stomach pitched as he drew back and she could see his eyes again. The wall felt cool to her bare back, and for a second she considered stomping her three-inch heel into his boot to get him to back off. But every sane thought fled her mind as she studied him.

Lord, he looks good.

Tremors rippled through her at Zack's nearness, and she wondered how she would begin to walk away from him when that one dance was over. Her body hummed as he stood close—not quite touching, yet not far enough away.

"How'd you end up running your dad's cattle ranch?" he asked, that smoky gaze fixed on her.

"I love ranching." Sky swallowed, wishing for a drink of water to soothe her dry throat. "I guess you could say it's in the blood." She flattened her palms against the wall behind her. "Your turn. Tell me what you've been up to."

"Had a nice spread in Texas, enjoyed my work as a fed, and did all right." Zack bent closer, invading her space. No, more like conquering it. "But I was lonely as hell."

She kept her tone light. "What? No friends?"

"I had friends." He reached up and traced the line of her jaw, his eyes intent. "But something was missing."

At the same moment, the lights dimmed and a slow tune started.

A shiver skittered through her as Zack trailed his finger down her neck. "How 'bout that dance now, Sky?"

Chapter 8

Sky hesitated, then nodded. The sooner they got this over with, the better. She'd give Zack one dance and then get away from him before she jumped right into bed with the man.

His hand burned the bare skin at the small of her back as he guided her. He stopped at the edge of the dance floor on the fringes of the other couples, where it was darker.

As Zack brought her into his arms, her nipples tightened. He swept his gaze over her breasts and gave her a slow, sensual smile that caused her mouth to go even drier. His hands settled on her waist and he moved his hips against hers until she felt his erect cock through her thin dress, pressing against her own softness.

A thrill blossomed inside her abdomen despite herself. Damn. It felt so good to have him pressed up against her.

He bent his head next to hers, and Sky automatically moved her hands to his shoulders, letting her body sway with his in time to the music. After the way he'd left her all those years ago, she shouldn't feel so turned on, but was she ever.

"Remember the first time we made love?" he murmured in

her ear, and she caught the scent of mint on his breath. She could imagine how good he'd taste and almost moaned at the thought.

Sky shivered at the feel of his mouth so close to her ear, and nearly melted when his lips brushed her earlobe.

"It was our hideaway." He pressed her closer along his solid length, all but making love to her on the dance floor. "It was a clear October day and we went horseback riding in the mountains with a picnic basket, a blanket, and a bottle of wine." His voice was raw, filled with desire. "The sun was shining, and it was still warm enough that you were wearing a pair of tight jeans with a T-shirt. No bra."

Her fingers tightened on his shoulders. God, yes, she remembered.

"I could even see your nipples through the shirt, it was so skimpy." Zack trailed one finger up Sky's bare spine and she shivered as he continued, "We went to our secluded spot, our own little hideaway, and it was like we were the only two people left in the world. Then you begged me to make love to you."

Sky pulled away and looked up at him with a frown. "I begged you?"

He brought her back into his arms. "Maybe we both did a little begging."

How Zack's kisses had unraveled her and how badly she had wanted him. *Needed him.* And it was true, she had begged him not to stop.

He had smiled, handling her so gently, as if he cherished every part of her. His mouth had teased her nipples, slowly working his way down to her folds. She couldn't believe he put his mouth on her clit, tasting her until she was writhing, and dying for him to be inside her.

Before he entered her, he had caressed her clit until he brought her to orgasm. And then he slid into her, taking her slow and easy. She'd cried out from the incredible pleasure rippling through her body once she got past the brief burst of pain as he took her virginity.

He had stopped, afraid he'd hurt her, but she had ordered him to keep driving into her, clenching his hips between her thighs. Harder and faster he moved within her, filling her, until he reached his own climax.

Zack's warm breath on her neck and his low voice brought her out of her memories. "I never thought I could want you more than I did that day. But every day after that, I couldn't get enough of you."

His hands moved from her waist, caressing her through the dress, down her hips, and back again to her waist, and she couldn't stop the shivers trailing along her spine.

His voice rumbled as he spoke close to her ear. "And somehow I want you now even more than I did then."

Damn the man. How could he do this to her?

Sudden anger flowed through her. "Hear me loud and clear, Zack," she said. "Nothing's going to happen between us. I agreed to be friends with you. Not fuck you."

Zack tried not to smile, but whether she realized it or not, her words were as effective as a dare. Like waving a red flag in front of a primed bull. Without a doubt, Zack knew she wanted him with the same fierceness he felt for her. Their one dance had already melded into a second, and if he had his way, he'd be dancing with her all night.

And then he'd get her home and in his bed.

Just the thought of what she was wearing under that scrap of a dress was enough to make him want to throw back his head and let loose a primal chest-beating howl, throw her over his shoulder, and take her home and bury himself inside of her.

When he'd arrived at the fairgrounds, Sky had pulled in and parked her Rover directly in the row in front of him. After a moment she'd slid out of her SUV and her tiny dress had climbed up her thighs to reveal garters holding up sheer stockings. Pure lust had bolted through him at the sight. All thoughts of work, smuggling, and rustlers blew away with the breeze.

Now she was in his arms, her scent of orange blossoms flowing over him, and it felt so completely right. He knew he'd been an idiot to leave her and he wasn't going to make that mistake a second time. And he'd be damned if he'd let her go any time tonight.

He lifted his head to look down at Sky, taking in her generous curves underneath that barely there outfit. Through the netting at the top of her dress, Zack could see the mole above her left breast. He yearned to peel away the material and run his tongue over that beauty mark, and every inch of her body.

Sky's green eyes met his, challenging him. "Your one dance is over."

He wrapped a loose strand of hair around one of his fingers. "Dance with me all night."

"I—no." Her voice was firm as she shook her head, tugging at the strand.

He brought his lips to her hair, traveling along her temple and down to her ear. His voice was a rumbling growl and his words came out as a demand. "Dance with me."

Sky gasped as Zack nipped at her lobe, hard, and when he raised his head he saw her eyes had turned a deeper green with sensuality and her lips had parted. He needed to kiss those lips again.

His mouth neared hers. She lowered her lashes and tilted her head back. Her scent was warm and inviting, arousing him even more.

"Zack." Their lips came closer as she spoke in a husky whisper that made his cock grow harder. "I—"

He didn't let her finish whatever it was she was going to say.

Her soft lips were his to take, her mouth his to taste. His hunger for her was so strong, so deep, that he took control of her body by dragging her close and pressing her tight against his erection. He cupped the back of her head, holding her so that she couldn't draw away, even if she wanted to.

And by the way she was kissing him that was the last thing on her mind.

She returned his kiss with the fervor he remembered from long ago. Much too long ago. Her mouth, lips, and tongue were the sweetest, softest things he'd ever felt or tasted.

Her moans and desperate whimpers grew loud enough for him to hear over the music and his body grew hot with such incredible need that he knew if he didn't have her right now, he would die.

Sky felt instantly robbed when Zack broke away from the kiss. The spinning sensation in her head and her belly made her almost dizzy from need. The place between her thighs ached and the crotch of her thong was soaked.

His features were harsh and hungry—dangerous—as he looked down at her. He grabbed her hand and started pulling her farther into the darkened part of the dance hall.

"Zack——," she started, but broke off when she realized he was headed to the back door.

"We need to talk," he growled as he jerked the door open and he dragged her into the near darkness behind the building. The carnival lights barely illuminated where they were and the sound of the crowd was dimmed.

He jerked her into more darkness, behind the trellis of some plant she didn't recognize—and didn't care about as he pushed her up against the building.

"Zack——," she tried again, but he pushed up the back of her dress and grabbed her ass at the same time he pressed her against the building, his cock like steel against her belly. Her ass was naked since she was only wearing a thong, and his hands burned her as he clenched her butt cheeks hard.

Sky gasped into his mouth as he took hers with the force of a man hungry for his woman. Her own hunger burned inside her so fiercely she answered his kiss with her own. God, her moans and whimpers seemed loud in the night, but she didn't care. Right now all she could think was that she wanted this. This moment with Zack.

He cupped her bare ass, drawing her up and forcing her to wrap her legs around his hips. He ground his jean-covered cock against her wet crotch and she grew even more light-headed.

Zack tore his mouth from hers and lowered his head to suckle her nipples through her dress at the same time he gripped her ass and rubbed his erection between her thighs.

Sky tried to keep her cries low so she wouldn't be heard—she couldn't stop them from coming from her mouth. She squirmed against him feeling such fire and need that she couldn't stand it.

"Hold on," he rumbled, and she wrapped her arms around his neck and crossed her ankles behind his back.

She was so light-headed and hot she was barely aware of what she was doing, just that she needed something. Now.

Zack. She needed Zack.

Sky clung to him as she heard something crinkle, then the sound of a zipper.

He pulled aside the crotch of her thong—

Then drove his cock deep inside her.

Sky would have cried out loud and long from surprise and pleasure if Zack hadn't clamped one of his hands over her mouth.

"I always loved that you're a screamer," he said in a low, throaty growl. "Next time I want to hear you scream my name."

With every thrust of his hips, Sky cried out beneath his hand. His cock was thick and long inside her, and he fucked her hard and deep enough that it felt like his cock reached her belly button.

The need to come was so intense that moisture gathered at the outside corners of her eyes. She couldn't take much more. She wanted to tell him, to shout at him to make her come, but he kept his hand over her mouth as he watched her eyes and took her.

Zack pounded in and out and she clutched him around his neck and hips as he pressed her up against the wall.

Oh, God, she was so close. So close that she whimpered and cried behind his palm.

He moved the hand that had been gripping her ass and slid it over her thigh. He drove into her again as he fingered her clit.

Sky felt like she'd just exploded. She screamed behind his

hand and as her whole body flushed with her orgasm. She jerked and cried out again, every part of her throbbing, her mind flying.

The walls of her core clenched his cock and every thrust drove her higher and higher until she came again. And again.

Then Zack came with a hard slam against her mound. He threw back his head, his jaw clenched as if holding back a shout of his own. His cock pulsed inside her, causing her to experience small aftershocks from her orgasm.

He finally released her mouth and pressed his body completely against hers as he rested his chin on the top of her head. His breathing was loud and harsh and she was having a hard time getting oxygen into her lungs, too. The night smelled musky— of his masculine scent and the smell of their sex. Whatever bush they were behind smelled sweet, like honeysuckle.

After a moment, Zack took a deep breath and let her slide down so that he drew his cock from inside her and her feet touched the ground again.

He placed his hips on her waist, letting her dress fall back over her ass, and kissed her again. "Goddamn, you make me crazy, Sky."

Slowly Sky became aware of her surroundings, the light-headedness slipping away. The sound of the midway and the throbbing beat of music from the dance hall brought her back to reality. She'd lost her clip and her hair was a mess around her face and her breasts cool from the damp fabric where Zack had sucked her nipples.

"I-I. Oh, God." She stared up at Zack in shock, her eyes wide as she pushed at him.

Zack allowed their bodies to separate and tucked himself away and straightened his clothes while she scrambled to do the same. He watched her, his eyes hooded but intense while she hurried to tug down her dress, run her hands through her hair, and try to make herself look like she hadn't just been fucked up against a wall. She had a feeling that she failed miserably.

"We need to talk, Sky," Zack said finally.

She wanted to laugh hysterically. Right. Look at where "we need to talk" had gotten them.

Sky shook her head, still feeling flushed and utterly and completely overwhelmed. "No, I-I can't."

Then she did the only thing she could do at that moment. Actually, it was one more thing on a short list of things she had promised herself that she wouldn't do this evening.

She ran.

Chapter 9

Sky halted just inside the dance-hall entranceway, her heart pounding as she frantically tried to remember where she had left her purse and her jacket. She glanced over her shoulder and saw Zack coming after her, like a wave about to crash down over her once again.

Ohmygod, ohmygod, ohmygod.

She plunged herself into the crowd on the dance floor, allowing all of the bodies to swallow her up. The crush of people, along with the sour smell of beer and cigarettes, was enough to make her claustrophobic.

She pushed her way through until she came out about where she thought she had left her things.

Sky almost sagged in relief when she spotted her jacket and purse, still lying on the table next to Zack's Stetson. She checked with the person watching everyone's belongings before she snatched her things up. As fast as she could, she thrust one arm, then the other into her jacket to cover her wet nipples, then whirled around intending to head straight for the door.

Instead, she ran smack into Wade Larson.

"Whoa," he said, catching her by her arms. "Where's the fire?"

"Wade." Sky pulled away from him and barely managed a smile. "I was just leaving."

"Leaving?" he said with a frown. "I was hoping that we could dance."

"Sorry." She eased away while her gaze darted around the room. She needed to leave before Zack spotted her. "I'm really all danced out."

Wade put a hand on her arm, halting her. "I'd like to talk. About you and me." His expression was serious.

Sky stared up at him in disbelief. Had all the men lost their minds tonight? "Wade, there is no 'us.' We haven't dated in months."

Wade slid his hands in his pockets. "Well, I'd like to change that, Skylar. I think things could be good between us if you give me another chance."

Sky closed her eyes and put a hand to her head. Why was this happening to her? Had she angered some god somewhere and was now paying the price?

She dropped her hand and looked up at Wade. "I can't do this right now. I really have to go."

Then she turned and fled. Again.

"Skylar, wait," Wade called.

She pretended not to hear and pushed her way through the crowd as if wild dogs were nipping at her heels.

Oh, God. I just let Zack fuck me. I fucked him.

The memory of Zack's hard body was still imprinted along her breasts, her stomach, her thighs. The feel of his hard, thick cock still inside her. She knew she would wake up in the middle of the night, her core still clenching at the feel of him inside her.

While she strode to the parking lot, Sky held the opening of her jacket tighter as she clutched her purse. Darkness closed in on her, the lights from the midway and the occasional floodlight barely enough for her to see where she was going.

Her high heels wobbled as she raced across the rocky lot, and then she stepped into a good-sized pothole.

She stumbled and barely managed to keep from landing on her backside. But the twist of her left ankle and the immediate, shooting pain of her injury were unmistakable.

Sky couldn't move, her eyes watering as pain screamed through her ankle. She almost dropped to the ground to hold her knee tight to her chest so that she could take the pressure completely off of it.

Terrific. Pain made her eyes water, the tears rolling down her face, no doubt tracking makeup over her cheeks. She hugged her purse as she hobbled to the truck closest to her and balanced herself long enough to wrench the sandal off of her good foot. She bit her lower lip to keep from crying out as she carefully slid the sandal from her other foot, trying not to move her injured ankle. Which was pretty much impossible.

More tears from pain trickled down her cheeks as she carried her sandals by the straps and hobbled toward her Range Rover. Rocks pricked her feet, and by the time she reached her SUV, her nylons were shredded, and her thong was riding the crack of her ass.

She'd lost her hair comb when Zack had fucked her, and the whole mess was probably tangled in the back from where she'd been pressed up against the wall. She managed to brush the tears from her cheeks with the back of one hand while holding her purse and shoes with her other.

Doing her best to balance on her good foot, Sky shoved her hand into her purse and dug out her keys. Just as she unlocked the door of her Rover, a male voice spoke behind her.

"Skylar."

Sky yelped and almost fell as she turned to face Wade Larson. The night darkened even more as she felt herself almost pass out from the shooting pain in her ankle.

Holding her free hand to her pounding heart and leaning against the Rover, she said, "Dammit, Wade. Don't sneak up on me like that."

"Sorry, hon." Wade looked her up and down, from her wild hair to her stocking feet. "You okay?"

Irritation ripped through her, borne on pain. "I'm not your hon, and I'm fine." Sky shoved her hair out of her face and glared up at him.

Wade stepped closer and put his hands on her shoulders. His tone softened. "Skylar, stop running from me and just listen for a moment. You know I care about you. I always have. I can make you happy if you just let me."

"Wade—"

"I've always been serious about you." Wade leaned close and she felt his warm breath as he murmured in her ear, "I want to be inside you again."

Sky flushed at the reminder of the few times they'd slept together. Why had she ever gone to bed with him? It was obvious he wasn't the type of man for casual sex—at least with her. And apparently the only kind of serious sex her body was interested in having was with Zack. Serious, sweaty, heart-pounding, mind-numbing sex.

Like what she and Zack had just done behind the dance hall.

"I can't deal with this right now." Sky gripped Wade's arms with both of her hands and gave a little tug, but he didn't loosen his grasp. "Not a good time. So just let me go, all right?"

He ignored her and moved his mouth close to her lips as if he intended to kiss her.

Just as she was about to wallop him a good one, Wade suddenly jerked away from her.

Sky stumbled back against her Rover.

Zack's expression filled her vision.

Total and complete fury.

Her heart seemed to stop for a moment. She couldn't breathe and her body froze.

Zack had hold of one of Wade's shoulders. "Stay away from my woman, you sonofabitch."

He slammed his fist into Wade's jaw.

Wade lurched back a couple of steps, surprise, then rage on his features.

Zack was already driving his fist toward Wade's cheekbone, but Wade blocked it. At the same time Wade punched Zack in his solar plexus.

Zack didn't even seem to notice. He hit Wade with an uppercut while blocking Wade's next swing.

For a moment Sky couldn't move. Horror tore through her at the sight of the two men fighting. Blood poured from Zack's nose, and Wade's split lip bled. Their hats were on the ground and they went after each other with punch after punch.

Sky came to her senses, her body no longer frozen, her heart now beating frantically, as she screamed, "Stop!"

Neither man seemed to hear her or they chose not to listen as she screamed so loud her throat hurt, "You bastards, *stop!*"

Tears came out of nowhere. They rolled down her cheeks as she cried at them again and again to stop fighting.

Sky did the only thing she could think of. Despite the pain in her ankle, she pushed herself away from the Rover, dropping her purse at the same time.

She hobbled over to the two men and thrust herself between them just as they each were reaching back to take a punch at the other.

"Fuck you. Fuck you both." The tear tracks on Sky's face were cold in the night as she looked from one man to the other as they lowered their fists. "I don't want to *ever* see either one of you again."

Silence fell and all she heard was the rough sound of their breathing and the fury at the two men in her head.

Her skin chilled as she turned away. She didn't look at them as she hobbled to her Rover, scooped up her purse, and gritted her teeth from pain as she climbed inside her vehicle.

"Sky—," Zack started, as Wade said, "Skylar—"

She slammed the Rover's door, locking their voices out. More tears flowed down her cheeks and she felt like she was going to throw up. She started the SUV and the tires spun in the gravel as she tore out of the parking lot.

Zack's muscles remained wound up like a loaded spring as he watched the red of the Rover's taillights fade. Larson stood a few feet away, his body stiff as he gazed in the same direction. So much adrenaline was pumping through Zack that he barely felt any pain from the blows Larson had landed.

Anger at Larson punched Zack's chest as hard as the man's fists had.

What the fuck is the matter with you, Hunter? Zack clenched his jaws as he wiped blood from his upper lip with the back of his hand. He rubbed his knuckles onto his Wranglers, smearing the blood on the denim. *You haven't changed a goddamned bit. You're still the same lousy sonofabitch who couldn't control himself ten years ago.*

You don't deserve Sky.

And she doesn't want anything to do with you.

Larson swung his gaze to meet Zack's. "I told you to stay away from Skylar." Even as his split lip was starting to swell and his face was already bruising, Larson took a step toward Zack. "Don't you go near her."

Zack clenched his fists at his sides, almost shaking from the desire to land another punch.

Instead, he met Larson's gaze for one long moment before he scooped up his hat off the ground, turned, and walked toward his personal vehicle, a Silverado.

"I'll tear you up if you even get close to her," Larson shouted behind Zack.

It was all he could do to keep walking.

As he saw Sky's horrified gaze in his mind, Zack's gut tied into so many knots he didn't think they'd ever unravel. It was the same way she'd looked at him the first time she saw him after he beat his stepfather.

You really fucked up, Hunter.

Chapter 10

Sunday afternoon, Zack stared through the sliding glass doors at the desert mesquite bushes and dried grass just beyond the apartment complex. His nose ached and had swollen, and the mirror had reflected one hell of a shiner last time he checked.

It had taken everything Zack had to stay away from Sky all day Saturday and most of today. He was going out of his friggin' mind.

He needed to apologize to Sky. He needed to let her know he wasn't giving up on the two of them.

Ah, fuck, Hunter. Who are you kidding?

Why should she forgive you?

Zack braced one hand against the wall as the afternoon sunshine cast shadows across the back deck. He tried to get his father's voice out of his head, but he kept hearing *"You're a worthless piece of shit,"* over and over.

Zack pounded the door frame with his fist hard enough to feel a satisfying jolt of pain.

Was he like Carter Hunter, the man who had fathered him?

No, goddamnit.

Zack pictured Sky's face as he'd entered her. After having Sky in his arms, after tasting her sweet lips, *after being inside her,* he'd known she was his again.

Seeing Larson come close to kissing Sky had sent Zack over the edge.

No way in hell was another man putting his hands on her.

No way in hell was Zack giving up on their relationship.

Zack turned away from the window. *Damned if I'm going to wait any longer to see her.* He'd given her some space. Given himself time to think things over. Now they'd talk.

He frowned as he thought about how Sky had been limping when she left. He didn't know what she'd done, but he wanted to make sure she was all right, too.

First things first. He'd better test the waters.

He located his small pad filled with notes and leads about the investigation and found Luke Rider's contact information.

Zack dialed Rider's number, and after a couple of rings, the man answered, "Rider here."

"Zack Hunter," Zack said as he scrounged for a pen in one of the kitchen drawers. "Wanted to check in with you on the rustling case."

"Anything in particular?" Rider said as a cow bawled in the background.

Zack finally found his pen and turned to a blank page in his notebook. "Did you figure out how Sky's dog got sick?"

"Vet called." Static crackled over the line like the wind was blowing. "That chunk of beef Blue got ahold of was laced with poison that could have killed him if Sky hadn't gotten to him when she did."

"Damn." Zack picked up the pen. "Do you think it was meant for Blue or to kill off some of the coyotes in the area?"

"With all the shit going on with the rustlers," Rider said, "my first guess would be intentional. But that begs answers to a whole lot of questions, and none of them make sense. At least not now."

"What's the vet's name and number? I'll give him a call."

"Hobgood." Rider rattled off the vet's phone number while Zack scrawled the information onto a page in the notebook. "If—*when*—we catch the sonofabitch," Rider went on, the slightest hint of amusement in his voice, "Sky's planning to personally cut off his balls."

"I bet she will," Zack said, and shook his head at the image. "Anything else?"

"Wade Larson's missing at least a dozen head of cattle, too," Rider said as one of the ranch hands yipped over bawling cattle in the background. "Larson reported the thefts today to Clay Wayland, the new county sheriff."

Zack whistled through his teeth. He couldn't stand Larson, but he didn't like to see the guy screwed like this. "I'll have to give Sheriff Wayland a call."

"Got any theories why the rustlers might be taking the cattle to Mexico?" Rider asked.

"Mad cow disease," Zack said, then explained what he'd come up with.

"I think you've got something there, Hunter." Rider had a note of approval in his voice. "That epidemic might be over a thousand miles away, but it's still too close to the U.S./Mexico border for comfort." He added over the static, "The Mexican government better get on stamping it out before it takes the whole damn country."

"How the hell do you transport herds of cattle across the line without anyone catching on?" Zack said, thinking out loud.

"The rustlers are possibly splitting the herds and using the same routes they're running drugs and illegal aliens," Rider said.

"Got a feeling you're right." Zack leaned his hip against the counter as he frowned. "You'd think with ICE, the DEA, the sheriff's department, and Border Protection on the job it would be possible to nail all these sonsofbitches before they cross the line."

"This is some huge territory to cover and the volume of illegals and drugs crossing the line—Jesus," Rider said. "Not to mention the routes change all the time. It's all the agencies can do to handle a portion of it."

An idea formed in Zack's mind.

"Hamburger," he said as he thought out loud again.

"You hungry or something, Hunter?"

"I'd bet a good portion of the beef is being processed somewhere around here." A feeling in Zack's gut told him he was on the right track. "Hell of an easier way to get it out of the country."

"Goddamned." Rider paused and Zack heard a horse whicker in the background. "Hell if that doesn't sound like you've hit it dead-on."

"I'll get on this first thing tomorrow when I hit the office." He'd have access to more databases there.

The line crackled. "I've got to head on out," Rider said.

Zack paused for a moment. Yeah, he'd wanted info related to the rustling, but he had another reason altogether for calling.

"Hold on a sec." He cleared his throat. "How's Sky?"

The bawling of cattle sounded louder, along with the sharp whistle of one of the ranch hands, as Rider said, "She sure did a number on her ankle after the dance. Doctor wants her off it for at least a week." He gave a frustrated sigh. "Keeping her down is going to take some doing. She's as stubborn as hell."

Zack rubbed his forehead. "I didn't realize she'd hurt it so bad."

"Yeah, she did." Rider paused for a moment before changing the subject. "I've never seen her so pissed." A note like suspicion was in his next words. "She's fit to be tied. Says she doesn't want any company. Especially you and Larson. Any particular reason for that?"

Might as well be straight up. "Larson and I got into a fistfight Friday night in front of Sky. I'd say she was beyond pissed."

"You might want to keep your distance," Rider said over the sound of the cattle that was growing louder. "Sky's got her claws out and she's spittin' mad."

"Is she laid up with that ankle?"

"She's in the living room and not exactly mobile."

Zack rubbed his jaw and winced as he touched a bruise from the fistfight. "I'll be right over."

Rider snorted. "They're your balls, Hunter."

"Check in with you later," Zack said before he ended the call.

He dialed information and got the number for the county sheriff's office. He placed a quick call to Clay Wayland and left a message asking the sheriff to return his call.

Zack clipped his phone to his belt, then braced his palms on the kitchen counter as his thoughts turned to Sky MacKenna.

Looked like he was headed into the lioness's den.

Sky eased back in the living room rocking chair, her foot resting on a hassock. Two ice packs surrounded her throbbing ankle and a pair of crutches leaned against the closest end table.

The prickling on Sky's arms, the heat flushing her body, drove away the cold of the ice pack. "Asses. Both of them," she nearly growled. Who the hell did they think they were, fighting over her as if they had some kind of claim on her?

But that wasn't the worst part.

No.

The worst part was seeing Zack's face when she screamed at him and Wade that she never wanted to see either one of them again.

Her chest suddenly hurt like she couldn't catch her breath.

Zack's expression had been the same as it had when she'd seen him the day he was released from jail. A flash of vulnerability followed by pain and self-loathing.

The heat of Sky's anger mixed with an ache for Zack, and her stomach twisted.

She didn't want Zack beating himself up like he had ten years ago. What he'd done was stupid, but that didn't mean he was anything but a good man.

She forced her thoughts away from Zack for the moment.

Last night, even through her haze of pain and fury at Zack and Wade, she'd realized she'd wrenched her ankle bad enough that she needed to have it examined. After she had been waiting for what seemed like forever in the ER, an X-ray tech had taken a couple of films of her ankle. Nothing broken, so they'd wrapped it in an Ace bandage, given her crutches, and told her to stay off it. Not to mention ice it, elevate it, and follow up with her own doc in a week.

Just fabulous.

Being cooped up inside was a slow form of torture as far as she was concerned. She wanted nothing better than to be out in the barn working with Satan, or riding Empress, her mare, or doing any number of things that didn't involve being stuck in the house.

Sky winced as she shifted her foot on the hassock. She leaned over the right side of her rocking chair and grasped the handle of her quilting basket.

"When are you going to finish this thing, Sky?" she said aloud. She'd been working on the same quilt since she was sixteen, when her mother passed away from breast cancer. While Sky's mother was ill, she'd taught Sky how to quilt one block. Sky had used it as an example as she practiced on a few blocks before she started working on some for a blanket.

Thirteen years later Sky was still working on the same damn quilt. She probably had enough blocks for two king-sized beds. For some reason she'd never been able to get herself to finish the project. Like it was the last link holding her mother to her.

Preferring to be outside, Sky only managed a few blocks a year when she couldn't do anything outside. But quilting did relax her when she was upset. She'd made a lot of blocks the first six months after Zack left.

She set the wicker basket on her lap. Quilting usually helped keep her mind off other things, too.

Like the fact I had sex with Zack.

Her stomach dropped. The illusion she'd had that she was less vulnerable than she had been ten years ago was completely and utterly shattered.

She wrapped her arms around her belly and shivered, and it wasn't from the ice pack on her ankle. It was from the realization Zack had stripped away all of her defenses.

He'd laid her heart and soul bare.

And I let him fuck me.

Sky hugged herself tighter, wishing to god she hadn't wanted Zack so bad at that moment. No matter how right it had felt to have him inside her, she shouldn't have let it happen. Zack Hunter had torn her apart once. She couldn't let him do it to her again.

Too late now, MacKenna. Now all you can do is regroup and push him as far away as possible.

Still, even though she'd told Zack she never wanted to see him or Wade again, she'd expected Zack to call anyway. To stop by. He was bullheaded that way.

But he already got what he wanted, didn't he.

Even as the thought came to her, she rejected it. Unless he had changed drastically, Zack wasn't the kind of man who used a woman and discarded her.

Yet he'd left ten years ago.

He left.

And this time he hasn't even called.

Sky's hands trembled a little as she gripped her quilting basket. Yes, she'd told him to stay away, but it still cut her inside that he hadn't made the effort.

She shifted in her seat again and tried to clear her mind of all things.

Yeah, like that's going to work.

Before she had a chance to grab anything out of the quilting basket, a knock sounded at the door.

Sky's heart stuttered before it started pounding. Maybe it was Luke.

The knock was louder this time.

Her heart knocked harder, too. *Ignore it, MacKenna. Don't answer.*

The catch on the door handle clicked and she could only stare at the door, holding her breath.

The door creaked open and Sky's heart creaked with it as Zack Hunter stepped over the threshold.

Chapter 11

For a moment Zack just stood in the doorway, watching Sky. Even after what had happened Friday night, he still had the power to take her breath away.

Damn him.

Zack stepped into the house, his dominating presence filling the room as he closed the door behind him. Sky felt like everything was off-balance, as if the house itself were tipping.

He said nothing as he walked toward her, his worn blue jeans hugging his thighs and his boots ringing against the tiled floor. A gray T-shirt stretched over his chest, the shade bringing out the steel of his eyes. His weapon was holstered at his side along with his cell phone.

No doubt from his fight with Wade, a bruise darkened Zack's cheekbone, his nose looked a little swollen, and he had a black eye. His dark hair was slightly ruffled and he gripped his Stetson in one hand.

Sky swallowed. Where were all the things she wanted to yell at him about? Why wouldn't her mind cooperate with her mouth?

When he reached her he towered over her for a moment and it looked like he was trying to read her frown. Then without invitation he moved to the couch near her rocking chair and sat on the end closest to her.

"I told you to stay away." Her mind finally was able to transfer the words to her mouth as she deepened her frown. "Starting a fistfight with Wade—that was inexcusable."

Zack looked down at his western hat that he now held in both hands. He raised his face again and met her gaze. "Was it?"

Sky looked at him with incredulity. "You think that charging in, acting like you own me, and trying to beat the crap out of another man is excusable?"

"After what we shared, I couldn't let another man touch you, Sky." Zack's deep voice was low, almost soft. "The sight of him trying to kiss you—there was no way I was going to let that happen."

"What you and I did—that was a mistake." Fear of Zack destroying her defenses any further made her voice quaver. At the same time, the memory of him taking her up against the building sent heat flushing through her.

He shook his head. "Being inside you again was right. Perfect."

"No, it wasn't." She clenched the edge of the quilting basket in her hands as she could almost feel him thrust in and out of her slick core. "It should never have happened."

Zack glanced down at his hat again that he was slowly turning around by its brim. "I'm not going to apologize for something that was meant to be."

"Then what are you here for?" She let the words out with a bite to her tone. "I've already made it clear you're not welcome."

"I fucked up." His voice had a harsh edge to it. "I shouldn't have lost control with Larson. I should never have let you see me like that."

Sky didn't know what to say as she looked into his gaze.

"And I don't know how to fix this." He glanced at his hat before looking at her again. "I don't know how to fix *us*."

She could feel her heart crumbling. Why was he doing this? To let him into her life again . . . she couldn't let him hurt her like he had before. She *wouldn't* let him hurt her again.

When she could speak, she said, "How many times do I have to tell you there's no *us* to fix?"

He looked away and when he turned back she was startled by the pain etched into his features. She had the instant desire to wrap her arms around him and draw that pain away. His expression filled with so much self-loathing that something hard twisted inside her belly.

"I saw it in your eyes when I was arrested for beating the shit out of that bastard." Zack got to his feet and looked down at her. A muscle in his jaw ticced. "You were revolted."

Sky was shaking her head. "Never—"

"That's why I left like I did." His gut churned as her eyes widened. "You deserved better than some out-of-control bastard like me.

"A decade later I thought I'd changed." His skin felt stretched tighter with every word he spoke. "God, when I saw you again, I thought maybe we had another shot." Zack pushed his hand through his hair, wanting to rip a chunk of it out just to feel the welcome pain. "But Friday night I proved I'm the same stupid sonofabitch."

"Zack!" Sky's shout, the red flush in her cheeks, and the anger in her eyes brought him to a complete halt. "I knew then and I know now that you'd never hurt anyone—except that worthless scum who deserved it."

She looked like she was ready to come out of the rocking chair despite her messed-up ankle as she went on, "Ellis Kerrigan was a lousy sonofabitch who deserved every damned punch you laid on him for what he did to your mother."

Sky's voice escalated as she tossed the basket she'd been holding onto the floor. "You never gave me a chance. You were so wrapped up in your own pity party that you couldn't see anything past your own misery."

Cold prickled Zack's insides as he continued staring at Sky, suddenly not knowing what to say or do.

Her green eyes glittered with moisture right before a tear rolled down her cheek. "Goddamn you, Zack Hunter. I loved you." More tears followed the first as she yelled, "I. Loved. You."

For a moment he didn't know what to say. Ten years ago she'd told him she loved him, but he hadn't let himself believe her. But the way she said it now, the hurt and anger in her voice—it was like a punch to his gut.

A wash of pain hit him like a tidal wave, for what he'd done to Sky. And to himself by leaving her. "God, I'm sorry."

Zack knelt in front of her rocking chair. He reached for her hands, but she folded her arms across her chest and looked away. "Save it," she said, her voice shaking. "Just go home."

He leaned forward and slipped his hands behind her back, drawing her close to him and pressing his face into her hair. "Listen to me."

She tried to shrug him off, still hugging her arms tight to her chest.

"I'm the world's biggest ass." His gut churned from the strength of his pain for having hurt Sky then and now. He drew away, caught her chin in his hand, and forced her to look at him. "I'm sorry."

"That's supposed to make it all better?" She closed her eyes while more teardrops slipped from beneath her eyelids. "I loved you so much," she said in a voice hoarse with pain.

All this time lost. *Goddamnit. I'm a fucking idiot.* He stroked her wet cheek with his thumb. "I was young and stupid."

"What do you mean, *was?*" She opened her eyes and tried to pull away from his touch as he rubbed his thumb across her cheekbone. "You're still stupid. You're still an ass."

"I know." Zack slid his fingers from her face into her hair and lowered his face. He kissed her forehead and drank in her orange-blossom-and-woman scent. "Can you forgive me for then? And now?"

When he drew back, her eyes met his. "I don't know." She wiped the back of her hand across one of her cheeks. "I can't afford to lose my heart over you. Especially not to you. You'll just take what I have to give and leave me again. Disappear into the sunset, or whatever."

"I'm not going anywhere." He brought her head against his chest and squeezed her to him. "And I intend to make up for every lost minute."

Sky didn't know what to think. How to feel.

Except for the fact that no matter what promises Zack made,

she wasn't about to give him her love again. Been there. Done that. Had the boot prints on her heart to prove it.

"Come here," Zack said, and somehow she couldn't protest as he gently scooped her out of the rocking chair.

He carefully moved her with him onto the couch so that she was sitting on his lap. She winced as pain shot through her ankle when he arranged her foot on the couch and he frowned. "You okay?"

She nodded and he brought her tighter into his embrace and held her close. She sank against him and let out a shuddering sigh. He felt so good. So, so good with his hard muscled body cradling her softer form. And the scent of him. Warm, masculine, spicy.

Despite the fact that she planned to keep an emotional distance, she wanted him. Wanted more than his arms around her—she wanted him inside her, too. Rocking in and out in a steady rhythm as he took away every bit of the pain of their loss and replaced it with the love she knew they could never have again.

Chapter 12

For a long moment Sky's breath caught as Zack's gaze held hers. His gray eyes seemed to drink her and his expression was hungry.

He brushed her hair away from her cheek with his thumb and the gentle touch sent a shiver through her. Slowly he skimmed his fingers along her jaw, down the curve of her neck, continuing on until his palm rested above her breast, right over her pounding heart.

Sky barely noticed his bruises as her gaze moved to his firm lips. She could almost feel the imprint his mouth had made on hers twice since he'd come into the barn and back into her life.

She breathed in his scent that was an aphrodisiac to her senses. At that moment she could practically taste him on her tongue, feel his hard body against hers as he took her and his cock thrust deep inside her core.

Zack's lips were inches from hers, but he didn't move closer. He just studied her as if looking for answers she couldn't give.

Right now she'd give him anything. Anything but her heart. God, she had to have him if only for now.

Sky raised her free hand and fire flashed in Zack's eyes as she drew him to her. Tingles spread through her belly and she gave a low moan that was like a soft purr as their lips met.

He groaned as he held her close and she sank farther into him as they tasted one another. It was so incredible being with him and all that he was. Spice and man and everything erotic and dangerous. He felt so good.

Need built up inside her like an oncoming storm. Her nipples tightened beneath her T-shirt as he moved his lips from hers and kissed her forehead, then nuzzled her hair. He started to draw back, but she kept him close by tightening her grip. His eyes turned slate gray as he studied her with hunger and need as obvious as her own.

She didn't know how she had endured ten years without feeling his length and thickness driving in and out of her. At this moment Friday night seemed so long ago and she couldn't have him fast enough again.

It was clear that he was ready and willing—she didn't even need his large erection pressing against her ass to tell her that. His expression was definitely perilous to her libido, and he gave a low growl that sounded primal and filled with need that matched hers.

Thoughts of him taking her again made her clench her thighs together as ripples of desire traveled from her belly to her now-damp folds.

Zack gave a throaty groan as he looked at her. "Controlling myself with you—damn, Sky. I want to be inside you. Now."

Sky moved her mouth closer to his. "Yes," she said before she kissed him again. It was a demand she was more than happy to fulfill.

The instant Zack's lips touched Sky's, his hunger grew, so deep and fierce he knew he'd never be satisfied.

All he wanted was to bury himself in her as he covered her soft body with his and possessed her in every way possible.

While clenching his hair in her fists, Sky ran her tongue over his lips. That sweet, sexy tongue that always drove him wild was now about to make him insane.

Soft moans came from her throat as she nipped at his bottom lip. He groaned and her tongue darted into his mouth.

Oh yeah, he had to taste her. Had to feel her. His arms tightened around her as he explored her mouth with his tongue, plunging and retreating and plunging again, showing her how badly he wanted her and what he'd like to be doing right now.

He slid his fingers to the back of her head and took the tie off the end of her braid. He speared his fingers into her hair, unraveling her braid until a silken mass tumbled over his hands to her shoulders. He picturing them both naked, her hair like burnished copper against his skin.

Sky squirmed in his lap as she kissed him, her round little ass rubbing against his erection. He was so damn hard the pressure of her movements and the tightness of his jeans nearly strangled his cock.

She dragged his T-shirt out of his jeans, then pushed it up and slid her hand over his abs. She trailed her fingers across his chest and down, down to the waistband of his jeans.

Before she could go any lower, he caught her hand and broke their kiss.

"I need to feel you," she whispered.

Zack released her hand to run his finger along her jawline, feeling her tremble at his light stroke.

Her eyes focused on him, Sky took his hand from her face and moved it to her breast. "Touch me, baby," she murmured in that husky voice he loved, using the name she'd called him when they used to make love all those years ago.

Baby.

The way the word came out of her sensual mouth and the feel of her nipple pushing against the lace beneath his palm just about undid him. The softness, the warmth, the fullness of Sky's breast sent a bolt of lust through his body.

With his thumb and forefinger he teased her nipples through the thin fabric of her T-shirt and her lace bra. He moved his mouth to her breasts, replacing his hand. She gasped and arched her back as he licked and sucked her through the cloth.

When her shirt was wet over her nipples, Zack pushed her T-shirt up to expose her lace-covered breasts. "God, you're gorgeous."

He caressed the swells with his gaze and his hands, circling the mole above her left breast with his finger. Sky had beautiful breasts, large and full, her nipples a deep rose and so hard they were like pebbles. And yes, she felt like satin as he touched her, just as he remembered. "You okay?" he murmured.

"More than okay." Sky's eyes were such a deep green from passion they almost looked like emeralds. "This isn't even close to being enough." She glided her fingers into Zack's hair again and pulled him down to her breasts.

He grinned, remembering how uninhibited she always was when they made love. Such a willing and apt lover. It was like she'd been born to love him and only him.

Trailing his tongue over her cleavage, Zack tasted her salty flesh as he leisurely made his way above her breast to the beauty mark. He circled it and then continued his exploration of her body.

Sky moaned and squirmed in his lap, her backside rubbing against his cock. He used one hand to tug down her bra, releasing both her breasts. As he moved his mouth from one breast to the other, Zack moved his palm down her flat belly, her skin soft to his callused palm. He stopped to tease her navel, running a finger around it.

"Baby, you're driving me crazy," Sky whispered while he slowly drew his finger along the silky skin above the waistband of her jean shorts.

He lifted his mouth from the nipple he was devouring and looked at Sky. "You've always made me crazy."

Her eyes were heavy lidded, her lips still swollen from his kisses. "I want your cock inside of me."

Instead, he took possession of her lips, kissing her hard, thrusting his tongue into her mouth as he slid his hand down her jean shorts. "Spread your legs," he murmured.

She opened for him, and he trailed his fingertips over the denim crotch of her shorts. He traced lazy circles over the warmth, imagining that he could almost feel the dampness of her folds through the heavy material.

Sky shifted her hips against his hand, but he deliberately took his time. He rained kisses over her face as he moved to unbutton her shorts, and then eased the zipper down.

He brought his lips to her ear as he ran a finger up and down the lacy black underwear. "You're so damn sexy, I can hardly stand it." He dipped his tongue in her ear and then nipped at her lobe. "Every time I'm near you I want to throw you over my shoulder and take you. I want to take you until neither one of us can walk straight."

"My fantasy." She laughed, soft and husky. "Being thrown over a desperado's shoulder and taken away to be ravished."

"Desperado, huh?" Zack watched her react to his voice, then kissed her smile. He slipped his fingers beneath her underwear to tease the curls just within his touch.

"Sí, señor." She squirmed as she moved her hand to the bulge in his pants. "What's your fantasy?"

"You. And those garters." Zack's voice caught at the memory. "Damn, but you looked so hot." He trailed kisses down her neck. "You're hot in anything. And nothing."

Zack drew away and smiled when she gave him a pout of protest. He played with the button of her shorts. "I want you to lift your hips a little if you can do it without hurting your ankle."

She gave a sexy smile. "What hurt ankle?" she said as she rose up and then helped him push the shorts down to her knees.

Zack lifted his head to look at Sky's almost naked form in his lap. She was so beautiful he could hardly stand it. Only a scrap of black lace panties covered her.

He stroked his thumb along the warm center of her panties, his cock hardening more just by feeling how damp they were. Moaning, she moved against his hand. He hooked a finger under the waistband as she lifted her hips, and he drew her panties down until they rode across her legs, above her shorts.

Trailing his hand along the inside of her leg, he groaned at the sight of the triangle of copper curls. His fingers glided into the hair and he cupped her mound with his palm.

"I can't wait anymore." She brought her hand to his chest and slipped it inside his shirt. "I *need* you inside me."

Goddamn, the way she said it made him hot.

Zack studied Sky's face intensely and she bit her lip as his fingers penetrated her soft, slick folds. She was so wet, so ready. Her eyes widened as he slid two fingers into her hot core. He thrust them in and out, just like he'd love to be doing right at that moment, driving his hard cock inside her.

"Zack, *please.*"

"I want you to come for me, sweetheart," he murmured as his fingers moved to her clit.

She gasped and arched her back as he caressed her, crying out when his mouth captured her nipple again. He flicked his tongue over it and then the other. At the same time, his fingers coaxed her, urging her to climax.

When Sky tensed in his arms and Zack knew she was going to climax, he lifted his head and watched her face. Her lips were parted, her lids lowered, her gaze fixed on him.

With a shudder and a soft cry, she came. He continued stroking her, not letting up until she cried out that she couldn't take any more.

When the last golden wave of Sky's orgasm subsided, she realized that Zack was watching her with such an intense expression it made her shiver. He rested his palm on her belly but made no move to go any further.

It felt incredibly erotic with his jeans against her naked backside, her T-shirt up over her breasts. Her lips felt soft and swollen from his kisses and every part of her body tingled.

Zack looked so good, so sexy with his dark hair ruffled from her fingers, his gray eyes smoldering. Her nipples puckered as his gaze swept over her seminaked body and back to her face.

Sky caressed his cheek that wasn't bruised, his stubble rough against her palm. "Aren't you going to take me to the bedroom?"

"Mmmm." Zack kissed her, soft and sweet this time, his mouth gentle, his earthy smell surrounding her.

His lips traveled to her sensitive breasts and she moaned as his warm breath fanned over them. But instead of devouring her again, he pulled her bra up over her breasts and then tugged down her T-shirt.

"What are you doing?" She was still dazed from her orgasm and had no idea why he was covering her up.

She wanted his cock inside her so bad—the touch of his hands and mouth on her and that incredible orgasm had only whetted her desire. For a moment she tried to think of how they could manage it with her injured ankle.

Zack pulled her panties up, his touch sending shivers through her. He made her lift her hips as he did the same with her shorts. Then he brought the zipper up and buttoned them.

"What—" When she tried to sit, he only cradled her closer to his chest. She was frowning. "Why are you stopping?"

Zack's expression became serious. "Before we go any further, there's something I want first."

Sky stared at him in disbelief. She had just been about to give it all to him. "What?" she asked, feeling a bit wary.

He eased his fingers into the hair at her temple and stroked it away from her face. "I want you to be mine again. Exclusively."

She blinked. After all he'd put her through in the past he was asking her this? She shook her head. "Not happening."

Gently, he cupped her face, but she wasn't fooled by his calm. She could feel the tension in his body. "Start over with me."

Sky lowered her eyes, afraid that if she kept looking into that intense gray gaze she wouldn't be able to say no. But she couldn't allow him into her heart again. Couldn't afford to trust him that much.

As she remained silent, he shifted her in his lap so that she was sitting rather than cradled in his arms. "I'm not going to give up, Sky. I'll keep after you for as long as it takes to make you mine again."

Then he smiled like a man who had already divided and conquered.

Chapter 13

As Sky remained silent, Zack said in a low voice, "No matter what you think, I'm not giving up on us." He pressed his lips to her forehead, kissing her softly.

She still said nothing but relaxed more fully against his chest, her head resting over his heart.

"Hungry?" he asked as he nuzzled her hair. "If you've got the makings in the fridge I can throw together a sandwich."

"I could use something." She met his gaze. "Since I didn't get what I was really hungry for."

The corner of his mouth quirked. "*That's* all up to you, sweetheart."

"Humph," she said, and he gave a pain-filled smile as he carefully moved her ass off his still rigid jean-covered cock and eased her onto the couch.

He'd just gotten to his feet and had Sky's foot propped on the hassock when his cell rang.

Zack whipped the phone out of its clip on his belt. He wasn't surprised the display said "Unknown."

As he walked toward Sky's kitchen, he answered, "Hunter."

"Clay Wayland here," a deep voice said. "Returning your call."

"Sheriff," Zack replied as he looked back at Sky, who cocked her head with an interested expression on her features. "I called to see how your investigation was going on the missing MacKenna cattle."

"I understand you're with Immigration and Customs Enforcement." Wayland's tone was even as he spoke. "What's ICE's interest in rustling?"

"These rustlers might be transporting the cattle across the line into Mexico, which puts it right under our jurisdiction." Zack turned his back on Sky and went into the kitchen. "I'm assigned to the case. I'd like to see if we can work together to make some headway on this situation."

Wayland filled Zack in on what he knew and his own theories. He mentioned he'd had a similar discussion with Luke Rider.

"Do you trust the man?" Zack said in a low voice so that Sky wasn't likely to hear.

"You know as well as I do that in law enforcement you hold some of the cards close to your chest," Wayland said. "I have a feeling Rider's doing the same thing."

"Something about the man strikes me as off." Zack walked farther into the kitchen, away from Sky. "He's holding back more than a few cards."

"I cover my bases," Wayland said in a slow drawl. "And my ass."

"Smart man," Zack said. He imagined he was also being checked out by Wayland while the sheriff was looking into Rider's background.

After he ended the call with the sheriff, Zack opened the fridge and pulled out whole wheat bread, ham, tomatoes, lettuce, mayo, and mustard. "You ready for that sandwich?" he called out to Sky.

"Sure."

As he threw together their lunch, he asked, "How about some of that iced tea you've got in the fridge? And maybe a couple of ibuprofen to go with it?"

She gave a soft groan. "Make that a double on the meds."

When Zack was finished, he picked up the paper plates filled with thick ham sandwiches and barbeque potato chips he'd grabbed out of the pantry. He carried them to the living room and handed Sky her plate while setting his own on the ironwood coffee table. After he retrieved the pain reliever, paper cups of tea, and paper towels to use for napkins, he sat at the opposite end of the couch.

"So what was that call all about?" Sky asked in between bites of her sandwich. "Why were you discussing the rustling situation?"

"I'm going to meet with Wayland on Monday," Zack said. "Got a couple of notions that I'd like to discuss with him." He crunched a potato chip before he spoke again. "Wayland mentioned someone went after your bull, before the dance."

"Yeah, that's what it looked like." Sky gave a scowl.

Zack went into his theories with her and she listened intently while eating her sandwich and drinking her iced tea.

When he finished, Sky said, "I can see the rustlers slaughtering the cattle they've been stealing." She shook her head. "But I bought Satan at top dollar to help build my herd and my ranch's reputation, and now someone's trying to take him. And for what? Hamburger? Not likely."

Sky set her plate down on an ironwood end table and crossed her arms over her chest. "I think they want him because he's valuable," she continued. "Of course Satan's registered with the American Angus Association. His pedigreed name is Black Ice Hellfire's Satan. He's the offspring of Black Ice on High Lonesome and Donovan's Apache Tears from Flagstaff—one hell of a match." She shook her head and uncrossed her arms. "But Satan's not worth a damn thing if the thieves don't have his pedigree papers.

"Oh, shit." Her jaw dropped and it felt like an icy wind rushed over her. "Maybe—maybe that was why Blue was poisoned, so someone could get by him and into the barn office. That's where I keep all the pedigrees."

Zack focused his attention on Sky, his eyes now gunmetal gray.

Sky felt like she was babbling as a sort of jitteriness took hold of her. "I'm usually in and out of the office during the weekdays, but what with Blue getting sick, going to the dance, twisting my ankle, the cattle rustling—" Christ, the past two days all she'd been able to do was think about Zack and the dance. "I've been preoccupied." She glanced down at her ankle. "This week I never had a chance to make it into the office.

"That's why they might have tried to take Satan Friday night," she went on. "If they have his papers . . ." She forced herself to release her clenched fists. "God, I hope I'm wrong and the office wasn't hit the night Blue was poisoned. Like I said, too much has happened this week and I just didn't make it to the office."

Zack had a grim expression. "We need to check it out just in case you're right."

Sky tried to push herself up by bringing her injured foot off the hassock and onto the floor.

"No, you don't." Zack's big hand caught her around her upper arm. "Whether you like it or not, I'm going to help you so you don't hurt that ankle any worse than you already have."

"Oh." She hadn't been thinking clearly. As bad as her ankle was, she couldn't climb down the stairs without a little help, even with her crutches.

While he grabbed her crutches, her heart pounded. Had someone been in her office? Taken anything that was valuable to her?

"Hey," she said as he lifted her into his arms while she held on to her crutches with one hand. "I just need help down. You don't need to carry me."

"Shut up and enjoy the ride."

"Yeah. Enjoy the ride," she said as she pictured her office.

He got her down the steps before resting her on the ground on her good foot and helping her balance on her crutches. She made her way to the barn as fast as the crutches allowed her to, gritting her teeth as she moved.

The usual smells of hay, sweet oats, dust, and manure hit her as soon as she stood inside the doorway. Her horses whickered on their side of the barn and Satan bawled on his. Sky let her eyes adjust to the shadowed barn before Zack supported her the rest of the way on to the hard-packed earth floor.

When they reached the office door, Sky felt a hint of relief when she tried the antique brass doorknob and found it locked. "I've got a key hidden nearby," she said as she pointed toward an old U.S. Cavalry feed bag hanging from a rusted meat hook, next to several other antique items she kept tacked to the wall by the office. "No one knows about it."

"Anyone else have access?" Zack said as he helped her balance while she dug into the bottom of the feed bag.

"Just Luke." She clasped her hand around the key in seconds and Zack got her back to the office door.

Zack took the key from her, inserted it, and twisted the knob. He pushed the heavy oak door open on its well-oiled hinges.

Her heart took a nosedive at the same time his voice dropped, anger inflected in every word. "Looks like you've had a visitor."

"No." Sky felt like ants crawled up and down her spine as she grabbed the door frame and looked inside. "Oh no."

As always the rich oak-paneled room smelled of lemon oil that she used on the solid oak desk that had been around since the days of the Old West. The office also smelled of leather from the oxblood brown overstuffed leather couch and chairs, as well as halters and saddles hanging in the back.

Sky could barely process what she was seeing. Instead of the clean, well-cared-for office, the place was a disaster. The computer's flat-screen monitor lay facedown on the glossy surface of the desk. Broken glass from the family photos glittered in the dim light. Paper was scattered over every surface from the coffee table to the floor.

She cut her gaze to the huge metal file cabinets that were normally locked and closed—only now every single drawer was open and folders were tossed everywhere.

"Christ." The word came out like an explosion from Zack. He wrapped his hand around Sky's upper arm and held her back when she tried to enter the room. "Don't touch anything. We've got to call this in and have the county sheriff's office dust the place for fingerprints and check for any clues the bastard may have left behind."

Zack withdrew his cell phone from its clip on his belt with his free hand. Sky felt almost dizzy from the shock of the violation.

She held her palm to her queasy stomach and eased back on her crutches, out of the doorway.

She barely heard Zack's voice as he got through to Sheriff Wayland and rattled off the information with unemotional professionalism.

After he'd fed the sheriff what little information they knew right now, Zack reholstered his phone and released his hold on Sky to wrap his arm around her shoulders. "Let's take you inside the house."

"No, Zack." Sky tried to shake him off. "This is my property the sonofabitch destroyed. And I want to know what he's taken."

Zack studied her for one long moment with narrowed eyes and his lips drawn tight. "All right," he finally said, "but we're going to get you off your feet."

He guided her toward several bales of alfalfa and she didn't protest. Her ankle throbbed and the pounding in her head began to match the tempo.

When they reached a hay bale, he grabbed a clean saddle pad out of a large trunk and stretched it out on a bale. She let him help arrange her so that her leg with the injured ankle was resting on the pad covering the bale. Her ankle screamed with pain and her eyes watered. She definitely could use some of the pain reliever the ER doc had prescribed. Too bad she hadn't had the prescription filled.

The smell of the fresh alfalfa was strong as she stared into Satan's stall, where thankfully the bull was still tethered. The yearling was too difficult to control and had bashed the stall door open three or four times, so they'd been forced to tether him. The thick nylon rope was long enough for him to be comfortable to sleep, eat, drink, and move around but short enough to keep him from slamming his head into the stall door and maybe even hurting himself.

His eyes flashed like black diamonds in the barn's low lighting as he stared at her. He bawled, probably ready for his feed. It was right about the time she fed the barn stock. The hands took care of the rest of the ranch.

Sky called Luke on her cell and he was at the barn in no time. The man's expression was virtually unreadable as she spelled everything out, but he gave off such an intense aura of anger that it almost made her shrink back from him.

Luke got on his cell and called in every ranch hand to be questioned once the sheriff and his deputies arrived.

It wasn't long before Sheriff Wayland, Gary Woods, and three other deputies made it to the ranch. They wore the traditional county sheriff department's tan uniforms, tan felt western hats, and boots. Thick belts held their guns along with other things—pepper spray, she supposed, and extra rounds. Batons, handcuffs, cell phones, and radio microphones were clipped to their shoulders.

Sky had been introduced to Clay Wayland, the new sheriff, not too long ago. He had crystalline green eyes, sable hair and mustache, and was built like a quarterback. Broad shoulders and a powerful frame, but lean and athletic.

Of course she knew Gary fairly well. She'd also run into the young and dark-haired Deputy Quinn two or three times. He reminded her of a currently popular country-western star out of Nashville.

The other two men she'd never met. Deputy Blalock was blond, thin, wiry, and sported a goatee. Deputy Garrison blinked a whole lot, like he wore contacts that were bothering him, and had a small paunch that rolled over the top of his uniform pants.

"Why do you need so many deputies for one little break-in, Sheriff?" Sky asked after she'd been introduced to the deputies.

"Call me Clay." The sheriff dragged his hand over his mustache before he answered. His green eyes turned almost jade in color. "There have been a couple of similar occurrences and we're working to determine whether or not the rustlings and burglaries are related or separate issues."

Garrison and Blalock set to fingerprinting the office and searching the scene for other evidence while Quinn took photos.

Gary Woods and Sheriff Wayland interviewed everyone at the ranch to find out if they saw or heard anything, and to find out where everyone was during the time they thought the break-in had occurred.

Sky thought she was going to go out of her mind while she waited for the men to be done in her office so that she could see what was missing.

When her back started to ache and her ankle throbbed, she leaned against the hay bale behind her. The alfalfa at her back pricked her through her T-shirt and a light coat of perspiration from the late-summer heat made her whole body feel sticky. She wanted a shower in the worst way.

Grouchy, hungry, and thirsty, Sky decided she was going to get up despite the blaring pain in her ankle. According to the time on her cell phone, over an hour had passed since the sheriff and his men had arrived.

Just as she started to swing her leg from on top of the bale and onto the ground, Zack took her by complete surprise when he showed up with a thermos of lemonade and a paper sack.

"Figured the guys might be hungry," he said as he set the jug and sack on the bale. Turned out the sack was filled with more ham sandwiches. He'd also brought out of the house enough plastic cups and plates to go around. "Only took me fifteen minutes to throw this together, so don't expect anything special."

Zack handed her a filled cup. After she drained her icy cold lemonade she gave a satisfied sigh. "You might be worth keeping around," she said before she knew what she was saying.

Zack's dangerous smile had her biting the inside of her cheek. She looked away and looked toward her office.

Damn the man.

After the sheriff and his deputies were finished with their interviews, and had arranged for everyone to go to the station to be printed, they gathered around where Sky was seated.

"Found quite a few prints," Blalock said. "We'll need to compare them to yours, Ms. MacKenna, to weed them out from potential suspects."

"Didn't see anything else too unusual." Quinn held up a plastic bag containing a chunk of yellow dirt. "But we'll check out this clump we picked up near the doorway."

"Doesn't match the soil around here," Zack said as he studied it. "Yellow instead of reddish brown."

The sheriff launched into a discussion about the intruder in the barn Friday night and how he figured the two had to be related.

The men enthusiastically chowed down on their sandwiches and drank their cups of lemonade. Outside it had turned dark, and a cooler breeze swept in from one end of the barn to another.

It was Sky's turn to figure out if anything had been stolen. Zack handed the crutches to her before she went into the room.

Her stomach turned at the sight of the wrecked office. At the same time, anger rose up in her so fast her ears burned. Whoever did this was so going to pay. She'd make darn sure they did once they were caught.

Payroll and accounting pages had been tossed on the floor along with other ranch records dating back to her great-grandfather's time. The old papers had been kept in leather-bound binders and had always meant a lot to her. "I should have put these in a bank safe," she said as she carefully scooped the papers into a pile.

For some reason she'd been saving looking at her pedigree papers for last—maybe because she already knew what she'd find.

"Yeah, Satan's are gone." Her throat ached as she rifled through the file folders and she had the sudden urge to cry. "The papers for my thoroughbred Quarter Horses, too." God, this was all too much. She looked at Zack. "Why did they take those papers? Are they going to start going after my Quarter Horse breeding stock, too?"

"I don't know." Zack gripped the edge of her file cabinet drawer. "The way your ranch's old records were shredded—that wasn't just theft or vandalism. That was deliberate."

Zack slammed his palm on the filing cabinet that gave a hollow ring. "And it was personal."

Chapter 14

Monday, the afternoon following the discovery of the break-in, Sky frowned as she sat behind the ancient desk in the ranch's office. Her crutches leaned against one of the oak-paneled walls and Blue had taken up vigil next to the office's open door.

On the desktop, next to an egg salad sandwich, she had a chilled plastic bottle of water sitting on a coaster made from old bottle glass. After finding the office ransacked, she was making sure she had her S&W with her. It was in the small holster at the side of her denim shorts beneath a shirt she'd left untucked.

If it weren't for her ankle, she'd be off riding on her property in the afternoon sunshine. Whenever she needed to escape, she took off with Empress and Blue after filling the saddlebags with lunch and treats for her and the horse and dog. They'd head out at a gallop. Sky would feel the teasing play of the wind whipping her hair, the power of the Quarter Horse beneath her, the freedom of riding across the range.

But no. Not only did she have to worry about her ankle, she had things to attend to.

Like this whole freaking mess.

Normally the scents of lemon oil and citrus air freshener made the office brighter, cheerier. Today some kind of dark smell seemed to hang over everything. Like the invasion had tainted the room.

The leather chair springs squeaked as she twisted a little to the side—an action she immediately regretted from the renewed throbbing in her ankle. She bit her lip, then sucked in her breath. She had some painkillers in the first-aid kit in the office's bathroom. Unfortunately that meant getting up and she didn't feel up to it.

God, she felt so violated from the break-in. It tore at her insides like a garden rake to see so much of the ranch's past reduced to piles of shredded pages and broken artifacts that included a hundred-year-old kerosene lantern and a collection of Apache arrowheads that had been discovered right on the Flying M Ranch.

She picked up the framed portrait of her mother, Nina MacKenna, taken when Nina had been so vibrant and alive. She'd had a full, round face and rounded curves, and a smile that had always made Sky feel like everything was going to be okay.

Until the End.

Sky brushed the back of one hand over her eyes. The photo was nearly destroyed the way the glass had been smashed.

Zack was right—this had been personal.

Who the hell did I piss off?

"If I knew I'd *so* kick their asses," she said in such a sharp tone that Blue raised his head and looked at her.

Did this have anything to do with the rustling?

Sky had never been one for too many tears, but she found herself fighting them back. She smoothed her fingertips over the worn and now-destroyed binding that had held ranch records from the late 1800s. Detailed income and expense reports had been kept in the ledgers. Her great-great-grandfather had handwritten purchases and sales of livestock, equipment, and feed, as well as breeding records and pedigrees.

In the 1990s, Sky had convinced her father to start using computers, and eventually they didn't keep any handwritten or manually typed records. With her urging, they'd constantly updated the computer software the ranch used as well as their hardware.

The computer monitor drew her attention. Its cracked LCD screen made her want to flinch and clench her hands. She didn't want to damage the papers she was holding, so she kept her grip relaxed.

With a sigh she twirled the end of her long braid with one finger. She glanced down at the Scotch tape dispenser beside one of her hands, and at the page she'd been attempting to put back together.

"It's hopeless," she whispered, then shook her head and released her braid. "No. The pages won't ever be the same, but I'm not going to simply throw a part of my family's history into the garbage."

Sky looked at the monitor again. She'd have to purchase a new one and update their cattle records to show the loss. They wouldn't know until roundup exactly which cattle were missing.

Her Black Angus herd had been over three hundred strong before this mess started. The ranch hands had a fair idea, though, of several that had been taken. You couldn't be around cattle for a significant amount of time without recognizing a good portion of them.

Damn, damn, damn! Every loss was like a punch. Not only was it a violation, but it would affect the ranch's revenues for the year and would impact every year for some time.

She'd already contacted the USDA inspector along with the American Angus Association. If any of her registered breeding stock showed up or if another rancher tried to register them, she'd be notified at once.

Blue gave a sharp bark that startled Sky into almost knocking over her water. The dog bolted out the office door as he continued barking and her heart started pounding. She wasn't expecting company, but it wasn't uncommon for a neighbor to stop by. The thrum of her heart had to be nerves from all that had been happening.

Blue stopped barking at the same time she heard the sound of a powerful truck engine. The dog's quieting was a good sign it was someone he recognized. Tires crunched the driveway's pebbled dirt before a vehicle came to a stop and the engine cut off.

Sky wheeled her chair over the polished wood floor, closer to the window, and winced as she bumped her ankle. She peered through the red-and-white-checked gingham curtains.

Zack.

The curtain slipped from her fingers as she sucked in her breath and her heart pounded for a different reason. She moved away from the window, placed her palms flat on the desktop, and released her breath in a slow exhale. She felt that telltale tingling in her belly and the pleasure warming her because Zack was here.

Before he could come in and catch her looking unnerved, she

picked up the tape dispenser and stared at the yellowed page she'd been trying to put back together. Only problem was that she was looking at the pieces without seeing them, her senses on fire while she waited for Zack to find her.

It didn't take him long. Blue apparently led Zack straight to the office.

Sky took another deep breath and looked up when she heard the thump of boots on the office floor. Zack stopped in the doorway, hitched his shoulder against the door frame, and shoved his hands in his front pockets as he looked at her from beneath his black Stetson.

His powerful presence never failed to make her heart pound. The bruise on his cheekbone and his black eye didn't distract from his rugged features and the steel gray of his eyes. She could never get enough of the way his T-shirt and Wrangler jeans fit his body the same way she wanted to wrap herself around him.

Blue stood beside Zack's legs, panting slightly, and looking pleased with himself.

"Zack. Why are you here?" she asked, trying to keep her voice casual.

He glanced at her crutches, then back to her. "You shouldn't be out running around."

"Oh, brother." She set down the tape dispenser and rolled her eyes to the open-beamed ceiling before meeting his eyes again. "I'm fine."

"Like hell." He moved from the doorway, placed his palms on her desk, and leaned close. He smelled of sun-warmed skin and mint, a heady combination that sent her senses reeling. "Do I have to tie you to your bed to keep you off that damn ankle?"

There was a thought that made her blood warm in her veins. Zack tying her to the bedpost. Naked.

Heat flushed through her and she raised her chin. "You didn't answer my question, Zack. Why are you here?"

His face was so close she wanted him to kiss her. Then take her. Right there on her desk.

Down, girl.

"Satan." Zack's voice was low, drawing her back from her fantasies. His eyes focused on her mouth, but then his gaze met hers. "Figured you might need some help taming the little shit."

Sky swallowed, ready to pounce on him from lust. "I can manage."

"Uh-huh." He pushed away and stood, and air rushed back into her lungs. "When are you going to figure out it's all right to ask for help when you need it?"

She flipped her braid over her shoulder. "I don't need your help."

"One thing hasn't changed." His look was dark and assessing. "You're still stubborn."

She snorted. "Says the jackass."

The corner of his mouth quirked, but then his expression went serious. "I'm concerned about what's going on around here—the break-in, the rustling." He jerked his thumb to the mountains behind the ranch. "Do you have any idea how much narcotics trafficking goes through that range? How many undocumented aliens are smuggled across all the ranches?" He raked a hand through his dark hair. "Damnit, but I don't like you being here alone."

Sky frowned. "What do you want me to do? Pack my bags and just leave everything?" She waved a hand toward the bunkhouse and corrals. "This is my livelihood. This is the way those cowboys make their living. You can't just expect me to turn my back on it."

His jaw visibly tightened. "You don't seem too concerned about your safety."

"I'm plenty concerned." A sigh left her in a rush. "And not just for myself—for all the other ranchers and folks who live in these parts. But all I can do is take it a day at a time and hope the law handles the problem."

He nodded, but his expression remained tense.

Zack grabbed her crutches from where they rested against a wall. The now-familiar possessive feeling gripped him as he helped her out of her chair. As she arranged her crutches he kept one hand on her for support. She paused and he heard her catch her breath when he nuzzled her hair to take in her scent of orange blossoms and summer storms.

He could almost feel her relax when he released her and she used her crutches to hobble to the door.

"Watch your step," she said when they exited the office and entered the barn. "One of the ranch hands did everything but rake the manure in the aisle and muck out the stalls. Another hand will take care of it before nightfall."

Blue followed them out into the barn, trotting at Sky's side as if protecting her.

The sorrel stuck her head over her gate and whinnied. On an alfalfa bale Zack stretched out another horse pad from the large trunk. He helped Sky sit on the bale. Her hands slid away from his arms, the light brush of her fingers making him hotter than Arizona in July.

Blue parked himself at Sky's feet and the border collie stared at the yearling's stall.

Sky turned her gaze from Zack and also looked at the stall where the bull glared through the slats. "The brat only lets me get close."

"Can't say that I blame him," Zack murmured.

Sky acted like she hadn't heard. "Satan goes berserk if Luke or one of the ranch hands tries to go near him."

Zack shook his head at the memory of Sky on her ass with her blouse half-undone. "If you have any control over him, what do you call what I walked in on last week?"

She raised an eyebrow, a slight smile on her lips. "Gonna try to handcuff him again?"

"Only as a last resort." Zack went to the rusted and scarred fifty-gallon drum where the sweet oats had been kept back when he'd dated Sky.

When he lifted the lid, the scent of molasses, corn, oats, and barley rose up to mingle with the dust, straw, and manure smells of the barn. Using the tin can inside, he scooped out some of the cob feed, closed the barrel, and returned to Satan's stall. The bull was the same color of black as the stones called Apache tears, his coat smooth and sleek.

"He's a beaut." Avoiding fresh horse droppings scattered in front of the stall, Zack crouched and set down the can of oats. He eyed the yearling, then glanced back at Sky. "How long have you had him?"

"Little over a month. I bought him from a rancher up north. Like I told you, he's champion stock." She shook her head and smiled. "Right now he's a champion pain-in-the-ass."

"If this guy gets much bigger before you gentle him, he's going to do more than knock you on your butt." The image of the bull hurting Sky was enough to make Zack's muscles tense and his jaw tighten.

Sky leaned back, bracing her hands on the hay bale at both sides of her hips. The movement caused her breasts to rise and her buttoned shirt to gape, exposing black lace.

All thoughts of the bull left Zack's mind as a vivid fantasy came to him. Sitting on the bale with Sky on his lap. Her wearing nothing but that black lace bra and a pair of garters. Her head tilted, eyes closed, copper hair falling over her shoulders. Him thrusting into her core and her riding him hard and fast.

"I just need to spend more time with him," Sky was saying, her husky voice breaking into the erotic video running through Zack's mind.

"Ah, yeah." He barely reined in a groan as he turned his attention back to the bull.

Sky was killing him. She wasn't aware of how erotic she looked spread out before him. And he would have taken her up on the invitation except that he had said he would help her with this damn bull. If he didn't, she would try to do it herself. The thought of the bull doing damage to Sky was enough to sober his lust.

Stubborn woman. But she was his woman and he'd do what he had to do to protect her, even if it meant spending every afternoon with this beast.

He spoke to Satan in a low, soothing tone, trying to get the yearling used to him and the sound of his voice. Satan butted the side of the enclosure, his eyes blazing. His tether wouldn't allow him to come all the way up to the stall's door. But he was close enough that when he snorted he splattered snot on the back of Zack's hand. Sky snickered.

Zack wiped the snot on his jeans while he continued to talk nonsense. When the bull had calmed a bit, Zack stood and located the bull's halter.

The Border Collie took position nearby, no doubt his herding instincts kicking in.

Zack tied the end to the stall, then lowered the halter onto Satan's head. The bull's eyes bulged. He fought and tugged, throwing his weight from side to side. It was a good ten minutes before he finally settled down. His sides rose and fell like a pair of bellows stoking a fire, a wild glint still in his eyes.

"You and I are going to be good friends," Zack said to the yearling, and then glanced over his shoulder at Sky. "No matter what you might think."

She frowned at the bull, her hand moving to her throat. "You're asking the impossible."

"Nah." He turned and unlatched the gate, then eased it open. "If there's one thing I've learned since I met you, sweetheart, it's that nothing's impossible."

"You always did have a large dose of overconfidence," Sky muttered.

Zack picked up the can of feed and entered the stall, moving slow and easy. He reached into the can for a handful and held his palm under the bull's nose. Satan's eyes glittered, his body seemed to swell, and he craned his neck.

As Zack started to step back, his boot slipped on a pile of

manure. At the same time, Satan rammed his thigh and a hard throb of pain shot through Zack's leg.

The feed can flew out of his hand as he lost his balance. He fell back, landing hard on his ass. The cob feed scattered, the tin can rattling across the ground.

Blue moved closer to the bull, obviously ready to jump into action if he needed to.

Zack heard more laughter behind him as he sat on his stinging ass.

"So much for friends," Sky said.

Zack glanced over his shoulder and saw she wasn't even trying to keep a straight face. "I'm not done by a long shot."

Sky continued to grin. "Spoken like a man who doesn't know when to quit."

"Got that right." He went to brace his hand on the ground, only to have his palm land in something cold and squishy with an unpleasant smell. "Ah, shit."

"Um, it sure is. Are you all right?" Sky asked between giggles.

He looked up and gave her a wry smile. "Nothing a shower won't cure."

She jerked her thumb south. "Just past Dancer's stall there's a sink and a bar of soap."

Blue continued his vigil while Zack washed his hands. When he returned from the sink, he spent another hour with the bull, determined to make some headway in their relationship. He ended up with a couple more bruises than the one on his thigh and the ones on his face from the fistfight, but he still got a kick out of working with Satan. Literally.

Every so often he'd glance at Sky and catch her watching him with expressions ranging from amusement, to concern, to frustration.

And yes, longing, too. But she was trying to bury that longing, trying to deny it even after their explosive, all too brief encounters. She was too scared to do anything else.

Ah, hell. He'd hurt her bad all those years ago, but he wasn't going to hurt her again. He'd make her see that and he'd have her trust again. There was no other alternative.

For now, he was concerned she'd try to tame this damn bull on her own and end up with more than an injured ankle.

After he worked with Satan, Zack mucked out the stalls and raked manure out of the aisle, despite Sky's protests. She'd started to get up to help him, and he'd threatened to turn her over his knee.

That shut her up.

Immediate erotic images came to Sky's mind—Zack's threat kinda turned her on.

More than kind of, MacKenna, she admitted to herself as she watched the powerful play of his muscles. He had shucked his shirt a while ago and she had immediately gone breathless and her panties had dampened at the sight. She figured Zack knew just what he was doing, deliberately putting on a show for her. Letting her get a good, long look at what could be under her hands and between her thighs—again.

Sky tore her gaze away before she came just from watching him. She shifted on her bale of hay, trying to relieve some of the ache in her pussy.

"Bastard," she muttered under her breath, and thought she heard him give a low chuckle.

When Zack was finished, Sky was already up and on her crutches. He helped her climb the steps to the front door and grabbed the door handle. "I want you to promise me something," he said.

A wary feeling came over her. "Depends."

He opened the door and Blue slipped inside the house.

"Don't mess with Satan until your ankle's better. Give it a good week."

Sky rolled her eyes again. "You're kidding, right?"

When he got her inside, Zack helped her sit on the leather couch so that she was comfortable and then he sat and moved close enough that their bodies nearly touched. Sky felt a jittery sense of panic rising up inside her.

"I'm dead serious." He held her gaze with his. "That bull is a strong bastard, and he's liable to knock the shit out of you. He could do some real damage."

Sky shook her head. "But—"

"No buts. If I have to tie you to your bed, I will."

Sky felt a rush of moisture between her thighs. *Please,* she wanted to beg him. But instead she gritted her teeth and told her hormones to shut the hell up.

"I can't ignore Satan for a week." Sky shifted on the couch and raised her chin. "That would undo what progress has been made with him."

Zack scrubbed his hand over his stubbled jaw. "I'll come over every day after work."

Sky blinked. "I—that's not necessary."

"I start early and my day usually ends in the late afternoon." Zack stroked her leg, causing a twisting sensation in her belly as he added, "I may not make it until later, depending on how things go. But I'll be here."

Another volley of protests pinged through her. Before she could say another word, Zack put his hand over her mouth. His fingers felt rough against her lips and he gave a low groan.

Her eyes widened as he moved his hand to her opposite hip, caging her, and he leaned close enough that their lips were barely apart.

Chapter 15

"Zack," Sky whispered as her heart pounded and her nipples ached to be touched by him. To be licked and sucked before he moved farther down until his mouth was on her folds.

"Just a kiss," he seemed to be saying to himself before he brushed his lips over hers.

"You can't do that to me again." She slid her hands into his hair and pushed off his western hat as he kissed the corner of her mouth. The hat tumbled to the floor, where it gave a soft thud. "I need more."

Zack nipped her earlobe and she clenched her fists in his hair and arched her back. "You know what I want," he said in a low rumble that sent thrills through her despite her instant mental rejection of his condition on their relationship. He palmed her breast with his warm hand and pinched her nipple. "I want everything again, Sky."

She went still as Zack glided his lips toward hers and he repeated the same words he'd said yesterday. "Start over with me."

It took all she had to move her hands to his chest and push

him away. She had a hard time getting the one word out as their eyes met. "No."

Zack looked at her for a long moment before brushing his knuckles across her cheek. "I'll wait for you to say the words." He trailed his fingers over her lips, "But you're already mine."

Damnit. She pushed harder against his chest. "We're not going there, Zack. How many times do I have to tell you that it's not happening?"

He drew away from her but clasped one of her hands in his. It felt strangely more intimate than any touch he could have made at that moment. He squeezed her hand and smiled. "Too late for that, sweetheart."

A knock at the door startled her and she pulled her hand from Zack's.

"Yo, Skylar?" Luke's voice said from behind the closed door.

"Come on in," she said as she tried to separate herself a little more from Zack.

Zack got to his feet, scooped up his hat, and was standing face-to-face with Luke when the man walked through the doorway.

Sky pushed her braid over her shoulder as she tried to get her mind off of what just happened between her and Zack. "What's up?"

Luke glanced from Sky to Zack, his expression intensifying into a frown. "The fence was cut along the north pasture and another dozen Angus are missing. Your herd's down to two-thirds in size."

Sky put her fingertips to her forehead, as if it would force away Luke's words. She felt all energy drain from her body at the news. "We can't afford this," she said as she rubbed her temples. "And we certainly can't afford to post twenty-four-hour guards around the entire perimeter of a couple thousand acres."

"Found these where the fence was down." Luke reached into a back pocket and pulled out a plastic bag with a pair of wire cutters that had a red nubbly rubber grip.

"Let me have a look." Zack held out his palm and took the bagged tool from Luke. "Damn, with this kind of grip, our labs couldn't begin to get a print," Zack said. "Unless he touched the metal. But most men who know how to cut fences use work gloves."

Luke nodded, his mouth drawn in a taut line. "My thoughts, too."

"Pretty common make and obviously used regularly," Zack said. "The rust indicates the man doesn't take real good care of his equipment—apparently leaves his tools out in the weather rather than putting them away." Zack turned the cutters in the plastic bag and examined the blade. "By the wear on this, I'd guess he's right-handed."

"Or she," Sky interrupted. When Zack turned his gaze to her, she gave a halfhearted smile. "Hey, I believe in equal-opportunity rustlers, too."

"Could be." Zack gave her a little smile in return before he turned back to Luke. "I'll take these pliers in," Zack said. "I remember seeing Wade Larson using a pair like this to fix his fence a few days ago."

Sky frowned. Wade had told her how much he cared for her when he tried to kiss her after the dance. Even if she had told him she never wanted to see him or Zack again, she couldn't imagine Wade doing something like this.

"Wade wouldn't be involved with the cattle disappearing," she said. "He's pushy and outspoken, but he's just not the kind of guy who would pull crap like that. Besides, the rustlers are swiping his cattle, too."

"I have to admit in the past I'd always known Larson to be an honest man, even if he is a sonofabitch," Zack said. "Anyone else having problems with these rustlers?"

Luke shook his head. "Only Larson, according to Sheriff Wayland." Luke hooked his thumbs through his belt loops. "The rustlers seem to go for Black Angus. Wade Larson's the only other rancher who's lost a few head, but nothing like Skylar."

Zack focused on Sky. "It could be a way of striking out at you for rejecting him."

Her cheeks burned at the fact that Zack had brought the subject up, and in front of Luke, too. "I already said I don't believe it's Wade. There are plenty of other people out there who could be suspects."

A thoughtful look crossed Luke's strong features as he said, "Some neighboring ranches have Angus, but most have Hereford and Brahma. None of the ranchers have reported any stock gone missing."

Leaning back on the couch, Sky propped her throbbing ankle on a hassock. "Maybe it's only a matter of time."

"You could be right," Zack said.

"I'd better head on out." Luke tipped his hat to Sky. "Got stock tanks to check."

After Luke was out of the house, Zack leaned over from where he was standing and brushed his lips across Sky's forehead. A faint shiver went through her. "I'll see you tomorrow."

* * *

The following morning, Tuesday, Sky watered the houseplants on her front porch, taking care not to bump her ankle as she tried to shove thoughts of Zack to the back of her mind. And failed.

The memory of every kiss, every touch, of him *being inside her,* caused her hand to tremble as she tipped the watering can. Water splashed off the spiked leaves of the spider plant and onto her blouse. She lowered the can and brushed the droplets off her breasts with her free hand, and lightly caressed her wet nipples. The material went transparent, showing her black lace bra and skin.

Sky smiled at the thought of what Zack would think if he saw her damp shirt, and then wanted to smack her forehead. She had to get over thinking about Zack that way, because she wasn't giving in.

Starting fresh with Zack. Yeah, right.

She limped on down the line of houseplants and showered the philodendron, the last plant at the farthest edge of the porch. Its green heart-shaped leaves reminded her of the gift Zack had given her their first and only Christmas together. The peridot heart pendant she'd tucked away all those years ago.

Stop thinking about him, MacKenna!

With a sigh, she set the watering can down on one of the plant-filled tables. She found a spot on the low porch wall that wasn't taken over by a houseplant, and eased onto it, taking care not to bump her ankle. Leaning against a pillar, she allowed herself to relax and enjoy the beauty around her for a few moments.

She had surrounded herself by beautiful living things that she could give love to and nurture. Things that couldn't reject her.

Couldn't leave her.

Wind chimes dangling from the porch's exposed beams made a musical tinkling sound as a light wind kicked up. The breeze teased loose strands of Sky's hair and cooled her breasts where the water had splashed, causing her nipples to harden like diamonds. Smells of rich soil and of fall just around the corner teased the air.

The sound of a horse's hooves brought Sky's attention to the front yard. A broad, imposing figure on an Appaloosa gelding was coming toward her home.

"Wade." Sky groaned. "What's he doing here?"

She gripped the edge of the low wall, clinging to it to keep her balance. Wade dismounted and looped the reins around the saddle horn. Her hold tightened on the wall.

He strode toward the porch, his walk purposeful. His eyes were hidden by his straw western hat until he met her gaze when he pushed the brim up.

"Skylar." He reached the top step and paused to peruse her wet blouse and the black lace bra showing beneath it. Desire was strong in his gaze when he looked at her. "How's your ankle?"

"Fine." She was relieved at his lack of commenting on her attributes, something he was prone to doing. "What can I do for you?"

Wade paused a moment. "I came to check in on you and see how you're doing with that bum ankle." He frowned and braced one hand on a porch railing. "But I expected a little warmer welcome."

She cocked her head to the side. "Even after I told you and Zack I didn't want to see either of you anymore?"

Wade's mouth tightened into a frown. "Did you really mean that?"

"At the time, yes." Sky gave a low sigh. "Now . . . I just want you to understand that there's nothing between us."

"It's Hunter," Wade stated as his frown turned into a scowl. "He dumped you, but you're just going to take him back when he shows up out of nowhere?"

A slow burn flushed over Sky. "Whether or not there's anything between me and Zack is none of your business."

Wade crossed his arms over his chest as he narrowed his gaze. "So that's it. You're screwing Hunter."

The burn in her body turned into fire. "I think you'd better leave."

"We had something, Skylar." Wade's gaze darkened even more. "You're going to throw that away because that sonofabitch is back?"

She curled her fingers, pressing her nails into the aging wood of the low wall of the balcony. "Leave."

Wade startled her by grasping one of her upper arms with his hand. "I care too damn much about you to see you hurt again."

His hold was tight enough that Sky felt a jerk in her gut, the fleeting thought that he might hurt her passing through her mind. "You've said enough for today," she said as she tried to pull away from his grasp.

He abruptly released her, causing her to falter on her perch and give her ankle a slight twist. Her eyes watered a little from the pain and she gritted her teeth.

"What's wrong?" Concern edged his words.

"My ankle is hurting like hell, and I've got to lie down." She could use a few glasses of wine. It was five o'clock somewhere.

He glanced at her bandaged ankle and back to her face. "Didn't realize you'd hurt yourself so badly."

"Yeah. Well. I did." She gritted her teeth as she pushed herself up and reached for her crutches.

He reached for her crutches, too. "Let me help you."

"I can take care of myself." She grasped her crutches and positioned them below her arms. "And that goes for everything else we've talked about."

"Skylar," he said in a rough voice as she turned away. "I'm sorry."

Sky grasped the door handle, then pushed the door open. "Too late for that, Wade." She looked at him over her shoulder as she paused at the threshold, letting her crutches bear her weight. "What you said was inexcusable."

The look on his face turned so dark she felt a harder twisting sensation in her belly.

He tugged down his hat, turned, strode down the stairs, and headed back to his horse.

Chapter 16

Tuesday, the afternoon following the too-brief intimate moment with Sky, Zack stood in his group supervisor's office. Zack barely held back a scowl as Denning went on one of his rampages.

Denning spit his chaw into the garbage can beside his desk before meeting Zack's gaze again. Denning's brown eyes were narrowed and his wiry, athletic body rigid.

He braced one hand on his desk and the other on his belt as he continued, "So tell me, why haven't you figured out how the goddamned smugglers are getting the cattle across the line?"

Zack sucked his breath in through his teeth and did his best to keep from telling Denning to fuck off and just let him do his job.

Instead, Zack told Denning, "You read my reports. Like I suspected, packaged American beef is appearing in southern Mexico, and we're working on finding out how the rustlers are smuggling it over the line," he said. "Torres and I are meeting with an informant Agent Travers is hooking us up with. I'll have more after we have a little conversation with him."

"You goddamn well better." Denning brushed Zack off with a wave of his hand. "Now get your ass out there and I want to see some goddamned results."

Zack didn't bother to answer as he turned and headed out of the supervisor's office into the mass of cubicles, and past several other offices. He nodded to the Assistant Special Agent in Charge and wondered how the ASAC put up with Denning's bullshit.

As Zack walked up to his truck and unlocked the vehicle, he drew out his mobile phone. He called the assisted-living center his mom lived in, and got ahold of Theresa, Molly's caregiver.

"How's my mother?" Zack asked Theresa as he opened the door and climbed into his truck. "Is it a good day to stop by and see her?"

"Her relapse is lasting longer than any other since she's come to the center." Theresa sighed and Zack's gut sank as he thought about what his mother was going through. "I don't think she's up to visitors."

Zack shut the door of his Silverado, his personal vehicle, and leaned back against the leather seat. "She still thinks my father is alive and he's after her?"

"Yes," Theresa said. "She's pretty much inconsolable."

Zack clenched his fist on his thigh. Damn his father, the bastard who'd done this to his mother. The sonofabitch who'd been his stepfather had compounded her condition. "Are you sure it wouldn't help if I stop by?"

"She wouldn't recognize you, honey." Theresa's voice held the quiet comfort of a caregiver skilled in her profession. "Hopefully tomorrow will be a better day for her."

"Yeah. All right." Zack looked up at the ceiling of his truck. "I'll call then," he said before he told Theresa good-bye.

Zack didn't start the truck. Instead he called Cabe.

"Goddamn," Cabe said when Zack let him know how their mother was doing and that she believed their father was trying to kill her again. "That fucking bastard."

"Even after he's dead he's hurting her." Zack added quietly, "That evil sonofabitch got what he deserved, Cabe. Don't you ever think otherwise."

Cabe was silent for a moment. "I know he did."

Just like he said he would, Zack stopped by after he got off work to help Sky with Satan.

Balancing on her crutches, Sky was standing in the entrance to the barn as she watched Zack drive up in his 4×4. The moment she saw him, her stomach did that stupid flip-flop thing that caused her to bring her fingers to her throat in her nervous habit. She mentally scowled at herself as she brought her hand down and grasped the crutch at her side.

After he got out of his vehicle, Zack strode toward her, a frown on his strong features. God, he looked good. Why did her heart have to flutter every time she was near him? It was dangerous, too dangerous, to be around the man, his powerful presence nearly overwhelming her even from a distance.

Seeing him come toward her, she found she hardly could catch her breath. Why was it he looked so good all in black? From his black Stetson to his T-shirt, overshirt, jeans, and boots he reminded her of a panther with its fluid, predatory movements. He was masculine perfection—even with his hard features, his bruises, and the scar on his left cheek, he was gorgeous.

"You'd better not have started without me," he said in a deep, rumbling voice that caused more flutters in her body.

She clenched the handgrips of her crutches. "I keep my promises." Before she could stop herself, she said, "Unlike you. You promised we'd always be together and you left."

Regret and pain flashed through his eyes and she immediately wished she could take the words back.

"You're right," he said quietly. "But that's not going to happen again."

Sky looked away. "Satan's in fine form today." With awkward movements, Sky turned, using her crutches. She moved toward the inside of the barn and tried not to meet Zack's gaze.

Zack moved beside her, matching her pace. They didn't say anything, even when they reached the hay bales that Zack covered with horse blankets. When she sat, she had to admit it was a relief to get off her feet despite her crutches.

While he worked with Satan she marveled at the progress Zack had made in a short amount of time. It was clear he had a natural ability to tame little demons like the yearling. Zack was patient and persistent. He was gentle, yet he made it clear who was boss—and it wasn't Satan.

Zack broke the ice that had formed between himself and Sky by asking her questions about her breeding stock and what plans she had for the future of the ranch. It wasn't long before they were chatting comfortably, as if what she'd said before hadn't happened.

When Zack stopped to take a breather, he sat on the hay bale beside Sky. He downed a bottle of water he'd taken from the small fridge by the sink in the back of the barn. She always kept it stocked with water, considering this was Arizona and it was easy to become dehydrated. Sky took a drink of her own water.

"Did you ever finish that quilt you started with your mom?" Zack asked with a little grin as he looked down at Sky.

"Uh, no." Sky's cheeks heated a little. "I'm making more squares."

He gave a low laugh. "Twelve years later and you're still doing that?"

"Thirteen." She gave him a sheepish look. "I think I might have enough made for six quilts."

"Why don't you finish it?" Zack asked, and he looked like he was genuinely interested.

Sky shrugged. "I guess it's because it's a part of my mom and I just don't want to let go."

"You still miss her a lot," he said quietly.

Sky looked down at her shoe as she swung her good foot back and forth. "It was like a flame was suddenly doused when she passed on. I keep wanting to relight it." She sighed. "But there's no going back and trying to change the past. All we can do is work on the future."

"That's what I've been trying to tell you," Zack said, and another tingle spread throughout her. She felt his body heat while she drank in his masculine scent of a warm summer's day. His scent was almost heady.

She stared at her bandaged foot. Desperate to change the subject, she looked up at him and asked, "How's your mother?"

He turned away and stared straight ahead. "She'll never be the same after what my father did to her."

Sky frowned. "You mean your stepfather?"

Zack continued staring down the barn pathway, as if seeing something Sky didn't. "No. I mean my birth father."

"You've never said anything about him before." Sky felt a twinge in her chest like something bad had happened.

Zack gave a mirthless laugh. "The man who fathered me

nearly destroyed my mother, and her second husband pretty much finished the job."

Sky reached out and touched his arm. "Whatever happened, was it in Flagstaff? Before you moved to Douglas?"

The tension in him radiated through his hand and he still didn't look at her. "I don't like to talk about it."

"Why not?" she said softly.

Zack was quiet for a long moment before his gaze met hers. "Maybe it's because I've gone over and over it in my mind so many times that I can't stand to say it out loud."

The twist in Sky's chest became a deep ache. "Your father beat your mother?"

"From the time we were kids. Probably longer." The pain in Zack's eyes made her want to reach out and hold him tight. "And if he wasn't knocking the crap out of her, it was my brother and me." Zack's throat worked as he swallowed.

Sky squeezed his hand harder, the ache in her chest increasing so much that she wondered how she could breathe. This was a part of Zack she'd never known, and she had no idea what to say.

"When we were old enough to understand what was happening, Cabe and I tried to get the bastard to take it out on us instead of on our mother." Zack took off his hat and set it on the hay bale before he pushed his free hand through his hair. "It never mattered, though. He beat the shit out of her anyway."

What Zack had gone through . . . Sky couldn't begin to imagine. She wanted to cry for him. For that abused child who'd had to see his mother beaten, too.

He heaved a sigh. "When I was around twelve and Cabe thirteen, we started trying to fight back, but our father was a big sonofabitch."

Sky moved closer to Zack so that her thigh touched his. She leaned her head against his shoulder and turned his hand over so that she could lace her fingers with his. She was almost afraid to ask her next question, but she got it out. "What happened to your father? Is he still alive?"

"He was killed while hunting deer with my brother and me." Zack's throat sounded hoarse. "Cabe shot my father by accident."

Sky sucked in her breath and raised her head from his shoulder. The tears inside her were getting harder and harder to hold back. "Oh, my God."

As his gray eyes met hers, Zack said, "The old man deserved it."

Zack looked away from Sky again. "As usual, he'd kicked us around when he made me and Cabe camp out with him the night before he died."

Sky laid her head against Zack's shoulder and this time closed her eyes as his pain washed through her. She couldn't remember him ever talking so much.

"He wasn't drunk, so we knew he was serious when he told us how he'd had it with our mother. Called her a whore and said she screwed around and we weren't even his. Not that we hadn't heard that one before. But this time he said he was going to kill her when we got home."

Sky felt wetness behind her eyelids as her eyes stung, and she kept them shut tight.

"Cabe and I didn't talk that night," Zack continued in his hoarse voice. "But I'm sure that like me, he was thinking about how we could protect our mom when we got home."

A tear rolled down Sky's cheek as they gripped each other's hand tightly. "It didn't matter anymore after the accident," Zack said. "She was safe."

Sky raised her face and looked at him as a few more tears made their way down her cheeks. "I'm so sorry."

Zack cupped her face in his hands and brushed her tears away with his thumbs. "Don't cry. Please."

"Why didn't you tell me about this back when we were together?" she asked as another tear escaped.

"What you and I had—it was so clean and beautiful." He pressed his lips to her forehead before looking at her again. "I didn't want to smear what we had with dirt from my past."

The awful words she'd said earlier to him about not keeping his promises came back to hit her like a slap. She was such a bitch. He'd had an awful life as a child and had kept it from her because he'd cared. And here she'd gone and said something so mean.

Zack brought her close so that he held her face against his chest. "What you said earlier was true, Sky. There's no going back and trying to change the past. All we can do is work on the future."

Sky paused from mucking out Satan's stall with a rake to wipe sweat from her forehead with the back of her hand. A cool October breeze stirred the loose hair at her cheeks and chilled her skin.

It was Thursday, almost one week since her injury. Her ankle still felt a little stiff and sore, but as far as she was concerned, she had recovered and didn't need help from anyone—no matter what Zack might think.

Satan stirred beside her in the stall, but thanks to Zack's help, she didn't have to worry about the little shit mowing her down. What Zack had done in a week—she had to admit it would have taken her two or three weeks.

Thank God there'd been no more attempts to take Satan or any of her other prize stock over the past few days. As far as they could tell from her ranch hands' checking fences and the herd, rustlers had left her cattle alone for the time being.

Unfortunately, neighboring ranchers, whose herds had been untouched before, had now lost several head of cattle. Wade had stopped by a couple of times, but she always cut him off.

She'd talked with Sheriff Wayland once and he'd said they were ramping up the investigation but had nothing concrete as of that time.

In other words, they didn't know anything, or wouldn't tell her if they did.

When she'd asked Zack if he'd had any news, an expression of frustration had come over his features and he'd shaken his head.

She'd taken that as a resounding "no."

While she raked manure out of Satan's stall, it was like dust motes and sunshine tickled the inside of her belly as she realized Zack would be arriving soon. At the same time she felt a twinge of regret that they'd come to the end of their agreement. He wouldn't be coming over daily to work with Satan now that her ankle was pretty much healed.

No. Not regret. She was thrilled that she didn't have to put up with Zack's hero routine any longer. Sky grimaced and swatted an insistent horsefly away from her face. *Yeah, right.* In truth, she'd miss having him around.

Satan butted her thigh and she paused raking to scratch the bull behind his ears. "You'll miss him, too, won't you?" she murmured. The devilish spark was still in Satan's eyes, but he was no longer bent on plowing down anyone who came near him.

Sky sighed and got back to work cleaning the yearling's stall.

Barn smells of hay, horse, and manure comforted her. Much more so than Zack's masculine scent. When she was near him she felt at ease, yet she also felt wild and restless, and more than a little reckless.

Every day Zack had shown up any time from dusk to dark, depending on how his day had gone. Sky had expected—had *wanted*—him to take advantage of the time they'd spent together by trying to get her clothes off.

But to her surprise and dismay he hadn't.

She'd asked him a couple of times if he wanted to go into the house for a glass of iced tea. He'd look at her and ask if she'd changed her mind about giving their relationship another chance.

"No," came to her lips each time so fast, so automatically, that she hadn't even paused to think his question over.

"Then there's your answer," he said the first time, then went to the back of the barn and got a water bottle, and brought her back a bottle, too.

She'd wanted to throw it at him for being so stubborn. They didn't have to have a serious relationship to enjoy each other's company a little more intimately.

Sky gripped the smooth wooden handle of the rake tighter as she paused in cleaning out the stall and tried to figure Zack out. He seemed so serious, wanting a relationship with her and refusing to take it any further until she agreed.

Instead, he'd spent time with Satan, made sure the stalls and aisles were mucked out, and asked her if there was anything else she needed help with. Then Zack would brush his lips across hers and go.

And she'd missed him. Wanted to be with him intimately but wanted to enjoy his companionship, too.

But promise to start their relationship over? She just hadn't been able to do that.

While he'd spent time with Satan, they'd talked about everything and nothing at all. Zack would share his day at work and talk about his mother, whom he'd stop by to check in on as often as he could. Every now and then he'd bring up his brother, Cabe, and tell Sky about some of the stunts they'd pulled as kids.

They never talked about his father again.

Sky in turn would talk to him about her sister, Trinity, and how she seemed to love her job in England. Sky would confide in Zack her concerns about the rustlers and tell him more about her plans for upgrading the herd and breeding championship stock.

Talking with him was easy and natural. It made her realize how immature their relationship had been ten years ago. They'd talked, yes, but their relationship had been fiery and passionate, based more on sex than substance.

She sighed and leaned on the rake for a moment as her eyes unfocused and she could only see Zack in place of everything else.

This past week, about the only thing they hadn't talked about was the future of their relationship.

Friendship, she reminded herself.

"Bad girl," Zack's deep voice rumbled behind her.

Sky yelped and spun around, almost clobbering him with the rake. "Don't scare me like that!" She punched him in his muscled biceps.

"The deal was a whole week, sweetheart." He took the rake from her hands and set it against the side of the stall, then placed his hands on her shoulders. "I've got one more day."

His stormy gray eyes captured her, and she felt as if she was hovering on the edge of a precipice. Just one step and she'd throw herself over.

She swayed toward him, intoxicated by his earthy scent and potent sexuality. "My ankle's fine," she murmured, amazed she'd found her voice.

He rubbed her arms through the light material of her T-shirt, setting her skin on fire. "Humor me."

Oh, she'd like to humor him all right. In the barn, in broad daylight—anywhere.

Zack brushed his lips over her hair and released her to grab the rake. Muscles in his arms and back bunched as he worked, and she barely contained a sigh.

She frowned and moved away. While Zack worked with Satan, she busied herself brushing down Empress. The sorrel mare whickered her pleasure and lipped Sky's braid. She couldn't help glancing at Zack, watching how gentle he was with the yearling.

For the first time in the week she and Zack had spent together, they said little. It was a companionable silence, but because he wouldn't be coming over every day to tame Satan she already missed Zack.

When they were finished, Sky walked him to his truck. She only had a limp now.

A breathtaking sunset rode the horizon, gold, pink, and purple streaking the sky above the Mule Mountains.

They stopped in front of Zack's truck and he leaned against the hood and into her line of vision. "Why don't we celebrate?" he said in a low rumble.

Sky snapped her gaze from Zack's truck to his face. "Celebrate what?" She slid her hands into the back pockets of her jeans and tilted her head.

"Taming Satan. Your ankle being better." Zack reached around her to catch one wrist, easing her hand from her pocket and clasping it. His touch electrified her through what felt like every single nerve ending.

"Dinner, tomorrow," he said, his voice deep and serious. "I'll pick you up at eight."

She swallowed. "As friends?"

"Whatever you say." Zack squeezed her hand. "How's Mexican food sound?"

"O-okay." Sky pulled her hand away from his, afraid he'd feel her trembling. She made her tone light and teasing. "Don't be late, cowboy. I'll be hungry."

He gave her a dark, sinful look that turned her stomach inside out. "I'm already starving."

Chapter 17

Friday night, Zack drove the last mile between the ICE office and Sky's door. He and the junior agent he worked with, Eric Torres, had spent the day tracking down leads on the rustlers, but they just kept dead-ending, frustrating the hell out of both of them.

When Zack had called Clay Wayland, the sheriff had been out of the office, and Zack had ended up talking with Deputy Woods instead. Woods hadn't been much help. The deputy was far too relaxed about the whole rustling situation.

But the memory of Woods dancing with Sky at the rodeo dance had Zack grinding his teeth. Would he ever get over this desire to pound every man who even looked at Sky?

Zack parked in front of her house wondering if any of the local ranchers could be involved in the rustling. Or was this strictly an outside job?

Whatever the answer, he couldn't give it any more thought. For the moment, his mind needed one thing and one thing only.

He got out of his Silverado and headed up the steps, determination in his stride. He had waited long enough. Tonight, Sky was going to give him what he wanted. All of her. No holding back.

The past week had been hell, forcing himself to keep a certain amount of distance from Sky. He had intended to take things slow and easy this time. Give her a chance to trust him again. But he saw that wasn't going to work. Sky was damn stubborn and he was going to have to remind her just who her man was.

Zack paused for a moment before he knocked on the door. The rapping sound echoed in the evening air as his knuckles hit the wood.

Yeah, he damned well was going to get that promise from her if it was the last thing he did.

But when the door opened and he saw her standing there, almost every shred of his good intentions vanished and all of the blood in his body went rushing to his cock. He clenched his hands and swallowed real hard.

Sky smiled, her green eyes wide. She'd piled her copper hair on top of her head and immediately he wanted to set it free and bury his face in the silk of it to draw in her scent and hold it inside him forever.

The tiny black dress she wore only reached mid-thigh, revealing her long, sexy legs. Legs he wanted to have clamped tight around him as he thrust his cock into her wet core. From head to toe, his entire being vibrated as he held himself back from grabbing her, pushing her inside her house, and taking her now.

As if she could read his thoughts, Sky sighed and ran the tip of her tongue over her bottom lip.

The woman has no fucking mercy.

He reached up and hooked his finger under one of the delicate straps securing her dress. "God, but you're gorgeous, sweetheart."

Sky's smile was seductive. "You clean up pretty nice, too."

Her hand went to that sensitive spot at the base of her throat. His gaze followed, then dropped to the very generous amount of exposed cleavage. Her nipples peaked below the thin material, and he had to force himself not to let his hand wander from her shoulder to her breasts.

"Just a sec." Her voice was low and husky as she drew away from his touch. "Let me get my purse."

When she walked to the kitchen, he just about groaned out loud at the sight of her sheer black stockings hugging her shapely legs. A line ran down the back of each stocking—stockings that were probably outlawed in forty-six states for what they did to a man. Not to mention those high heels she was wearing. Her outfit screamed sex and he had the erection to prove it.

Trying to gain some control over his body, Zack took a deep breath and thought about as many things as he could that would cool him off. The cattle rustling and the frustration of nothing but dead ends. Someone trying to steal Satan. The asshole group supervisor of Zack's new duty station.

Yeah, that did it.

Relief relaxed his tense muscles as those images made his lust fade. It allowed him to breathe, and as his erection lessened, the pain of his swollen cock against his zipper eased.

But the moment Sky returned to the living room and smiled at him, no image of any kind came to mind to replace the erotic ones of her.

God, he was going to die if she didn't agree to his condition. Like now.

Sky's skin tingled where Zack touched her elbow as he guided her into *Los Dos Hermanos,* a popular restaurant in Douglas. Sounds of laughter and voices, clinking plates and mariachi music filled the air. Tantalizing smells of Mexican food caused her stomach to growl.

The place was crowded, but they didn't have long to wait before the hostess escorted them to a corner booth. Serapes and sombreros decorated the walls, strategically arranged baskets of colorful gourds complemented the room, and piñatas swayed from the ceiling's exposed beams.

Zack slid onto the bench next to Sky, his presence solid and virile. When she glanced up, he gave her a sinfully devastating look, and she quivered with awareness from head to toe.

He looked so delicious dressed all in black from his western shirt to his boots. He'd already taken off his black Stetson when he'd walked into the restaurant and had set it on the bench seat beside him.

After they had ordered and the waitress had returned with their drinks, Sky took a long sip of her margarita. The mixture of salt from the rim and the citrusy taste rolled over her tongue. She needed to relax and enjoy the evening, and she was hoping the margarita would help her mellow a bit.

Zack's eyes swirled stormy gray as he watched her, filled with passion—and something else. Something that made Sky wonder if there could be a happily ever after.

Not likely. She wasn't Cinderella.

Though lately Zack had been kind of like a Prince Charming. A devastatingly handsome, untamed cowboy of a prince.

A smile teased the corner of her mouth.

He trailed his finger over her lips. "What's that smile for?"

She shook her head. "It's silly."

"Tell me." His tone was both coaxing and demanding.

Sky dropped her gaze to her margarita, picked it up, and took a healthy swallow. She rarely drank, and she could already feel her body relaxing from the alcohol. Maybe it would loosen her inhibitions, too, and she'd get Zack where she wanted him.

In bed. Naked.

Heat flushed her cheeks as she looked back to him. "I was just thinking you've been a cowboy Prince Charming this past week."

His mouth curved into a slow smile.

Oh, God. Zack rarely smiled, and whenever he did it put her senses into overdrive—causing her nipples to ache, her belly to flip, and the place between her thighs to throb.

Sky's face grew even warmer. "Told you it was silly."

"Cinderella." His voice was a husky murmur as he stroked her shoulder, drawing lazy circles on her bare arm with his fingers. "Does that mean if I find your glass slipper, you'll be my princess?"

His touch was sensual and hypnotic, stirring her blood, igniting flames throughout her body. She shivered, so acutely aware of him. Wanting him.

Her nipples tightened more, pressing against the taut silk of her dress. Her naughty stockings and garters felt erotic, and she wanted Zack to explore her body and discover exactly what she wore beneath her dress. She needed his touch, his kiss.

"Watch out," a voice said, breaking Sky's lustful trance. "It's hot."

I'm hot. So hot.

Sky blinked, reality seeping in as she realized the waitress was setting their plates in front of them. Zack gave Sky a look like he knew exactly what she was thinking and how she was feeling. He eased his arm from around her shoulder and started eating his combination platter of enchiladas, tacos, and refried beans.

Oh, God. Oh, God.

Being around Zack was so not a good idea.

Ignoring her own plate, Sky picked up her margarita and took a long draught, peeking at Zack from beneath her lashes.

It wasn't food she was hungry for.

Zack's groin tightened as Sky climbed into his Silverado and scooted next to him. Her orange blossom and rain scent mingled with the smell of his leather upholstery.

As he backed the truck out of the restaurant's parking lot, Sky rested her head on his arm, her body snug against his. The next thing he knew, her hand was on his thigh. Slowly tracing patterns with her fingernail down to his knee, and then higher. Not quite up to his hip, and then back to his knee again.

His heart punched his chest as he guided his Silverado through Douglas, his body on fire, his cock so hard he could use it as a gearshift. He drove with one hand and captured her exploring fingers with his other. Fuck, yeah, she wanted him. And he sure as hell wanted her.

She sighed and snuggled closer. "Thanks for the wonderful dinner."

He glanced from the road to her. "You hardly ate."

Sky's voice came out in a husky purr. "I'm not hungry for food."

Zack was so hard, he was seeing stars. He wanted to bury his cock inside her more than anything. He wanted to touch her and taste her, and make her scream when she came.

Damnit, this whole evening was going straight to hell, along with all of his carefully laid plans.

When Sky couldn't dislodge her hand from beneath his, she shifted in her seat, pressing her breasts against his arm. He groaned as she started an erotic assault, nipping at his shoulder through his shirt. She moved her other hand to his chest, sliding her fingers down to his belt.

"Sky," he grumbled in warning and desire combined.

Pausing, she looked up at him. "What?" she asked in an innocent voice.

He had a hard time forming coherent words. "If you don't stop, I'm liable to have an accident."

"Mmmm." She ran her finger over the bulge straining against his zipper, lightly stroking his cock. "Now that would be a shame."

Zack wasn't sure how he made it to the ranch without coming in his jeans. Sky hadn't let up and his cock was so hard for her that the minute he reached her house he wanted to shove that tiny dress to her waist and take her in the cab.

As soon as he parked his truck and killed the engine and the lights, Sky laced her hands in his hair and pulled him toward her. She kissed him with such hunger that he felt it straight to the soles of his boots.

Lust consumed him as she thrust her tongue into his mouth. God, but she tasted good. Her own unique taste, combined with the citrus of the margarita she'd had.

He wanted her to straddle his lap. Now. With a little seat adjustment, there was plenty of room between him and the steering wheel. *Hell, yeah.*

Sky tore her lips from his and rose up on her knees, putting her breasts at the same level as his mouth. "Touch me," she whispered.

Zack couldn't think straight. He bit her nipple right through the silky fabric of her black dress. She moaned as he bit, licked, and sucked the nipple and it hardened even more against the now-damp material.

His hands roamed her body, learning her curves all over again as he moved his palms from the swells of her breasts down her waist and on down, down.

Dear God.

He shoved her dress up and groaned when his fingers discovered her garters and the tiniest wisp of panties that were tied with small bows on either side of her hips.

"I need to feel you," he murmured as he caressed her hips through the silk underwear. "I've got to taste you."

"Please, baby," Sky moaned as he moved his mouth to her other breast, nipping at it, soaking the thin material. He slid his hand over the cloth covering her damp folds and she gasped as his fingers stroked her.

While he caressed her, Sky clenched her hands in his hair and rocked her hips. "I want you inside me again."

"Sky," he groaned. He had a wild woman in his arms, and he wanted to drive his cock into her now.

If she pushed him any further, he didn't know if he could hold on to his so-called good intentions.

She squirmed against him and squeezed his erection. "Fuck me," she demanded.

Shit. He was a goner.

Chapter 18

The rumble in Zack's chest was deep, untamed. He made her feel wild. Crazy. Dizzy with lust.

He captured both her wrists in his hands and held them between his and Sky's bodies.

She squirmed on his lap and he groaned. She tried to free her wrists so she could touch him, reach between them, and unfasten his jeans and wrap her fingers around his cock. God, she had to have him.

"Hold on." His voice was rough, almost feral. "Before we go even one step further, you have to answer one question. And you'd better give the right answer, sweetheart."

Sky stilled. She wanted him so bad she could barely comprehend what he was saying at first. Then she realized it had all come back to the question he'd asked her every time she'd invited him into her house over the past week.

She swallowed and couldn't move.

Zack released her wrists and slipped his fingers into her hair on each side of her head. "I want you to be mine. Not just for sex. I want *all* of you."

He brushed his lips over hers and she shuddered from need— the feelings racing through her were only desire and lust, right?

"Give me another chance," he murmured against her lips, then drew away so that he was looking into her eyes. "Give *us* another chance."

Sky held back a groan as she felt the hardness of his jean-clad thighs between hers, the stiffness of his cock pressing against the little bit of material covering her folds. "You so do not play fair, Zack Hunter."

He brushed his thumb across her cheek, his eyes and expression dark in the cab's light. "No, sweetheart, I don't."

All of the time they'd spent together over the last week flowed over her in a smooth wave. She'd enjoyed being with him every moment. It had been more than lust she'd felt when he was near. Comfortable companionship and a feeling that grew deep in her belly every single day just knowing he was on his way to her home to work with Satan—and to be with her.

With a sigh, Sky leaned her forehead against Zack's chest. The intensity of his masculine scent heightened her arousal as she breathed in deep.

"You win." She rubbed her face against his shirt. "I'll give it a try."

"Hey." He caught her by her chin with his fingers and forced her to look at him. His expression was hard, serious. "I don't want some half-assed attempt at this. All or nothing, Sky."

"Just how serious are you?" she asked as she looked up at him, wanting to see it in his eyes.

"I told you," he said. "I want it all." Zack reached behind her head and pulled out the clip, setting her hair free and letting it fall around her shoulders. He tossed the clip onto the seat next to them and nuzzled her hair. "I want that sweet body and I want your heart again, Sky MacKenna."

"Oh, God." She let her breath out in a rush. "You don't ask for much, do you?"

He kept his fingers in her hair as he drew away. "Yeah, I do." His expression looked more serious than she had ever seen it. "I made the biggest mistake of my life when I walked away from you, from us, ten years ago. I intend to make up for every lost moment."

"I missed you so much." She brought her hands to his face and traced the scar with her fingertips. "I'm scared, Zack. What I went through—it was like a nightmare. I don't want to have you and then lose you all over again."

Zack's throat threatened to close off. *Goddamn.* Every time they talked he found he'd hurt her even more than he'd realized.

"You're not going to lose me." Zack wrapped his arms around her, brought her tight into his embrace, and buried his face in her hair. The ache in his throat grew even more intense as her orange blossom scent filled him. "I promise," he murmured while he rubbed one of his palms in a circle on her back.

She gave a shuddering sigh against his chest, then drew back from his embrace. Her smile was a little shaky, but it was a smile.

"Okay." She moved her mouth closer to his. "I'll give us another chance."

Relief rushed through Zack like he'd never felt before. Relief measured with something more. More than triumph and more than hope that he'd win Sky's heart again.

Rain had begun to drizzle lightly on the front windshield. He helped her out of the Silverado, handed her the purse she'd left on her seat, and locked up his 4×4.

Her hand felt small and delicate in his as he took it before walking side by side through the misty rain with her toward her house.

The crazy pounding of his heart grew and he almost didn't notice the difference between the blood thundering in his ears and the rumble of thunder over the mountains.

Sky glanced up at the dark clouds as lightning brightened the sky, and her face was wet with moisture. The air stirred with the scent of a serious oncoming storm. "Damn, but we need the rain." She sounded a little nervous, as if she was trying to think of something to say as they walked.

Zack squeezed her hand and she looked up at him, this time with a more confident smile that made his heart flop over like an egg, sunny-side up.

Fat drops of rain burst from the sky and wind whipped around them in a sudden rush. Zack scooped Sky up and she laughed and clasped him around the neck, almost hitting him in the face with her purse.

They were drenched by the time he'd hurried up the steps and reached the porch, before setting Sky on her feet. She shook her wet hair out of her face as she handed him the key and he unlocked the door before guiding her through the doorway and into her home.

Zack closed the door behind him and Blue greeted them with enthusiasm. Sky paused to rub the Border Collie behind his ears and tell him hello before she straightened and focused her eyes on Zack.

His blood stirred hot as Sky's gaze met his. She took a deep breath, then looked at Blue long enough to order him to go to his bed by the fridge in the kitchen. If dogs could glare, Blue did, but he did as she ordered. His toenails clicked across the kitchen floor and then were silent once he curled up in his bed.

Zack's heart pounded harder as he held Sky's hand again while she led him to her bedroom. She flipped a switch by the door, and twin lights came on to either side of the bed. She tossed her purse on a chair beside the doorway. In the distance the sound of thunder rolled over the desert, and a gust of wind rattled the windowpanes.

For endless seconds they held each other's hands and stood face-to-face, just looking at each other. Her rain-soaked hair clung to the sides of her face, and the water had plastered her dress to her body.

She'd never looked more gorgeous than she did at that moment.

Sky kept her gaze focused on him as she reached up with both hands and pulled the straps of her dress over her shoulders. The wet material whispered down her body as it fell to the floor. All she wore were black garters, those tiny panties, stockings, and a bra, along with high heels.

Zack felt like a fist pressed against his Adam's apple and a thousand strong hands held him in place. He couldn't move. He could only watch as she reached behind herself and unclasped her bra and it landed by her feet, too.

It was like he was in a daze as she untied each side of the tiny black panties and dropped them, too, baring the copper curls of her mound.

Jesus. His knees were going to give out.

He tried to swallow. Tried to touch her. But still he couldn't move.

A dream. It was a goddamned dream, and he was going to wake up and pump several hundred pounds of iron to get control over his mind and heart.

Her clear green eyes were wide, drinking him in the same way he was watching her. Her lips parted and her nipples were hard as she took a step closer to him. His gaze slid over her fair skin. The sprinkling of freckles across her bared shoulders. The patch of copper curls on the mound between her firm thighs.

"Damn." He swallowed, the fist pressing into his throat making it hard to speak. "You're so beautiful. I don't know if I can breathe anymore."

"Come to me, Zack." Her voice was a caress and a demand all in one.

He finally found the strength to take a step forward, meeting her so that they almost touched.

The fog stayed in his mind as she helped him undress. He shed his boots and every last bit of his clothing. He surprised himself by actually remembering to pull out his wallet and drag out a foil-wrapped condom that he tossed on the nightstand beside the bed.

She stroked his cock, wrapping her fingers around it and looking at it almost in fascination. Zack groaned, grasped her by her waist, and forced her to release his erection by picking her up and placing her on the bed.

She smiled as she lay back on the bed and held her arms out to him. Her wet hair was a shade of auburn against the white of her pillowcases. He eased onto the bed beside her, trying to catch his breath.

Zack propped himself on one elbow as her gorgeous face mesmerized him. Looking at her was making him insane. At the same time, animal instinct to take her hard and fast warred inside him with the desire to make love to her and cherish every bit of her body.

He smiled and allowed himself to caress her cheek, then brushed his lips over hers. She sighed, her warm breath fanning over his mouth. He ran his tongue along her lower lip, then caught it gently between his teeth.

Soft cries rose from her throat as he released her lip and his tongue moved into the warmth of her mouth. Just the taste of her was enough to set off a thunderstorm in his mind.

As Zack kissed Sky, he trailed his fingers down her shoulder and arm to her waist and over the curve of one hip. His fingers skimmed her flesh, light brushes that caused her to shiver and goose bumps to roughen her soft skin.

In turn she stroked him, her nails lightly raking him from his back to his hips. "Make love to me," she murmured as her hand slid up his back and into his hair.

He pushed a strand of wet hair from her face. "I am, sweetheart."

Slowly, Zack kissed and licked, and explored every part of her body he could reach, using his lips and tongue and hands. Sky's palms continued to stroke his muscles and his cock as he kissed the tender spot below her earlobe, then moved to the hollow at the base of her throat where her hand always crept when she was nervous. His tongue found the soft skin of her shoulder, the mole above her breast, the curve of her waist, and her navel.

Lower and lower he worked downward until he reached the copper curls of her mound. He nuzzled the soft hair of her folds and drank in the scent of her musk.

Zack looked up to see her watching him, her eyes so green with passion, her chest rising and falling.

He kept his eyes focused on her as his tongue dipped into her folds and he tasted her. Her eyes widened and her body jerked at the contact. "Zack!"

Oh, God, she tasted better than he remembered. He slid two fingers inside her warm core and moved his mouth over her clit. He licked and sucked it, enjoying her flavor on his tongue and breathing in her scent.

When her body tensed, he slipped his hands under her hips and pressed his mouth harder against her, driving her toward her climax. Her body arched up off the bed and she cried out as her orgasm tore through her.

Even then, he didn't stop. "Zack. Baby," she moaned. But then she was too helpless to do anything more than ride the next wave sweeping through her.

Rain pattered on the windowpane, a distant sound that somehow made their joining even more intimate.

Before she had completely come down from the summit, Zack rose above Sky, somehow managed to sheathe his cock, and thrust into her. He fought for control as he took her slow and easy, reveling in the sensation of being inside her and wanting to prolong it as long as possible.

Sky wrapped her legs around his waist, her hands clenching his hips, her eyes closed.

"Look at me." Zack's voice came out in a rough growl. "Watch me while I'm inside you."

Her desire-filled green eyes met his. He couldn't hold back any longer. He pounded into her, like the rain that was now pounding down on the house. She begged him for more, urging him on, like parched earth begging for moisture, until she cried out with another orgasm.

Zack shouted Sky's name as he climaxed, buried so deep inside her that he never wanted to find his way back.

Chapter 19

Sky reveled in the feel of Zack between her thighs, the weight of his big body pinning her down, his sweat-slicked skin against hers, the feel of him inside her.

It was almost like a dream, almost surreal.

Zack. In her arms. Again.

She squeezed her eyes tight and had the absurd desire to cry. The moment felt too good, too precious to be real.

"Hey." Zack brushed his lips so lightly over her forehead that it was almost like she'd imagined it. "Let me see those beautiful green eyes that I've missed so much."

The tears really wanted to come then, but she wouldn't let them. She'd cried all she ever would over Zack. No matter what he'd said about a fresh beginning for the two of them, she wasn't getting her heart stomped all over again.

Zack slipped out of her and rolled onto his side, bringing her with him so that he had one of her legs pinned between his. She opened her eyes and met his gaze as he squeezed her to him with one of his muscled arms, making her feel secure, like nothing could ever hurt her.

Lightning flashed close enough that the brightness through the window cast light and shadow over his features. The long scar running down his cheek and his expression gave him an almost harsh look.

"No regrets?" he asked in a low rumble.

The words came more easily than Sky expected. "I don't regret a minute of what we just shared." She managed a smile, a real one. "I didn't remember us being so incredibly good together." Zack raised his eyebrow, and Sky stumbled over more words. "I mean, it was good before, but this time . . ."

"I don't know what's going on in that exceptionally intelligent head of yours, but I know one thing." Zack ran his palm up and down her upper arm as another flash of lightning let her see his gray eyes. "You mean more to me than good sex."

Sky's cheeks felt warm and her core started aching to have him inside her again. "Let's try the good-sex part again. Just to make sure we're getting it right."

Zack growled and she gasped as he rolled her onto her back, braced his hands to either side of her arms, and stared down at her. Small bursts of lightning seemed to go off in her belly at the dark, intense look he gave her. "This time we'll get it *all* right."

She squirmed beneath his big body, not wanting to answer, just wanting *him.*

Sky reached up her arms to bring Zack down for a kiss when an insistent beep came from somewhere in the room. For a moment she was confused, her thoughts too filled with lust for Zack.

"Not mine," he murmured as he nuzzled her ear and she realized it was her cell phone. "Leave it."

At the same time, Blue started barking. Loud, sharp barks outside the bedroom door.

"Blue doesn't sound like that unless something's wrong." The sparks in her belly died away and changed to a heavier weight of concern. "And no one calls on the ranch line this late at night— it's got to be important. Really important."

Zack rolled off her and she could feel the abrupt change in the atmosphere. A switch from lust to professionalism in virtually an instant. "Where's your phone?"

"My purse." She scooted off the bed, almost catching her foot in the bedcovers. "I left it on the chair—"

But he was already there and he handed the purse to Sky. Her phone stopped ringing at the same time she opened the purse. She grabbed the cell and pulled it out. For some reason her hand shook, as if she already knew something was desperately wrong.

She looked at the missed caller's name on the display screen. "It was Luke," she said, already hitting redial as she spoke.

Luke immediately answered. "Got a situation. Hector Ramirez has been beat up real bad." Sky's heart exploded into a panicked beat as Luke continued, "Sheriff Wayland, paramedics, and an ambulance are on their way."

"Oh, God." Sky scrambled in her dresser drawers for a pair of jeans and a T-shirt—screw underwear. "Are you with Hector? Where?"

"The bunkhouse." Voices rose in the background as Luke spoke. "Saw Hunter's truck, so I'm assuming you've got company. I still don't want you unarmed anymore, so keep that S&W on you."

Sky glanced up at Zack, who was already getting dressed. He had his jeans on and he'd taken his weapon off the nightstand

and was tucking it into the holster inside the waistband of his jeans. "We'll be right there," she said before she pushed the *off* button.

While Sky shoved her feet into a pair of tennis shoes she grabbed off of her closet floor, she gave Zack a quick rundown on what Luke had just told her.

Her heart thrummed as she stuffed her cell phone into her pocket and ran from her bedroom door to the living room. Blue was already there, still barking, his hackles raised.

Sky's heart pounded as she pulled out the secret drawer from beneath the end table and withdrew her S&W before slamming the drawer shut again. With Blue at their sides, she and Zack bolted out into the pouring rain.

Sirens cut through the storm and the night as Zack and Sky ran toward the bunkhouse. Red and blue strobes flashed eerily through the wet night from oncoming law enforcement vehicles, and the yellow and red flashes came from the approaching ambulance. Considering how far outside of town the Flying M Ranch was, the response time had been amazingly fast.

Blue barked as Sky and Zack splashed through mud puddles. It was so dark, even with Zack's high-powered flashlight. Water soaked through her tennis shoes, mud splattering her jeans. The bunkhouse was at least a football field's length from the ranch house and the sheriff and ambulance were almost to the bunkhouse at the same time Zack and Sky made it.

She bounded up the steps and past a tethered, muddy horse and a couple of the ranch hands who stood like grim sentinels outside the door. Blue stayed outside with the men, his gaze darting across the dark landscape as he gave low growls.

Bright light caused Sky to blink as she entered the large

common room of the bunkhouse and at once spotted Hector sprawled on a couch. Luke studied Hector with intent concentration as he crouched at the ranch hand's side.

With a gasp, Sky came up just short of reaching the two men. Hector looked like he'd hung out a red flag and tangled with a fighting bull. Both of Hector's eyes were red and purple, and swollen shut, both his lips split and bleeding, several gashes slashed his cheeks and forehead, and his jaw was swelling along with a huge knot on his forehead. His clothing was ripped and bloody and one of his arms was obviously broken as it lay at an impossible angle by his side.

"Shit." Zack's voice filled the room as he moved past Sky and crouched next to Luke and Hector. "What the hell happened?"

"Not sure. Ramirez hasn't been conscious since he made it to the bunkhouse." Luke's blue eyes burned like hot ice as he looked from Zack to Sky. "He barely made it back on his mount. Probably only because the mare knew her way home and Ramirez held on just long enough to get here."

Loud boot steps clunked on the wooden floor and Sky looked over her shoulder to see Sheriff Wayland and Deputy Garrison enter the enormous common room. The two men stepped aside as paramedics pushed a stretcher from a ramp leading up to the door and into the room. Zack, Sky, and Luke moved off to the side while the paramedics started taking Ramirez's vitals.

The voices of the paramedics echoed in Sky's ears as she heard their reports. "Pulse thready, pupils dilated, respiration shallow . . ."

She felt as if her surreal moment earlier had magnified and the moment had turned from a pleasant dream into an outright nightmare.

As the sheriff and deputy joined her, Zack, and Luke, Sky's stomach churned and for a moment she thought she was going to have to run outside and retch. One of her men had been beaten, might even be close to death.

Why?

As they stood out of the way of the paramedics, Sky rubbed her arms with her palms. She looked up at Zack before turning to Luke, then the sheriff, feeling like someone had a choke hold around her throat. "Do you think Hector stumbled across a group running drugs or illegals across my land?"

"Shit." Wayland dragged his palm over his face and his mustache. His crystal green eyes were darker and assessing. Although he was hard to read, Sky was pretty sure he was as pissed as everyone else was. "Yeah, it could be drugs or undocumented aliens."

"That, or the rustlers," Luke said with an even grimmer expression than he'd had before.

Sky noticed the deputy taking notes and glancing up every now and then when there was a slight pause in the conversation.

"Was Ramirez alone?" Zack's gaze narrowed on Luke. "What was your man doing out so late?"

Luke rubbed his temples with his thumb and forefinger and glanced at Joe, another one of Sky's ranch hands. Joe stood nearby with a look of self-disgust on his face that reflected in his mannerisms.

"Normally the men go out in pairs, but Joe got held up and Ramirez went off on his own." Luke scowled. "Apparently Ramirez heard a calf bawling its damned head off and was worried it was caught up in a fence line."

Joe came closer, his face still twisted in a way that told Sky he was way pissed at himself. "I told the asshole to wait till I got off the damn phone, but he left anyway." Joe clenched his fists at his sides. "I should've made sure Ramirez didn't go off without me."

Luke said nothing, but his muscles tightened beneath his shirt. "Right now we've got to figure out who the hell did this."

Another deputy skirted the paramedics and went straight to the sheriff and said something Sky couldn't hear.

"Just about enough men are here now so we can start combing the southeastern pasture," the sheriff said to them.

Luke nodded. "My men can join you."

Sheriff Wayland glanced back at the deputy. "Where the hell is Woods?"

The deputy shrugged. "Hasn't answered his cell or his radio."

Footsteps told Sky someone else had entered the common room. "Right here, Sheriff," Gary said, his voice carrying over the din. He came in dripping wet and stopped to stomp the mud from his boots. "Just took a quick look around."

He looked somber as he moved past the paramedics who were now lifting Hector onto the stretcher. Sky swallowed past the tight clamp on her throat as she saw the oxygen mask on Hector's face and IV taped to the back of his hand. The paramedics had been shouting out one thing after another, but everything was a blur to Sky.

The lawmen and Luke looked angered by the situation but calm and professional, whereas Sky wanted to puke.

When everyone was out of the way of the door, the paramedics, along with a couple of the deputies, wheeled Hector from the bunkhouse, into the rain, and to the ambulance.

"I'll want a word with all of you," Wayland said to his deputies and the ranch hands as well as Luke, Zack, and Sky, "after we conduct our search to see if we can find any sign in this god-damned rain."

"The fireworks have moved on." Zack had gone to the door and was looking outside. Sky realized the lightning and thunder had stopped even though the rain hadn't. "We just have to deal with the rain, which is likely washing away evidence as we speak."

Luke made a frustrated sound. "We'll have to do the best we can with what we've got."

Wayland gave a short nod to Luke. "Call all the men you have into the bunkhouse." He turned to Gary. "I want the deputies back in here now."

When the twenty or so ranch hands and deputies returned to the room, Wayland's gaze moved slowly from one deputy to another before landing on Zack. "Hunter and the rest of you know what to do."

They nodded and the sheriff turned to Deputy Blalock and said, "Question the ranch hands while we get started searching for evidence."

As the deputies headed toward the door, Sheriff Wayland, Luke, and Zack stopped Sky, an imposing barricade of three huge men.

Blue came into the bunkhouse, settled on his haunches at her side, and looked at the three men as a low rumble rose in his throat.

"Ms. MacKenna, I need you to stay put." Wayland's lips were tight, his expression one of a man who expected to be obeyed.

Sky braced her hands on her hips and scowled at the men. "I can help search just as well as any one of you."

Blue barked as if to emphasize her point.

"I don't doubt that," Wayland sounded firm but sincere, like he wasn't just feeding her a line. "But we need someone here. I'm going to leave you with Deputy Blalock in case anyone turns up. You can stay here while Blalock questions the ranch hands."

Sky started to argue, but the three big men headed out the door. The goateed Deputy Blalock moved to Sky's side at the sheriff's order.

"I run an entire ranch and can handle a weapon with the best of them," Sky muttered.

"I bet you can," the wiry deputy said. "But—"

"Someone's got to stay here," Sky repeated in a mocking tone. She moved past Blalock, plopped down on the common room couch, and crossed her legs, and folded her arms across her chest. "Bullshit," she said as she sat like a good little woman.

But cursed the entire time like a sailor.

The relentless rain made working across the southeastern range frustrating as hell. Zack clenched his high-powered flashlight in his fist as he swept it across the ground, hoping to find a sign of where the incident had taken place and maybe some kind of clue that would lead them to the bastards who had beat the shit out of Ramirez.

Anger burned in Zack's gut. He'd like to work over the men who'd done a job on Ramirez. Zack sucked in his breath. *Shit.* He hadn't felt so personally involved in any case as he was with this one. Anything and everything to do with Sky—whatever affected her in any way—was his business and he was taking it personal.

What if Sky had been out on the range?

What if it had been her tonight?

The thought made his anger turn to nearly blinding fury, and he had to force himself to shove personal thoughts aside and think like a fed. Not like a man ready to kill for his woman. Right now she was safe at home with one of the deputies and Zack had to concentrate on his job.

Joe worked at Zack's side as his partner during the sweep. The ferocity on Joe's features never ebbed as he searched. It was easy to see just how hard the man had taken Ramirez's beating.

The pale gray of predawn had just started to lighten the sky when the heavy rain all but stopped. Relieved the constant downpour had turned into barely a mist, Zack mumbled, "Christ, it's about time." Then something glinted in a patch of flattened grass ahead of him and Joe.

"Well, *fuck* me," Joe said as they carefully stepped up to a large area beside a piece of downed fence line—obviously cut.

Deep tire prints had pressed into the claylike mud and in one place it was clear the rear tires of a horse or cattle trailer had been stuck. Wooden planks had been left behind that had obviously been used to get the trailer out of the muck, and mud had spattered across the ground where the wheels had spun trying to gain traction.

Zack squatted and pointed to a metal pipe that had rolled under the edge of one of the planks, out of the rain. "Fifty bucks that pipe was used on Ramirez."

The growing dawn glinted on the smooth steel of a two-and-a-half-foot-long, three-quarter-inch pipe. "If I'm not mistaken," Zack continued, "that's blood on the far end." He glanced up at Joe, who was eyeing the pipe that was under the plank. "Better let Rider and Wayland know."

Joe drew out his cell. "On it."

At the same time Zack focused on the scene, he pushed Joe's conversation to the back of his mind—but out of training and experience still listened to what Joe had to say. Might not be important, but, hell, you never knew.

Taking care not to disturb the scene, Zack bagged and tagged the bloody pipe as evidence. He took in the bent grass, and what remained of three sets of muddy shoe prints and a horse's hoof-prints.

In the background, Joe was speaking to Rider or Wayland in a surprisingly efficient manner that made him sound like a cop himself.

Zack filed that information away with the dozens of other questions filling his mind.

After the investigation had been conducted and the scene fully documented and photographed, Wayland, Rider, and Woods each took a look at the piece of evidence Zack had recovered.

Wayland listened to Zack as he examined at the pipe.

Rider's mouth had tightened in a thin line. "Sonsofbitches beat Ramirez with a metal pipe. We'll make damn sure they pay."

"Now don't go off all vigilante on me," Wayland said, the look in his eye hard. "You let law enforcement handle this."

Something hard flashed in Rider's eyes. "Wouldn't dream of it," he drawled in a way that made Zack wonder if Rider was talking about being a vigilante or letting law enforcement handle the situation.

Chapter 20

"Ready, Torres?" Zack asked the following Monday as he stepped into the two-desk office he shared with the younger special agent.

Torres pushed back his chair and got to his feet. "Talked with a guy from Customs and Border Protection."

"CBP tell you anything new?" Zack picked up his western hat from where he'd left it on his squat filing cabinet beside his desk.

"Yup." Torres pointed to an aerial map on his desk. "The CBP officer I spoke with said in the San Bernardino area they found a few cattle and human tracks headed into Mexico rather than out."

"Enough to account for the large numbers of cattle being rustled?" Zack asked as he stood inside the doorway leading out of their office.

The younger agent shook his head. "Not at all."

"Time to check in with the informant Agent Travers hooked us up with." Zack headed out the door as he mentioned Travers, one of the other senior agents in the office. "Grab your hat and we'll get the cash we requisitioned to pay off our informant."

* * *

Zack sized up the man as they met in the darkened lot behind the old Dairy Queen. Marlin Jones didn't have the shifty-eyed, nervous look of a lot of informants. With his arms folded across his chest and a pleasant expression on his face, Jones leaned casually against a new model black Nissan sports car. Zack wondered just what Jones did to afford the higher-end vehicle—other than sell info to the feds. Likely selling *a lot* of info to the feds.

The air smelled faintly of cigarette smoke and Zack noticed the glowing embers of a butt rested on the gravel next to Jones's shoes. Traffic was light on Douglas's main strip, G Street—if you could call it traffic. Car lights flashed by occasionally and a nearby traffic light glowed green, then yellow, then red in the night.

After Zack had confirmed Jones's identity, Zack verbally identified himself and Torres.

"Travers says you have information on the missing cattle," Zack said as they got down to business.

"Good profits to be made," Jones drawled in a distinctly Texan accent. "About a fourth of those stolen are driven across the line—only the breeds of cattle that'll blend in better with Mexican cattle than Black Angus."

Zack studied Jones's hazel eyes. If it weren't for the gut sensation that ate at Zack's consciousness, Jones could have been any good ol' boy.

"The other three-quarters of the cattle stolen?" Zack asked. "What's being done with them?"

Jones braced his hands behind him on the shiny hood of the Nissan. "Another quarter—all Black Angus—are being sold to ranchers in Texas and New Mexico. Prime stock with papers to go along with them."

Of course. The theft of Sky's pedigree papers and the theft of papers from other ranchers according to the USDA Inspector. "So the last half?" Zack asked, trying to keep the hardness out of his tone.

"Processed." Jones smiled and he looked like they could be chatting at a barbeque. "It's easier to smuggle into Mexico than a live herd. Roasts, steaks, hamburger, even sides of beef are being taken into southern Mexico. Beef is being sold at top dollar since mad cow disease wiped out lower Mexico's herds."

"You're not telling us a lot more than we already figured out," Zack said as he shifted his stance. "What I need to know is where the hell that beef is being processed, who's heading the operation, and where we can track them down."

"That info comes with a little higher price." Jones held out his hand. "In advance."

Zack narrowed his gaze but dug out his wallet that held his creds and pulled out the wad of cash that had been approved for this transaction—money for information. Zack didn't place it into Jones's palm, though.

"You're holding back, man." Zack kept the cash close to his chest. "I want some hard facts."

"San Bernardino Valley." Jones's expression tensed and hardened. "Look for an abandoned ranch."

"Care to narrow that down a little?" Zack clenched the cash in his fist. "You're talking about some pretty big territory."

The informant drew out a pack of cigarettes, shook one out, and put the pack away. Zack's body ached with the need to get this over with.

Jones lit the end of the cigarette, which glowed orange-yellow in the night. He tucked the lighter into his pant pocket before taking a long drag, then blowing smoke out in a cloud.

"I don't have time to fuck around, Jones." Zack began stuffing the wad of cash back into his pocket.

The informant regarded him for a moment. "Not far from the border, a couple miles west of Slaughter Ranch, you'll find what you're looking for." Jones took another pull on his cigarette before flicking ashes onto the gravel and dirt at his feet. "You've got a nice surprise in store, too."

Zack had a hard time keeping his irritation with Jones from showing. "Well, why don't you keep us in fucking suspense all night long."

Jones's pleasant expression faded into a scowl. "Listen, Agent Hunter, I gave you a hell of a lot to go on. Don't push me, or—"

Zack raised an eyebrow. "Are you threatening me?"

"Shit, no." Jones's scowl deepened. "I gave you enough to get your job done. The rest is up to you."

"I want to know what this surprise is."

The corner of Jones's mouth curved as he flicked more glowing ashes onto the dirt. "Someone close to your operation is in on it. Real close."

Hair on the back of Zack's nape prickled. "Care to give me a name?"

Jones shrugged. "If I did, it would cost you a hell of a lot more than you're paying me now."

Zack gave Torres a sharp nod. Zack eyed Jones steadily as Torres stepped in front of Zack and handed Jones a receipt for the cash, along with a pen.

Jones put the paper on the rooftop of his Nissan, scrawled his signature across it, and shoved the receipt back at Torres along with the pen.

"Counted the cash before I left, the agreed amount," Zack said as he handed the money to Jones.

"Fuck you," Jones said as he pocketed the money and strode to the driver's side of the Nissan.

"That went just great," Zack grumbled while he watched the Nissan's taillights as the vehicle's wheels spun in the gravel. The car pulled out of the driveway and onto G Street.

Torres didn't look concerned. "Agent Travers said Jones gets a little pissy sometimes. But he'll jump at the cash and he's completely reliable. Never had a case where his information didn't pan out in one way or another."

"Gotta pay for that snazzy ride somehow," Zack said as he opened the driver's side door of the SUV. "Now to see if his information is worth shit."

And who the hell is involved that's close to the operation.

Even though it was late, as soon as they returned to the office— what had long ago been dubbed the "house"—Zack and Torres got to work.

Thank God their dipshit group supervisor had left for the day. Zack didn't think he could deal with Denning right now.

They pored over the aerial maps of a section of the San Bernardino Valley just east of Douglas and west of Slaughter Ranch.

The junior agent glanced up at Zack. "Looks like a few places have potential. It would take us a week to set up surveillance on all of them."

Zack shook his head. "We're looking for easy access to the

border between this area and Mexico Highway Two." He pointed to a location on the map. "This acreage is damn close to the border, and significant herds of cattle could be held here for sale or processing, too.

"If you look close," Zack continued, "you'll see an awful lot of dark spots clumped together that are possibly cattle." Zack circled the area with his forefinger. "And here are two buildings large enough to handle meat packaging. We'll have to do a search to find out who owns that property."

Torres nodded, his expression thoughtful and assessing. One of the things Zack liked about Torres was how sharp the junior agent was and how fast he learned.

"Here we have what looks like a ranch with plenty of rangeland and what appears to be several buildings." Zack touched another place on the map. "One of which could be used to handle meat packaging, too." Zack glanced at the agent. "The property belongs to a well-known and well-respected rancher, Chuck Markson."

"Markson," Torres said. "Targeting him won't go over well if he's innocent. The man's got some serious clout in these parts."

"Hold on," Torres continued. He turned his attention to his large-screen computer monitor and his fingers worked like lightning as he maneuvered his way through a database. He leaned back and tapped his fingers on his desk. "The other ranch is currently listed as being in foreclosure." He looked at Zack with a shrewd expression. "No one should even be there."

"We'll still need surveillance on both locations." Zack studied the map, zeroing in on the tiny spots he suspected were numerous cattle that should be off grazing and not penned. His gut told him he was right on. "Since we're looking at desert rangeland, our boys are going to have to use any method possible to gather intel and stay out of sight."

"I want to be in on it." Torres pressed his finger on the ranch supposedly in foreclosure. "Starting with this one. We'll use spotting scopes, take a few photos, license plates of people coming and going, and run the tags."

Zack slapped him on the back. "In the morning I'll contact Billingsly at the USDA," Zack continued. "I'll find out if Markson has a USDA permit to process cattle at his location, and if there's any kind of permit on the other suspected location."

Zack tapped his fingers on the map. "I'll get ahold of Sheriff Wayland, too."

Chapter 21

Wednesday, Sky studied her reflection in her bedroom mirror and the revealing red dress she was wearing. "Maybe I should wear something else." She shook her head and grinned. "This dress says exactly what I want. 'Take me, baby.'"

Sky ran the brush through her hair, the copper waves falling wildly around her face and shoulders. For the thousandth time, Sky wondered if she had made a mistake in agreeing to a relationship with Zack. As much as a part of her wished for something more permanent, her heart held back from giving away too much of herself.

Zack had called earlier in the day and asked her out again. He'd sounded tired, but his voice was deep and sexy, a low timbre that traveled straight to her core.

This was crazy. But she had to admit after what happened last night with Hector she needed to get out and forget about everything for a while. And Zack would certainly make sure she didn't have time to think about anything but the two of them for tonight.

Sky took her purse off her vanity table and clutched it to her at the same time Zack's voice rumbled, "Hi, sweetheart."

With a yelp, Sky whirled toward the door. Heat flooded her as her eyes locked with Zack's.

"No one answered when I knocked, so I let myself in." He was leaning against the door frame, his arms folded across his broad chest, and his gaze focused intently on her. His sensual smile and smoldering gray eyes made her stomach flutter. He was wearing his black Stetson, an ivory western dress shirt with pearl snaps, snug jeans, and boots. And damn if she didn't want to eat him up whole.

"You're so beautiful," he said in a husky murmur as he looked her up and down again.

For some reason Sky's hands shook as she gripped her purse. God, was she *nervous*? She managed a smile. "Let me grab my sandals."

She went to her closet and picked out a pair of sandals that matched her little red dress. "I'll get these on and then I'm ready."

Was she *ever* ready.

Zack moved so close that she could feel his heat radiating through her. "Let me."

The heat in her belly traveled down between her thighs as she bit the inside of her lip. Before she could respond, he maneuvered her onto the edge of her bed, and knelt in front of her.

He rested his hands on both sides of her hips, his mouth so close to hers that she could feel the warmth of his breath on her lips. Blood rushed in her ears and her throat went dry.

His eyes slowly traveled down her dress, and her gaze followed his. From her nipples puckering the front of the dress, to her flat belly, down to the garters exposed below the hem of her dress that had hiked up almost to her hips.

Slowly, he slid one finger from one hip, over the exposed skin above the garter, and onto the sheer stocking. Sky gulped, her chest rising and falling as her breathing grew more rapid.

Continuing on down at that maddening pace, Zack trailed his finger over her knee, down her shin to her ankle. He caught her heel in his hand, tracing the ball of her foot, and then raised it to his mouth.

She gasped as he ran his tongue along her arch. The feel of him through her sheer stockings was incredibly erotic.

He nipped at her big toe, then sucked on it, and she thought she was going to climax from the feel of her toe in his warm mouth. She whimpered when he pulled away and he slipped the sandal onto her foot.

Zack let her foot slide out of his grasp, then tugged the other sandal out of her hand. The movement startled her. She'd been so intent on what he was doing, she'd forgotten that she was holding it.

Smiling, he ran his fingers down her other leg until he reached her stockinged foot. He caressed it as he had the other, with his tongue and his mouth, and then slid the sandal on. When he was finished, he brought his gaze to her face.

Nudging her knees apart, Zack moved between her legs and forced her back so that she was partially reclining and bracing her arms on the bed behind her. He pressed against her until the bulge in his jeans was tight against the crotch of her red thong. His face was an inch from hers, yet he made no move to kiss her. He ground his cock harder against her folds, spreading her thighs wider.

Sky moaned as he nuzzled her neck, the feel of his stubble against her skin lighting a fire inside her.

Just as she was about to beg him to take her, he drew away. "I made reservations in Bisbee. We'd better leave if we're going to make it on time."

Surprised and disappointed, Sky only nodded. She wanted him bad. And she wanted him now.

Zack held his hand against the small of Sky's bare back as the hostess led them to an isolated corner of the restaurant.

This time, the cell phone was off. He'd even left the damn thing in his car. Let the rustlers take all the cattle in the county. He had a shitload of work to do tomorrow. Tonight, his attention belonged to Sky.

Her skin felt hot against his fingertips, and he yearned to peel her clothes off and slide his cock into her.

Right on the restaurant floor.

It had been one incredible feat of self-control to not take her the moment he got to her house. But he didn't want her thinking this was only about sex, even though that's all she seemed to want from him.

As they walked across the plush burgundy carpet and through the maze of mauve-draped tables, he wondered what it would take to get Sky to trust him again.

A single candle flickered at the center of the table, barely giving enough light to see by. The restaurant was busy, but the way their table was hidden from view in the corner, they might as well have been alone. Which was just fine with Zack.

Sky set her purse and jacket down on a free chair, then tried to keep that scrap of a red dress from climbing up as Zack seated her.

Let it climb, sweetheart. Let it climb.

He sat in the chair closest to her, so close that his leg pressed against hers. "Don't worry about your dress," Zack whispered in her ear. "It's so dark no one can see, and the table blocks the view."

His gaze roamed over her, and then he added, "From everyone but me, that is."

"If you say so." Sky gave him a wicked smile and stopped trying to pull her dress down. Instead, she wiggled and let her dress hike up to the tops of her thighs.

Zack's cock had an immediate reaction to the sight of those garters, and he was real glad the hostess couldn't see either one of their laps.

The hostess handed them each a menu and told them their waiter would be there soon.

Color rose in Sky's cheeks as Zack studied her. "Why are you staring at me?" she said in a hushed voice.

"You're so damn beautiful." He reached under the table and squeezed her fingers as her features turned even more pink. "I can't stop looking at you."

Sky brought her fingers to her throat and he wondered if the rest of her was as flushed as her face.

A ponytailed waiter interrupted them and Sky requested a white zinfandel. Zack ordered a beer and the shrimp appetizer. A moment after the waiter left, a busboy placed glasses of iced water in front of Sky and Zack.

"Romantic." Sky glanced around the restaurant, picked up her glass, and sipped her iced water.

"Uh-huh." Zack's mind was mush and he could hardly take his eyes off her.

Sky's scent of rain and orange blossoms enveloped him, sharpening his senses. Her thick hair fell in a copper wave over her shoulders, resting on the tops of her breasts. Candlelight reflected in her eyes and her lips were glossy and slightly parted.

The thought of what she could do with those lips damn near made Zack groan aloud.

Before the waiter returned with their drinks, Sky glanced at her menu. Zack flicked his gaze over the specials, hardly able to concentrate, and practically chose the first thing he saw.

After the waiter brought their drinks and took their orders for their main course, he left them alone and vanished again into the restaurant's darkness. Zack found himself wishing the guy would stay away. At least long enough for him to steal a kiss from Sky. Or two.

To hell with the waiter.

Sky picked up her glass of white zin and smiled. Through the crystal wineglass he saw her tongue press against the rim, the rose wine rolling over her lips. Mesmerized, he watched her throat as she swallowed.

He swallowed, too. His throat was so dry he didn't think he could have spoken a word.

Forcing himself to move, Zack picked up his draft and downed half the glass before letting himself look at Sky again.

The sensual play continued until the smell of grilled shrimp alerted Zack that the waiter had brought the plate of appetizers they'd ordered. Sky picked up a shrimp and peeled off the tail. Then she held the piece between her thumb and forefinger and placed it in front of Zack's lips.

"Open up," she murmured, and slipped the shrimp into his

mouth when he did. Zack sucked her fingers as she withdrew them and he felt the slight tremor of her hand.

"The taste of you was the best part," he said before he picked out a shrimp. Her eyes focused on him and she parted her lips. As he put the shrimp into her mouth, she caressed his fingers with butterfly strokes of her tongue.

Just from what Sky was doing with that incredible tongue, Zack's cock was so hard his eyes almost watered.

She brought another shrimp to his mouth and his gaze strayed to her breasts. He suckled her fingertips like he wanted to be doing to her large nipples. Slow, lazy strokes and then harder, applying slight suction.

Too soon, or maybe not soon enough, the shrimp were gone. Sky licked her own fingers as she stared at him, the candlelight reflecting desire in her green eyes.

The waiter arrived with their meals, but they barely noticed.

Zack had never had a meal that was a sexual experience like this one. Every bite Sky took made him feel as if she was thinking about going down on his cock, licking her tongue along his length, and swallowing his come.

She continued to feed him bites of grilled chicken with her fingers, and he returned the favor, until their plates were clean.

"Dessert?" the waiter asked when he cleared their plates away.

Frankly, Zack wanted to get out of the restaurant and out to his truck. He'd never screwed in the cab before, but at the moment it was looking real good.

Sky glanced up from the dessert menu and licked her bottom lip. "Why don't we share a piece of chocolate cheesecake?"

Zack could hardly form a coherent thought, as all his blood had settled in his groin, so he settled for a quick nod.

In a few minutes, the waiter returned with the slice of cheesecake and set it in front of them with two forks. Raspberry sauce drizzled down one side of the dessert.

Sky dipped her finger in the sauce and sucked it off. "Mmmm, this is heaven."

Zack thrust his fork into the cheesecake. "I know what's even better."

She gave him a seductive smile. "Oh, you do?"

As he held the bite of cheesecake in front of her lips, Zack's right hand glided up her thigh, over the silky stockings, and to the bare flesh above.

Chapter 22

She gasped as his hand traveled beneath her dress to the wisp of satin thong beneath. "Zack," she whispered, but he slipped the bit of cheesecake into her mouth.

"Better than cheesecake." He skimmed the crotch of her thong, and smiled when he felt how damp it was. He found the edge of the fabric, and her eyes widened as his fingers brushed over the curls beneath.

Her hand trembled as she put her own fork into the dessert and she held it up to his lips. The cheesecake was smooth and creamy and melted over his tongue as his fingers glided into the wetness of her folds. He wanted nothing more than to taste her right now instead of that cheesecake.

"If you keep doing that," Sky said with obvious difficulty, "I'm going to come right here in the restaurant."

"That's the idea." Zack fed her another bite of cheesecake as he continued to rub his finger over her clit. "No one can tell what we're doing."

He looked into her eyes, the passion in them driving him wild. "I want to watch you come, sweetheart. Now."

In the next moment her hand was in his lap, caressing his cock through his jeans. His own hand shook a little from the feel of her palm on his erection. He thrust his fork into the cheesecake again, then slid the bite into her warm mouth just as she parted her lips and climaxed.

Her body shuddered with wave after wave of her orgasm. He didn't let up stroking her clit until the tremors stopped and she relaxed against the back of the booth.

"*Oh. My. God,*" she said breathlessly. "Unbelievable."

Watching Sky come had damn near put Zack over the edge. She continued to stroke his cock as she looked at him with heavy-lidded eyes. He slipped his fingers out of her thong and placed his palm over her hand, stopping the motion that was driving him out of his mind.

With a shaky sigh, she sat straighter in her seat. Her free hand trembled as she picked up her glass of wine. "I'll never think of chocolate cheesecake in quite the same way," she murmured over the rim of her glass, and then drained the contents before setting her glass down.

Zack focused on her lips and kissed her, licking away a bit of raspberry sauce from the corner of her mouth. She tasted of raspberries and wine.

The waiter approached and set the check on the table. "Anything else I can do for you?"

Sky shook her head and Zack said, "We're more than fine."

"Great. Come again."

Sky burst into a fit of giggles and Zack's lips quirked. "I'm sure we will."

With a puzzled almost smile, the waiter took their empty dessert plate and left. Zack pulled cash out of his wallet and put it in the center of the table with the bill.

Sky dabbed her lips with her napkin, and then tossed the napkin under the table.

Zack raised an eyebrow. "What did you do that for?"

She winked. "Oops. I dropped my napkin. Better get it."

Before he could say a word, she slid beneath the table-cloth.

Blood pounded in Zack's ears. Sky wasn't about to do what he thought she was. Was she?

"Ah, Sky?" he said as she disappeared.

She pushed the tablecloth out of the way and moved between his thighs. "I'm going to return the favor."

Zack's breathing became ragged and his hard-on positively ached. "Uh, I don't think—"

"Mmmm." Sky's nimble fingers found his belt and she unfastened it. "Weren't you the one who told me no one could see us?" she said. "The waiter left the check, so he's not likely to come back right away." Her words were slightly muffled, but the sensual tone was unmistakable. "But *you'll* come."

Zack felt a tug on his zipper, and then thrill and release as she freed his cock.

His eyes darted around the restaurant.

No one could see them.

Right?

God, he hoped not.

And then he couldn't think anymore as Sky's hot breath teased him. Slowly, she slid him into her mouth, flicking her tongue around the head of his cock.

He groaned, then bit the inside of his cheek, fighting to hold back the next groan.

As if sensing her advantage, Sky went down on him, taking him deep.

Her mouth was warm. Hot. Burning.

Zack slipped a hand beneath the tablecloth and clenched her hair in his fist. There was something about sitting in a restaurant and not being able to see what she was doing to him that made it all the more intense.

He chewed his cheek to the point of blood, holding back another groan as Sky stroked him with her hand and mouth, sucking and licking him. Her other hand caressed his balls.

Intense sensations flooded Zack. *"Sky . . ."*

He'd never felt anything like this. Not even close.

Fighting to keep his eyes open, to be sure no one was about to catch them and haul them straight to jail, he gave himself up to Sky's hot mouth.

He couldn't help it. Sweet Jesus. What was she doing to him?

Sweat broke across his forehead as Sky took him deeper in her throat. Soft. Wet.

In the next instant, Zack's body corded. He clenched his teeth to hold back a shout as he came. She grabbed his hips and held him at the back of her throat, swallowing his semen until the last surge of his orgasm ended.

His vision was still hazy when he noticed the waiter approaching. Sky started to get up, but Zack leaned closer to the table and pressed down on her head with his palm.

"Waiter," he mumbled, and heard her soft laugh from between his knees.

When the waiter reached the table, his gaze flicked to Sky's empty seat and then to the cash.

"Keep the change," Zack managed to say, his jaw twitching as he felt Sky's hand caressing his cock. Up and down. Slowly. Teasing him, wanting a repeat.

And damned if he wasn't getting hard again.

"Thanks," the waiter said as he picked up the money. "Have a good one." With a slight nod he turned and left.

"Oh, I did," Zack murmured under his breath.

His hands slid back to Sky's hair. He tried to pull her up, but she wasn't budging.

Slowly, her tongue worked him again, from top to bottom.

He was pouring sweat now, and his body jerked as she closed her lips over him again, making him fucking harder than before.

Her hands traveled to his hips, forcing him forward as her sucking became more demanding. More insistent.

Zack let go of her and grabbed the table.

"Damn," he whispered. "Damn, woman. Have you lost your mind?"

Sky purred, and the rumble of her voice against his now-throbbing shaft was too much to bear.

Zack closed his eyes.

Let the whole restaurant know. He couldn't care less. All that mattered was Sky's mouth. The rhythm of her ceaseless caress as she took him in, up and down, harder and faster.

The table rattled as he came and was unable to hold back a fresh round of groans. His face burned, and he coughed, trying to cover up the sound.

Thank God she only kissed him a few more times then

stopped. She tucked his still semihard cock back into his jeans, and he heard the hum of the zipper before she fastened his belt buckle.

Once more, his hands found Sky's hair and ran down her body as she rose from under the tablecloth to her seat. She grinned and dabbed her lips with the napkin.

"Found it," she said.

Zack opened his mouth, but all that came out was a rattling sigh of exhaustion. He felt like he could fall asleep on the table. Face-first. But he didn't dare. Who knew what Sky might do to him then?

She grinned at him, letting the napkin fall across his shaking hand. "Maybe you ought to be more careful starting things you can't finish in public, Zack Hunter."

"I'll keep that in mind." His voice sounded like gravel in a box.

Sky wrapped her arms around his neck. "You're still the most exciting man I've ever met."

He pressed his lips to her forehead. "And you're dangerous, sweetheart."

Her green eyes glittered, and she kissed the corner of his mouth. "I love how you taste." She released her hold around his neck and checked the zipper on his jeans. "You ready to leave, baby?"

Zack wasn't too sure he could walk straight but he cleared his throat and nodded. "Let's get you out of here before you drop anything else."

Chapter 23

Sheer contentment settled throughout Sky as Zack drove them back to the ranch. She couldn't believe how intense her orgasm had been, heightened by being in a public place and the danger of getting caught.

Sky grinned to herself. She'd so enjoyed giving Zack his due, taking his cock in her mouth under that table. The power she'd had over him had been intoxicating. It had been incredible feeling his release as he came in her throat, and how she loved making him come twice in one sitting.

She so wanted to ride that cowboy, and ride him good and hard.

A country tune played on the radio as she studied his features in the amber glow of the dashboard lights. So gorgeous. That rugged profile, the cleft in his chin, the strong line of his jaw, even the scar on his cheek made him dangerously exciting. Just looking at him made her entire body ache.

Zack turned his truck onto the dirt road that led to the Flying M Ranch. She abandoned her attack on his lap as they pulled up to the ranch house. He parked the Silverado and killed the engine.

The instant his hands were off the steering wheel, he cupped the back of Sky's head and brought her to him, in a hard, rough movement. She gasped as his tongue thrust into her mouth, his lips grinding against hers. He tasted of beer and the more intoxicating flavor of man.

His free hand captured her breast, squeezed and fondled it through the silky material of her dress.

When he lifted his head to look at her, his breathing was rough and his expression possessive. "God, I want you."

"You've got me, baby," she said as her heart pounded.

"Let's get in the house." With a jerk he opened the truck door and climbed out.

Zack might want to wait to get in the house, but Sky had other plans.

As she followed him out the driver's side door, she intentionally let her red dress slide up her hips while she climbed out of the cab. She was facing him, her garters exposed almost up to her thong.

Zack braced his hand against the truck door, staring at her thighs as if he'd lost his brains. Well, she knew right where they'd gone. South. The perfect place.

"Oops. Forgot my things." She turned and bent over the seat as she reached for her purse and jacket, her dress hiking up even farther. Cool air caressed her backside, which was bare thanks to her thong, and she knew she was giving him a great view. She wiggled her hips and parted her legs, letting the dress shimmy up a little more.

Thank God the ranch hands couldn't see what she was doing.

From behind she heard his groan, and then his warm hands pushed her dress up around her waist, completely exposing her naked bottom.

"Zack," she murmured as he caressed her bare flesh, his hands rough and possessive. "What are you doing?" As if he weren't doing exactly what she had wanted him to do.

"You drive me out of my mind, woman," he murmured as he pressed his groin to her ass, his jeans rough against her bare flesh.

His cock felt good and hard through his jeans and against her ass. It was totally delicious being bent over, half in and half out of his truck cab in her backless dress, high heels, stockings, garters, and thong.

He kissed her bare back, trailing his lips along her spine and sending shivers through her body. Easing his hands into her hair, he pushed it away from the neck of her dress and unfastened the clasp. One quick tug and he'd pulled the top of her dress down until her clothing bunched around her waist.

Zack cupped her nipples and she moaned as he fondled them. Her breasts ached and her folds were so wet for him she could just about scream.

"Let's get in the house," he murmured, his voice a low rumble and his warm breath tickling her back. "I've got to have you."

Sky pressed her hips back against his cock. "Take me here."

"Don't tempt me." A groan rolled from his throat as he kissed her nape and caressed her breasts. "We need to go inside."

"I want *you* inside. *Me.*" Sky covered his big hands and pressed them tighter to her breasts. "Take me *now*, Zack."

"Damn," Zack said. "The ranch hands."

"We're on the opposite side of the truck," Sky said. "The

bunkhouse isn't that close to the main house, so I doubt anyone could see us."

Pausing and giving him a mischievous grin over her shoulder, she added, "Not to mention it makes it all the more naughty."

"You're incredible." He removed his hands from beneath hers, and she heard the sound of him unfastening his buckle, and then his zipper going down. In the next moment his warm cock pressed against her.

Oh, God. That felt *so* good.

He kneaded and fondled her ass, then trailed his fingers down the crevice. Working his way lower, he teased the curls but didn't enter the wetness between her thighs.

"I'm going to strangle you if you don't move a little faster," Sky murmured as she moved her hips against his hand.

He slid a finger into her warm folds, stroking her clit, and Sky dug her nails into the leather upholstery. "Like this?"

"Yes. More." Sky gasped when he thrust two fingers inside her.

His strokes intensified. "You're so wet."

She couldn't wait any longer. She needed to feel him deep inside of her. "Now, baby. *Now.*"

He slipped his fingers from her fold. She heard the rustle of a package and she knew he was slipping on a condom. A moment later he hooked his fingers around the waist of her thong and eased it down almost to her knees.

While he gripped her hips with his hands, he pressed his sheathed cock against her. He teased her with slow thrusts between her legs but didn't enter her.

Sky clenched her hands in frustration. Bent over like she was, she couldn't reach him—a definite disadvantage. She wanted to be touching him, tasting him.

But did it ever feel incredible. The smell of his leather upholstery surrounded her, along with the scent of cool desert air and
sex.

He used both hands to part her folds and pressed his cock
against her opening. Oh, thank God. This was what she'd been
waiting for. She needed Zack inside so bad she almost had tears
in her eyes.

Sky whimpered and moved her hips back, wanting him to
hurry. But he only teased and tortured her, entering a little bit
at a time and then pulling back out.

He gripped her hips. "You really want me to take you right
here?"

"Yes, damnit. Now, Zack!"

With one powerful thrust, he buried his cock inside her.
Sky cried out, so close to going over the edge and they'd only
started.

He plunged in and out, slow and steady.

Too slow.

"Faster, baby. Harder," Sky begged.

In reply he pounded into her, the sound of his flesh slapping
against hers filling the night. "You feel nice and tight around
me."

Sky moved her hips back as he thrust into her. Her breasts
chafed against the upholstery as incredible sensations built up
inside her. Knowing that she'd need something to hold on to,
she clenched the steering wheel with one hand, while she dug
the fingers of her other hand into the soft leather seat.

The intensity of her climax took her completely by surprise.
It stormed through her like a thunderstorm, and she couldn't
help letting out a long, loud cry. Her body rocked against the

seat, her orgasm stretching out in endless waves as Zack continued to thrust into her.

And then he growled deep in his throat and shuddered. His cock pulsated inside her and she clenched the muscles of her core, wanting to feel every bit of his release.

He sank against her back, slipping his hands around her waist and trailing kisses across her shoulders.

"Mmmm," she purred, enjoying the feel of him, his cock still inside her. His shirt was soft as it rubbed her naked back, but his jeans were coarse against her bare skin.

He nuzzled her neck. "After that scream, your dog probably thinks you've been attacked."

Vaguely in the background she heard the sound of Blue barking from inside the house. "I think you might be right."

Zack pulled away and Sky almost whimpered from the feel of his still hard cock leaving her. Taking her by the shoulders, he turned her around, cupped her face in his hands, and kissed her.

Oh, could that man kiss.

He moved his lips over hers, gently devouring her in a sensual kiss that turned her body into a mass of melted chocolate, warm and gooey, and ready to pour herself back over him.

When their lips parted, he looked at her and smiled. "Did I mention how incredible you are?"

"Once or twice." Sky kissed the corner of his mouth, fighting the temptation to try for another time. The man probably needed some time to regenerate.

Good Lord, was she becoming a nympho?

Damn straight.

Before she knew what he was doing, he grabbed her around

the waist and set her on the front seat of the truck cab, then slid her thong completely off.

"What are you doing?" she asked as he spread her legs, staring at her mound.

His voice was rough as he replied, "I've got to taste you." He hooked her legs over his shoulders and buried his face between her thighs before she had a chance to form a thought.

"Zack!" Sky cupped her breasts, as he sucked and licked her clit. She squirmed, crying out when he plunged his fingers into her, his satisfied groan against her clit sending vibrations through her already sensitized body.

The leather seat was slick with her sweat as he devoured her, his cheek stubble rough against her soft skin. She pinched and twisted her nipples, clenching her knees tight around his head. A buzzing filled her mind and she no longer felt anything but his tongue licking her clit, his fingers thrusting inside, and the climax rising within her.

When Sky came, she dug her hands into the leather seat and shouted his name. Zack continued licking her, pushing his face against her until she climaxed yet another time. Her body shuddered with wave after wave of sensation.

When he stopped, she felt so sated and limp that she knew she'd never move again.

Zack pulled back and rested his head on her leg as Sky continued to feel aftershocks from her orgasms. "You taste so good, sweetheart," he murmured as he touched her clit with his finger, causing her body to spasm even harder.

"Doooon't," Sky moaned. "I can't take any more."

"You know what they say about revenge." Zack raised himself up and grabbed Sky's hands, pulling her to a sitting position.

"Revenge?" Her head was still fuzzy from the orgasms.

Pressing her close to him, Zack slowly kissed her. She tasted her own musk on his lips. When he raised his head, he smiled. "For that 'down under' experience at the restaurant."

"Oh. That." Sky ran her fingers along the scar that made him seem almost dangerous in the moonlight. "I like your kind of revenge."

After he fastened his belt and jeans, Zack helped Sky straighten her clothes. He closed the door of his truck, wrapped his arm around her shoulders, and walked her to the house.

The corner of Zack's mouth turned up and she went weak-kneed at the sight of his devastating smile. "What am I going to do with you?" he murmured as they walked up the porch steps.

They stopped in front of the door and she reached up and brushed her lips over his. "Anything you want."

He placed his hands around her waist and nuzzled the top of her head. "Anything?"

Sky gave a sigh, feeling so contented that she wrapped her arms around his waist and buried her face against his chest. The emotions rolling through her were making her dizzy. She couldn't tell one from another, and the thought of what they could be scared her, twisting her stomach into knots.

She couldn't be falling in love with Zack Hunter all over again.

Chapter 24

The next morning, Thursday, Sky shifted from one foot to the other in Hector's hospital room as she looked down at him. A twinge of guilt ran through her at the thought of how much she'd enjoyed herself with Zack while Hector lay in his hospital bed, his body battered and broken.

Outside the door stood the wiry, goateed Deputy Blalock, who was Hector's guard today.

Hector's fingers felt hot against Sky's as she squeezed them gently—the parts of his fingers that weren't covered by the cast.

Sky tried to ignore the hospital smell of disinfectant that didn't disguise the lingering odors of death left behind by other patients.

The smells reminded her too much of when her mother had passed away from cancer. Nina MacKenna had been a large woman with soft, full curves that were made for hugging. Sky had felt like she was the most loved child on earth whenever her mother embraced her. When her light had finally left the world, Nina had been nothing but a skeleton, a remnant of that once vibrant soul.

Just the memories made more tears try to fight their way forward. Throughout her illness, Nina MacKenna had gone from being a robust woman full of life to a frail, thin woman gripping the hand of death.

The last time Sky had seen her mother, her thin lips had formed a weak smile as she looked from Trinity to Sky. They each held one of their mother's hands as tears flooded their cheeks.

"*I love you,*" their mother had whispered before slipping away. Her last three words. *I love you.*

Sky bit the inside of her cheek and focused on Hector, trying not to cry from the memories of her mother's death.

"I'm so sorry, Hector." Sky pulled a green-padded chair close to his bed, then gripped his fingers again. "We'll get the bastards who did this to you."

Surprise jolted through Sky when Hector squeezed her fingers. He rolled his head to face her and his lips moved like he was trying to form words.

Sky's heart beat faster and she held her breath for a moment before she asked, "What is it? Who did this?"

The sound that rose from Hector's bruised throat was a horrible grating noise. His lips moved and she leaned closer as he tried to speak out of the side of his mouth where the jaw wasn't broken.

"Wu . . . wu . . ." His swollen throat worked as he swallowed. His eyelids fluttered as if the effort to speak was exhausting him.

"Water?" Sky said as she squeezed his fingers.

She thought for a moment he was trying to move his head from side to side.

"Deputy Blalock." Sky raised her voice. "Hector's trying to speak."

"Wu . . . ," Hector tried again just before the deputy entered the room.

Hector's body slackened and he fully closed his swollen eyes.

At first a burst of fear hit Sky full in the chest as the thought slammed into her that he could be dead. But she relaxed as she saw the steady rise and fall of his chest and the vital signs on the monitors didn't vary.

"Ms. MacKenna?" the deputy said as he looked down at her with concern.

Sky explained what had happened. "I imagine he was asking for water, but I'd hoped he'd be able to tell us who did this to him—that's why I called you into the room."

Deputy Blalock nodded. "I'll keep an eye on him to see if he wakes again."

Sky took a deep breath. "Thanks."

After the deputy left, Sky turned back to Hector. "You get some rest." She lightly settled her hand on his cast as the backs of her eyes stung. "We'll take care of everything."

She squeezed his fingers one last time before she left Hector's hospital room. The deputy guarding the room gave her a short nod, and she tried to answer it with a smile but failed and turned away to head out of the hospital.

Her sneakers squeaked on the county hospital's cracked linoleum floor. Sky stopped and spoke to the nurse manning the reception desk and let her know that Hector had tried to talk and that she thought he was asking for water.

Sky took the cell phone from the clip on her western leather belt and called Zack's number that he'd given her back when he'd been working with Satan.

A few rings and then she was directed to his voice mail. "Hey, Zack," she said as her gaze roved the parking lot through the glass front doors. "I just visited Hector Ramirez at the hospital. He tried to talk but was only able to get out a 'wu' sound. He was probably asking for water but I thought you might want to know he woke long enough to attempt to speak."

When she finished, she closed her cell phone and reclipped it to her belt. She took a deep breath and pushed open the hospital's glass front doors and stepped into the chilly but clear October morning.

After saddling Empress, Sky swung up and onto the sorrel mare. Leather creaked as Sky seated herself and loosely held the reins of the bridle. Blue stood calmly by Empress, waiting for them to head out.

Dust motes glittered in a shaft of sunlight, particles of hay floating with the dust. The familiar scents of alfalfa, manure, horse, and cob with molasses calmed Sky and the ongoing tightness in her belly relaxed. She could almost forget all that had happened over the past few weeks. This was normal. This was how things should be.

She smiled at the memory of the crazy-wonderful sex she'd had with Zack. Good Lord. Zack had given her an orgasm in a restaurant while feeding her cheesecake. And then she'd gone down on him *under the table,* making him come *twice.* God, and the sex half in, half out of the truck had been so *hot.*

Sky had woken at dawn just as Zack had been ready to leave.

He had to change at his place and get to work. Then she'd gotten up, showered, and gone to the hospital to visit Hector.

Her smile vanished into a frown and she couldn't help a deep sigh. *Damn, damn, damn.*

Sky clicked her tongue and pressed her knees into the sorrel's sides. "Let's go, girl." Empress tossed her head, the bit firmly in her mouth. "You, too, Blue," Sky added to her Border Collie. "We're escaping this place and getting some fresh air and sunshine."

Sky always found herself talking to Blue and Empress like they were people. They certainly were just as intelligent, if not smarter than a lot of people.

Blue trotted at Empress's side as Sky guided the sorrel out of the barn into the cool October afternoon. The copper-red Quarter Horse was one of the finest on the ranch and of Sky's best breeding stock.

In the house, Sky had tucked her S&W in its holster at her side, her long overshirt covering the weapon. The S&W was the only company she wanted right now, other than Blue, who was a damned good guard dog when she needed him to be.

Of course her cell phone was in its clip on her leather belt, the phone set on vibrate. She wished she could turn it off for a while. She didn't want any interruption to break the afternoon's peace, but she was the owner of a large ranch and if she was needed, she had to be available.

In one saddlebag she'd shoved a pair of pliers, her heavy-duty leather work gloves, and a small spool of baling wire in case she found any downed fence lines. She could do a temporary patch to keep the cattle in if she needed to and send one of the hands out to finish the job later. As usual when she worked, she had her utility knife shoved into the right front pocket of her jeans.

The other saddlebag contained her snack—a banana and a granola bar—along with some treats for Blue and Empress. Of course she had a couple of large bottles of water.

Sky's long braid swung across her back as she, Empress, and Blue headed out to the south pasture. The hay had been harvested in August and the bales now filled the southern end of the cattle barn.

It was the middle of October and the fields had turned yellow. The scent of fall was in the air and she was thankful for the overshirt to protect her arms from the slight chill. Overnight the weather could turn and she'd be freezing her ass off the next time she rode out onto her acreage to work or just to get some fresh air.

In another month roundup would begin so that her cattle could be vaccinated and wormed. Then part of her herd would be cut and shipped. The calves would be castrated, tagged, and branded with the more-than-a-century-old Flying M brand. She tightened her jaw. Luke would have a better idea at that time just how many of her cattle had been rustled. And damnit, she was afraid it was more than they had figured.

Blue bounded ahead of her, head down every now and then as he sniffed the path they were taking. Empress's hooves sank into the earth that was still damp from the rain the night Hector had been beaten.

Sky frowned and her stomach did an angry flip. Thank God Hector was going to pull through. "At least Hector's alive." Sky used her knees to guide Empress south. "That's what counts right now."

The mare whickered and tossed her head. Blue looked over his shoulder and gave a short woof. It sounded as if they both agreed.

Sky had to smile at that.

It wasn't long before they reached the fence dividing the Flying M and Wade's ranch, Coyote Pass.

A jackrabbit bounded across Empress's path, but the sorrel was so well trained she didn't so much as step sideways. Blue watched the rabbit, but he was just as well trained as the mare and didn't give chase. The Border Collie was trained to work cattle and obeyed Sky's every order.

For a while Sky traveled along the length of the fence line with her two companions. They reached the eastern pasture where her cattle grazed. The southern pasture had already been harvested or Sky would have had them herded there. As it was, the only grazing fodder was in the eastern pasture and they'd been forced to leave the cattle where they were, regardless of the rustlers.

Sky swung down from her saddle to open the gate from the southern to the eastern pasture. She guided Empress through with Blue following before she shut the gate behind them. She mounted the horse again, settling comfortably in the well-worn saddle.

Sky let out a huff of breath as she looked down the stretch of fence that had been patched in several places where it had been cut.

She scowled at the tire tracks and flattened grass that told her where the rustlers had broken through to take her cattle. Luke and Zack, along with Sheriff Wayland, had already investigated the area and were checking to see if the prints along this fence line matched those where Hector had been beaten.

If her ranch weren't a thousand acres, it might have been easier to patrol the eastern range, but as it was they didn't have the man power. Her ranch hands were at a minimum until roundup in the fall and spring.

Horse hooves hitting the earth hard caught Sky's attention. She glanced back the way she'd come. On the other side of the fence, a rider approached at a gallop and a whirling sensation tingled in Sky's belly. The man was large and rangy and she wasn't positive who it was. As for the horse, at first Sky just saw the head and chest, which were cinnamon red in color. But then she got a glimpse of the horse's hindquarters and saw that it was an Appaloosa.

Wade, she realized as he and his horse got closer. Just great. After his last visit she'd rather put him on the end of a stick and roast him on a barbeque spit.

A low rumble rose in Blue's throat and she glanced at the Border Collie. She turned back to watch the approaching man. "I did tell you that you had permission to bite him in the ass the next time you saw him."

Blue growled a little louder and Sky looked at the dog. "Let's hold off on the ass biting for a moment. Okay, boy?"

The border collie stopped growling but remained at Sky and Empress's side.

When Wade reached them he pulled his mount up short. His green eyes looked as fiery and obstinate as ever.

Empress shifted beneath Sky as if sensing her irritation—or perhaps because she was pressing her knees tight to the mare's sides without realizing it. Sky relaxed the pressure as she tilted her chin and met his gaze. "What can I do for you, Wade?" She said with a hint of ice to her tone.

Wade removed his straw western hat, his hair plastered to his forehead with sweat. His collar was soaked and perspiration glistened on his face. Despite obviously working a long, hard, sweaty day, he was still a handsome man. It was easy to see the sexual appeal in him that she'd found enticing. She'd grown up around Wade, but she'd been too much younger than him to really know him—four years was a big gap as kids. It wasn't until he truly turned into a man and she was older that she'd found him attractive.

She certainly hadn't found him too attractive when he'd been by last, though.

"I planned to come by your place later," Wade said as he wiped the back of his sleeve over his sweaty forehead. "But I saw you heading on out this way and I thought I'd meet up with you so that we could talk."

Sky narrowed her eyes. "I think you said enough."

His jaw tightened before his eyes met and held hers. "I think we could have had something if Hunter hadn't returned."

"You and I didn't have a relationship beyond being friends." A strange sensation swirled in her stomach as she watched his darkening expression. "We hadn't even dated for a couple of months."

"Only because you were too busy." His scowl deepened. "At least you said you were."

"I *was* busy," she said, suddenly feeling the need to be careful of every word she spoke. "But I also didn't realize you thought our relationship was more than casual."

"I've had a thing for you for years." Wade's gelding side-stepped and Wade brought the horse back in line. "You know that."

"You've always been a good friend." She gripped Empress's

reins. "I thought that would be enough for our relationship to go somewhere, but it never felt right to me."

Wade's knuckles looked a little white as he clenched the Appaloosa's reins. "You're making a mistake."

A crawling sensation tickled the back of her neck. Something wasn't right.

His voice came out harsh when he continued speaking. "Everything changes. Sometimes you gotta do what you gotta do."

Blue growled and the way Wade said those words sent a chill along Sky's spine. "What do you mean?"

His eyes returned to hers, his gaze hard now. "Nothing to concern yourself with."

A lead weight went straight to Sky's stomach. For the first time she noticed the Remington rifle secured on his saddle. His pistol was in the holster strapped to his thigh as usual, like a cowboy gunslinger from a century ago.

Wade used the horse's reins to wheel the Appaloosa around, facing his ranch. "Watch out for yourself, Skylar," he said before he snapped his reins and urged the gelding away at a steady gallop.

Sky swallowed as she watched the horse and rider fade from sight. Shit. Did Wade have something to do with the rustling? Did he have some kind of personal vendetta—maybe against her? What had that all been about?

She caught her breath. No way he'd be jealous enough to go after Zack, right?

"No," she repeated aloud as she stared at what was now just a pinprick of Wade and his horse. She'd had a hard time believing Wade would even be involved with the rustling. But she'd believe that before she'd even consider him capable of murder.

All of a sudden the scene in Hector's hospital room came back to her. What if he hadn't been asking for water but had been trying to tell her a name? The name of his attacker.

Wade.

"No, damnit." She said the words loud enough that Blue looked at her.

Was she being fricking naïve? She rubbed her forehead with her palm as she pictured Hector's battered body. Was Wade capable of that kind of violence?

Should she tell Zack? Or was she just overreacting? Wade hadn't actually come out and threatened anyone.

Still . . .

"Wu . . . wu . . . wu   "

"Wade?" she said as she stared in the direction he had cantered off with his horse.

Damn.

Maybe she should let Zack know of her thought that Hector could have been saying a name instead of asking for water.

Crazy.

But what if?

Sky sucked in her breath so deep her lungs ached. She decided to follow her instincts and tugged her cell phone out of its clip. Again she reached Zack's voice mail. She let him know about her run-in with Wade.

She felt silly, but she continued, "I'm wondering if Hector was trying to say a name that started with *W* instead of asking for water. I'm probably wrong, but the thought occurred to me.

"If you come over," she added, "I'm off in the eastern pasture checking the fence line. I needed some fresh air to sort things out."

Sky called Luke just to let him know where she was and when he could expect her to be back.

After she'd shoved her cell phone in its clip she said, "Come on, Empress. Blue. Let's get to work."

Spending time on the fence line this afternoon, and some good, physical labor, was bound to help her work out her frustrations.

Chapter 25

Zack made a stop at the assisted-living center and was glad that his mother was having a good day. She deserved so much more than the life she was forced to lead. Every time Zack saw his mother in the condition she was in now, he couldn't help but mentally curse his father and his stepfather.

Afterward, Zack spent the morning out in the field, doing a portion of the surveillance.

Looked like Markson was clean, but the foreclosed ranch wasn't. Plenty of activity going on there—they almost had enough probable cause for that search warrant they needed.

And the dirt was the same color of mud they'd found in Sky's office.

When Zack made it back into the office, it was late in the afternoon. He finally had time to check his messages, and one of them was from Sky. A warm rush of pleasure went through him when he heard the sensual tone of her voice as she said, "Hi, Zack."

She told him Ramirez had been conscious enough to make a sound, probably asking for water. That was good. Maybe Ramirez would be able to give them information soon and tell them who his attacker was.

But when Zack heard the second message from Sky, the warmth inside him turned into a chill.

She'd just had a disturbing run-in with Larson. Not only that, but her theory about Ramirez trying to say a name starting with a *W* had blood pumping faster through Zack's veins.

The informant had said someone they knew was involved.

"Wu . . ." Zack made the sound out loud as he looked out the window of his office and stared at the cars in the parking lot. Could Ramirez have been trying to say "Wade"?

Zack dragged his hand down his face. Shit. Could Larson have attacked Ramirez?

Was Sky in danger from Larson? But he hadn't done anything when he met up with her.

But . . . shit.

Zack had to think this through before he reacted. If it wasn't Larson, it might be someone else they knew, someone close to the operation like the snitch had said.

"Who have names that start with *W*?" Zack said as he pinched the bridge of his nose again.

In his mind he ran through those he could think of.

As the names churned through his mind only three came to him.

Wade Larson, Gary Woods, and the sheriff, Clay Wayland. All were close to the case and all had either a first or last name that started with *W.*

Shit.

Might mean something. Might mean nothing. But Zack intended to check out every damn possibility—and in a hurry.

Torres walked into their shared office.

"We need to do some quick research," Zack said. "We've got to find out everything we can on Clay Wayland, Gary Woods, and Wade Larson."

"The sheriff?" Torres said with raised eyebrows.

"I cover my bases," Wayland had said. Zack sure as hell was going to cover his.

Torres pulled his chair up to his computer while Zack stood behind him. With his arms folded across his chest, Zack stared at the computer monitor. Torres brought up TECS, the Treasury Enforcement Communications System.

Zack had Torres run Clay Wayland's name first. No history of violations, but he had a few Currency Transaction Reports.

"His CTRs show inflow and outflow of some damn good sums of cash, over ten thousand dollars," Torres said. "A lot of money movement for a sheriff on a modest salary."

"Seems I heard that buying, developing, and selling rural properties is how Wayland has made a good living." Zack shifted to get a better look at the record. "Certainly can't expect the man to survive on a county sheriff's salary."

NCIC, the National Crime Information Center, was just as clean. The man was golden.

Too golden?

And there was still Wade Larson to consider in all this.

They moved on to Larson next.

Even though Zack and Wade had never been what anyone would call buddies, Zack had a hard time believing that Wade was capable of crimes like these. But Zack didn't fool himself for a minute—he'd seen some of the most wholesome-appearing, all-American young men and women turn out to be big-time criminals. And Wade Larson was far from wholesome.

"TECS is clean on Larson." Torres rubbed his hand over his military haircut. "No history of investigations for smuggling of any kind—firearms, drugs, undocumented aliens."

"At one time his business apparently had some real good years," Zack said. "Multiple CTRs for well over ten thousand dollars associated with his ranch account."

Torres nodded. "Yeah, but the last couple of years don't look so hot."

"Is Larson hurting for money?" Zack said aloud, but to himself. Enough to get caught up in rustling and smuggling beef to Mexico?

"Check NCIC for a criminal history," Zack said to Torres, who had it up within in a few seconds.

"Underage possession of alcohol when he was eighteen and again at twenty." Zack ran his gaze down the screen. Twenty-one was the legal drinking age in Arizona. A man could die for his country at eighteen but couldn't legally drink until twenty-one. That was some screwed-up shit. "Hell," Zack said, "who hasn't been caught drinking before they were 'of age?'"

"The man's been in a couple of brawls." Torres pointed to the screen. "Disorderly conducts and assault charges."

Zack said nothing, but he rubbed the scar across his cheek that burned at the memories. His own NCIC record showed his arrest for just about beating his stepfather to death. The bastard had almost killed Zack's mother, but Zack was the one with the black mark on his record. Familiar heat and anger pounded in his head.

"You think Larson is capable of the kind of violence that was used against Hector Ramirez?" Torres asked.

"I'm not sure." Zack replied quietly. "We may have to dig deeper and chat with the Douglas P.D."

"I can contact Captain Zeke Black," Torres said with a wry grin. "The sonofabitch can find out anything and everything."

"Larson has motive with his ranch's cash flow currently at an ebb." Zack scrubbed his hand over his face. "And he's got one hell of a temper." Which Zack did know firsthand from their high school brawls, but in every case they'd come out about even.

Zack and Torres moved on to Luke Rider. He didn't have a *W* name, but Zack had a gut feeling he should check the man out.

Rider didn't have any history of smuggling charges but had a long list of large, unexplained transactions of over ten thousand dollars each. In one case over two hundred thousand dollars had been deposited into one of his accounts.

Torres leaned back in his chair. "That's a hell of a lot of money for a ranch foreman."

Zack's skin started to grow warm. "I don't like it."

When Torres pulled up Rider's information from NCIC, Zack narrowed his eyes and his skin went from warm to fire hot.

"I'll be fucked," Zack growled. "Embezzlement. Fraud. Theft." He looked at the page for a long time. "Shit. The bastard almost had me." He ground his teeth. "Who knows what he's done to Sky's ranch. Or her money."

Zack had the sudden urge to get to Sky's place in a hurry. But there was one more man left to check.

Zack leaned forward when Torres brought up Gary Woods in TECS. "Well, hell," Torres muttered. "Isn't that interesting."

Torres navigated the system as Zack whistled between his teeth. Woods had a hell of a lot of CTRs. Ten, twenty, thirty grand at a time in and out of bank accounts—most of it out, landing in a couple of casinos.

Zack braced his palms on Torres's desk as he leaned closer to look at the screen. "Our friendly neighborhood deputy has a bit of a gambling problem."

"I wonder just how much he owes." Torres navigated to the other system. "And now let's run him through NCIC. . . ."

Zack scanned the page. "No criminal history.

"My gut's telling me we need to dig deeper." Zack frowned. "Let's do a little Internet research on Larson and Woods."

Torres clicked a few keys and typed in an Internet search. "Here we go. *The Douglas Daily Dispatch* reported Larson's last altercations. According to this he came out on the winning side. Put three men into the hospital." Torres narrowed his gaze as he studied the article. "You think Larson is capable of the kind of violence that was used against Hector Ramirez?"

"Were the men as badly beaten as Ramirez?" Zack replied quietly.

Torres shook his head. "Nah. A broken nose in one case, otherwise just beat them black-and-blue. He sustained injuries but did a better job against his opponents than they did on him."

A warning in Zack's gut told him to keep pressing on. "Search for anything on the Internet regarding Woods."

"Whoa." A few moments later, Torres drew back from the computer. "Woods was investigated twice for excessive force when apprehending suspects while serving as a sheriff's deputy."

"Well, I'll be goddamned," Zack said as he stared at the screen that showed a newspaper article from the *Dispatch.*

"Creamed both of the men. Pretty bad." Torres shook his head. "But he got off on both counts."

"Wait." Zack frowned. "One of them was a woman. She just has a man's name. Alex."

Torres's face flushed as he was obviously pissed. "That fucking sonofabitch. According to this, she attacked him and his excuse was self-defense. Apparently he was a little beat-up himself, but he broke the woman's jaw."

Hair at the nape of Zack's neck prickled and his shoulders tensed. "When did this happen?"

"It's been two and a half years since the first time he was investigated." Torres pointed to the information on the screen. "But he had his run-in with the woman thirteen months ago." He glanced up at Zack again. "A couple of months before Wayland was elected sheriff."

"Shit." Zack's mind raced over the possibilities. "He was late getting to the bunkhouse when Hector was brought in." What if Woods had something to do with the rustling to pay off gambling debts?

And what if he decided to go after Sky like the woman he'd beaten up?

"As far as we know, with these kinds of histories, Woods, Larson, and Rider could all be in on the operation." Zack clenched his fists. "That would sure make it a lot easier to keep law enforcement from tracking them down."

The history of violence Woods and Larson shared caused the prickling on Zack's skin to grow more intense.

Sky.

Out on the range.

Alone.

Zack needed to get to her. And he needed to get to her now.

Chapter 26

Empress whickered as she picked her way along Catwalk Trail coming down from Sky's eastern range at the foot of the Chiricahua Mountains. She patted the mare's neck as they made their way through the growing darkness.

"Thank God for a little moonlight," Sky said as they headed down the trail, Blue trotting just ahead of them.

I can't believe we stayed out so late." Sky's stomach growled. "I should have brought us all something extra to eat." She sighed. "But the time away from the ranch did me some good. I feel like I can face whatever comes next."

Strangely enough, no one had contacted her on her cell phone all day, and she considered that a blessing.

The horse continued on, her gait smooth and fluid beneath Sky. The only sounds in the night were the creak of saddle leather, Empress's horseshoes' clonking against small rocks on the trail, and the yelp of coyotes in the distance. The scents of grass, horse, cattle, and mossy water met Sky's nose as they neared one of the massive metal water troughs next to a stock tank just beyond the rise.

Sky leaned low in the saddle, trying to peer at the water tower through the brush at the same time. The full moon hung low in the sky, giving a little light to see by whenever it wasn't hidden by clouds. She saw nothing but part of her herd at the trough, as well as brush and cacti.

It had been a while since she'd been on such a long ride. Despite being a seasoned rider, her legs ached a little. She looked at Blue, who glanced over his shoulder.

"Just need to stretch my legs." Sky dismounted and tethered the Quarter Horse to a paloverde tree and Blue wheeled around to return to her.

The crunch of rocks beneath her boots seemed loud in the night as she walked a little way down the trail. After she had stretched her arm and leg muscles, she made her way to a close outcropping of boulders. They were about a hundred feet from the water tower and she sat on one of the last remaining smooth, huge rocks before the rangeland. The boulders were large, and she almost felt like a kid, because her feet didn't touch the ground when she perched on top of one.

It had to be getting close to eight. Luke would be concerned if he saw her SUV and noticed she wasn't around. Zack would probably be worried about her, too.

She withdrew her cell phone and tried to dial both men, but she discovered she didn't have any signal and the calls wouldn't go through.

Sky slid the phone into its clip on her belt. "Damnit."

At the same moment, Blue's entire body stiffened and she immediately felt the dog's tension. His hackles rose as he fixed his stare in the distance.

"What is it, boy?" she said, as a low growl rumbled in his chest.

Then her heart pounded and her mouth grew dry as she heard the crunch of tires on the dirt road leading to the water tower and the low roar of an engine.

Headlights sliced through the darkness, becoming brighter and brighter as the sound of the vehicle grew louder. A rattling noise accompanied the sounds, as if the truck was pulling some kind of trailer.

The rustlers. It has to be the rustlers.

Her chest hurt from the increased thundering of her heart. Before whoever it was could have had a chance to see her, she slipped off the boulder and crouched behind it.

Blue growled again and she put her hand on his neck. He was so tense she could feel the tightness in his muscles. "I need you to slip into the bushes and remain quiet." Blue stopped growling and looked up at her. "Just in case something happens to me, I need you to wait until I call for you."

The Border Collie almost seemed to narrow his gaze like a human ready to argue with her. "Go," she whispered, and pointed toward a clump of bushes. When he retreated and obeyed, she held up her palm, facing him. "Stay."

Blue glanced at the approaching vehicle before looking back at her. Without another sound, he blended into the bushes. If these were the rustlers, they might shoot Blue on sight.

Sky took a deep breath, feeling like she might hyperventilate. She drew the cell phone out of her clip—still no signal.

Shit, shit, shit!

The vehicle's brakes squealed and its tires slid in the dirt as the truck came to a stop. The engine cut off and the lights went out.

Sky brought her fingers to her throat while she tried to slow her breathing. She forced herself to remain still beside the boulder. She was partially hidden by another paloverde and hoped whoever this was wouldn't see her.

She thought she heard a trickle of rocks behind her, and her heart slammed against her ribs. She looked over each shoulder but couldn't see anything in the darkness. In the distance coyotes howled again, an eerie chorus of voices that crawled along her spine.

God, she had to calm down instead of feeling like she was going to be jumped.

And maybe, just maybe, she'd see who the sonofabitch rustlers were and could tell Zack and the sheriff.

The sound of first one door slamming and then another met her ears, and she took a deep breath. Two men. She rubbed her sweaty palms on her jeans and slowly peeked around the paloverde.

A one-ton truck was parked maybe fifty feet from where she was hidden. Behind the truck was an enormous stock trailer. A couple of men in baseball caps walked around toward the back of the trailer, and one man stood at the front of the truck as he lit a cigarette. The small flame of the lighter lit up his features for a second, and then he turned and sauntered toward the stock trailer.

Sky's gut churned. She didn't recognize him, damnit. He had an arrogant look to his features, deep-set eyes, and a confident swagger. Her skin prickled and a hot rush of anger flooded her from head to toe. These men were stealing her cattle.

She crouched on her knees, still out of sight, and pressed her forehead against the cool boulder. Sky took a deep breath, while she tried to decide what to do next. Her good friend the S&W was in its holster, but the phone clipped to her belt was useless.

Deep breath.

Deep breath.

A click by Sky's ear sent ice shooting through her veins.

Her entire body chilled as the cool metal of a gun barrel slid along her cheek.

The government-issue SUV's headlights burned a path down the two-lane highway. Zack tried Sky's cell phone, but it went straight to voice mail again.

The tension that had gripped Zack's entire body since running the reports on Woods, Larson, Wayland, and Rider doubled. Tripled.

Mile markers and road signs flashed by, illuminated by the SUV's headlights. Zack tried dialing Sky again. No answer.

Immediately he contacted Eric Torres for backup in case he needed it. When Zack explained that he couldn't get ahold of Sky, Torres said he was heading out the door as they spoke and would be there as fast as he could.

After seeing the man's records, or lack thereof, Zack felt pretty solid about Clay Wayland, so he called the sheriff next.

"Wayland," the man answered after one ring.

"Sheriff, I'm concerned Sky MacKenna may be in trouble," Zack said as calmly as he could. "I ran NCIC and TECS reports on a few people, and I think I have a pretty good idea who's behind the rustling."

"Who?" Wayland asked. "What did you find that makes you think they're rustlers?"

"Might better be explained in person," Zack said.

Wayland paused a moment. "All right, Hunter, I'll trust you

on this one." The sheriff was in another part of the valley but told Zack he'd head on over right away. "I'm calling for backup."

Zack asked Wayland not to call Gary Woods in on this one and said he'd explain later. To Zack's surprise, Wayland didn't question him about this and only grunted in response.

Maybe the sheriff suspected Woods, too.

Zack thought about calling Rider, but after the NCIC report he'd run on the man, there was a good chance Rider was in bed with the rustlers. Could be how the bastards got into Sky's office—Rider had the only other key according to Sky.

Fraud. Embezzlement. Rider could already have taken Sky for all she had. He might even be ready to leave town.

Yet something . . . something wasn't right. Something wasn't clicking with Rider.

There was someone else Zack could check in with.

Zack hit one of his speed dial numbers on his phone.

"Cabe Hunter," came his brother's voice.

"Something might be going down with Sky." Just saying the words made Zack's heart pound harder. "I need you to tell me anything you know about Sheriff Wayland, his deputy Gary Woods, and Wade Larson. And Luke Rider. Know anything about Sky's foreman?"

Cabe seemed to recognize the urgency in Zack's tone and answered with calm professionalism. "Never met Rider," Cabe said, "and haven't heard much about the man."

"What about the other three?"

"Wayland's a good man." Cabe's voice made it clear he respected the sheriff. "I've known him a few years—met him before he was elected sheriff. We've played poker a few times."

Good—Zack's instincts about Wayland seemed to be right on. "Tell me about Larson," Zack said as he drove. "You think he'd get himself involved in anything dirty?"

"He's a hothead and can be a real ass." Cabe paused. "But other than that, can't tell you anything."

Zack's right front tire hit a pothole, jarring him. "Are you as up close and personal with that deputy, Woods, as you are with the sheriff?"

Cabe snorted. "Woods is a prick."

Zack's skin crawled. "What makes you say that?"

"Beat the shit out of a woman once. I think that says it all. I don't give a flying fuck if he claims it was self-defense. She had no weapon, no skills to protect herself, and was homeless." Hot anger radiated over the line. "Saw her myself, Bro. He messed her up pretty bad."

Zack took the turn that would put him on the road to the Flying M. "I've got a goddamned bad feeling."

"What's up?" Cabe's voice grew serious. "What can I do to help?"

Zack glanced in his rearview mirror, where there was only darkness reflected. "Right now you're about sixty miles too far away to do any good."

"I'll be here if you need me."

"Thanks, Bro."

As he severed the connection, Zack's SUV flew down the dirt road leading to Sky's ranch. Once he turned off onto the private road leading to her house, he slowed the vehicle to draw less attention.

He was probably overreacting.

His brother's words rang in Zack's head. More and more he had a bad feeling about all of this.

The tires on Zack's SUV came to quiet halt when he reached the ranch house and killed the engine. As much as he wanted to go charging out to find Sky, he had to think like a fed. Like this was another operation that he'd handle as coolly and professionally as any other.

He glanced at the dashboard digital clock before looking back at the house. After eight thirty and the house was dark.

Sky had better be back.

According to her message, she'd been on her way from Catwalk Trail at the foot of the Chiricahuas. Maybe she was in the barn by now dressing down her mare. The building was lit up like every light in the place was on.

Adrenaline surged through Zack as he got out of the vehicle. His SIG Sauer was snug in its holster on his belt beneath his overshirt.

Yeah, maybe Sky had returned. He hoped to God she had.

Yet Zack's gut told him something wasn't right.

The ranch was silent in the usual ways ranches quieted at night. A horse whickered. Satan bawled. Coyotes howled off in the desert.

But nothing overt. Nothing that sounded unusual.

Lights illuminated the windows of the bunkhouse, the door closed. Nothing unusual about that, either. But the barn . . .

Zack kept his hand close to his holstered SIG as he went up to Sky's darkened house, first. He knocked, the sound hollow and empty in the night. His heart rate picked up as he tried the door handle and found it unlocked.

He unholstered his weapon and held it as he crept through the house, turning on lights and checking every room. He searched the entire house.

No Sky.

Shit.

Because of the dread in his belly that wouldn't go away, Zack kept his SIG out and eased from the house, down the porch stairs, to the barn. He moved through moonlight and shadows until he reached the enormous building.

When he reached the building, keeping his back to the side of the huge entrance, he heard muffled voices. He peered around the corner.

Luke Rider finished cinching the saddle on his Quarter Horse as he spoke to one of the ranch hands who was standing next to a saddled roan. Tyler, Zack thought the ranch hand's name was.

Zack remained in the shadows and didn't make even the slightest of sounds, but Rider casually moved his hand close to his holstered gun. He kept talking to Tyler, but Zack knew Rider was aware of his presence, whether he realized exactly who it was or not.

Zack eased his SIG into its holster just as casually as Rider was doing, but Zack kept his thumb hooked in his belt loop, close to his gun. He gritted his teeth. If Rider was hurting Sky in any way, Zack would make sure the man paid.

Letting instinct drive him, Zack stepped from out of the shadows and into the barn. He detected the slightest release of tension from Rider, as if he didn't consider Zack to be a threat. Tyler eyed Zack with the same calm confidence that Rider wore.

"Where's Sky?" Zack asked as he strode into the barn, never letting his guard down. Instinctively he scanned the rest of the barn's interior for other people, while keeping his eyes on Rider's and Tyler's hands in case they reached for their guns.

"She left a message earlier that she was heading toward Catwalk Trail," Rider said with a steady expression. "That was a few hours ago. Tyler and I are heading out to look for her."

"How about I join you instead?" Zack said, approaching the second saddled horse.

Rider paused, then nodded. "All right, Hunter. Go ahead and take Tyler's mount." He turned to the ranch hand. "Find Joe, then saddle up Gray Dawn and Tracks." He met Tyler's eyes and something unspoken traveled between them.

Tyler nodded. "On it, boss."

The ranch hand headed toward the bunkhouse at a jog while Zack and Rider mounted the two horses. They were silent as they left the barn at a trot and guided their mares to the southern fence line and headed to the eastern pasture.

Tension and urgency was thick in the air between them.

They were going at a pretty good pace, but his horse's gait was smooth and fluid beneath Zack. Sky had some of the best riding stock in the country.

When they were away from the ranch buildings, Zack held his reins with one hand while keeping his hand close to his SIG. "Does Sky know about your history of fraud, theft, and embezzlement?"

Rider slowly looked at Zack. "Finally got around to running me through NCIC?"

For some reason, Zack wasn't surprised Rider knew about the criminal history database. "Just before I headed out to the ranch."

"Should have come clean with you a while ago," Rider said, "but I'd been watching you, too. Your own criminal history shows you were arrested for almost killing a man around the same time you were dating Skylar."

"Fuck." Zack pulled up his mount. "You *are* a fed."

Rider had to bring his mare to a stop and waited for Zack to catch up again. "DEA. I'll show you my creds once we take care of these bastards.

"Real name is Luke Denver," Rider—or rather Denver—said. "I've been undercover for a good long time, so we'll just keep it as Rider. We're closing in on a drug ring involving a Mexican drug cartel. The rustling's just a cover."

"You've figured it all out then," Zack said.

"Maybe." Denver nodded and Zack caught sight of something glinting in the darkness. "We're about to find out if I'm right."

Chapter 27

Zack eased through the mesquite bushes and brush on Catwalk Trail, blood thrumming in his veins as he kept an eye on the rustlers near the water trough and tower.

He glanced to where Empress was tethered, and his anger burned like fire in his head. The men must have Sky.

Before reaching the trail, he and Rider had guided their mounts on opposite sides, in wide arcs around the rustlers. Rider had silently cut the fence with a pair of work pliers so that he could come at the rustlers from the south while Zack skirted them on the north side. Both Zack and Rider were to keep far enough away to avoid being seen by the men now herding cattle into a trailer.

Instinct again kicked in and Zack realized he wasn't alone, but what was near him wasn't human, either. He glanced to his right where Blue crept from the bushes to his side.

"I bet Sky told you to stay here," Zack murmured as Blue let loose a low rumble. The dog drew his lips back to reveal his sharp canines as he studied the activity below. "There's a good chance you'd be dead if she hadn't." Zack shifted his position. "You're going to get your opportunity to help her, bud. Just hold on."

Zack briefly wondered when the cavalry would arrive. He and Rider had both made calls to their men before they split up, and Zack had contacted Sheriff Wayland again, who'd said he had just reached the ranch. Zack hadn't been surprised that Tyler was a fed, too, when he heard Rider contact him.

Clouds parted and moonlight brightened the scene enough that Zack could easily make out the large cattle trailer parked behind a one-ton pickup truck near the tower. He wasn't sure where Rider was but figured he wasn't far and that the agent was in position.

The men herding cattle into the trailer held Zack's attention. One man dogged the several head of cattle by horseback while three other bastards were on foot, using cattle prods to get the animals into the trailer. The men's shouts and whistles along with the bawls of cattle filled the night. The rustlers were at least a couple of miles from the nearest ranch house, so likely they had no real concern they'd be heard.

Zack had started to work his way down the trail when hair prickled at his nape. Someone was coming up behind him.

In one smooth movement he whirled while drawing his gun, at the same time keeping in a crouch.

"Hunter." A low voice came from the darkness. "Clay Wayland."

Zack's muscles relaxed and he lowered his weapon. "Thanks for joining the fun." He reholstered his gun and nodded toward the rustlers as Wayland moved closer and crouched beside him. "Not sure where Sky is." Zack clenched his jaw before he continued, "I'll bet these are the sonsofbitches who took Skylar's cattle."

"And everyone else's." Wayland nodded as he watched the men rounding up the herd. "Recognize any of them?"

"Hard to tell from here." Zack clenched his fist, imagining the pleasure he'd take in knocking the crap out of the SOB he was sure was responsible.

"They're finished loading the trailer," Wayland said as the rustlers slammed the gate behind the last cow they'd loaded. "Looks like we're going to have to go in without backup."

"Rider is here, too." Zack's mouth set in a grim line as he glanced at Wayland. "He's a fed. DEA."

The sheriff nodded. "The way the man handles himself, I'm not surprised."

"Sky's got to be down there," Zack said. "I haven't been able to spot her." His voice came out in a low growl as he added, "She'd better be all right, or whoever hurt her is dead."

Wayland glanced at him, a hard look on his face as he nodded. "Yeah, take care of Skylar first." Wayland's expression said he'd do the same thing if he were in Zack's shoes. "These guys aren't going anywhere."

"Let's do it," Zack said as the men had almost finished loading the stock trailer.

Both Zack and Wayland started forward when a furious shriek cut through the sounds of the cattle and men's voices and the blood in Zack's body surpassed the boiling point.

A woman.

Sky.

After tying her wrists in front of her with rough baling twine, one of the thieves threw her on the dirt next to the truck. The rustlers left Sky alone as they loaded up the cattle. She sat on the ground, her back against a truck tire, her tailbone and ass hurting from hitting the ground so hard.

The men were obviously stupid when it came to women being armed. They hadn't bothered to check her for more weapons after taking her S&W, so her utility knife was still in her right front pocket. While the rustlers were busy stealing cattle, she bent her knees so her hands couldn't be seen from where they were, bound in front of her.

Whistles, horse hooves, and the sound of bawling cattle echoed in the night as the men worked the cattle.

Sky set to trying to get the utility knife out of her right front pocket. It had worked down so deep she was having a hard time reaching it. Her fingers ached and the twine chafed her wrists as she maneuvered her hands. She was beginning to think she'd never dig the pocketknife out when she finally got a good grasp on one end of it.

The men's voices around her were loud and would easily have been heard by ranchers if they weren't so far from the nearest ranch house.

Her breathing came hard and fast and her heart pounded as she struggled to get the blade out. She was biting the inside of her cheek so hard she tasted blood.

Sky gave a huge sigh of relief when she managed to pull the knife out and into her palms. She fumbled as she worked to open the damned pocketknife.

There.

She didn't give herself a moment to appreciate the small victory. She was just about to see if she could cut the twine binding her wrists when she noticed one of the men approaching her. A man in a sheriff's deputy uniform.

Her eyes widened.

Gary Woods.

"Gary?" The closer he came, the greater the shock. "You're part of this?"

She barely had the presence of mind to hide the knife between her hands and her bent knees. She hoped Gary hadn't somehow seen the metal glinting in the moonlight.

Gary gave a low chuckle as he ambled closer, an arrogant look on his face she didn't recognize.

His expression turned hard when he reached her. "We've got a bit of lost time to make up for, Skylar."

She had a hard time shaking off the surprise at seeing him and learning he was one of the rustlers. "What are you talking about?"

He crouched in front of her and his handsome features seemed strangely twisted in the moonlight. "I wasn't good enough for you, was I?" he stated. "Wouldn't give me the time of day."

Sky's jaw dropped. She couldn't get over the stunned feeling that had temporarily overtaken her anger. "What the hell are you talking about?"

Gary's humorless laugh grated on her fraying nerves. "Like I said, not good enough for you to even notice me."

As the men continued loading the trailer, Gary reached out and caressed her cheek with his knuckles. She gritted her teeth and refused to recoil from the deputy's touch.

The smells of chewing tobacco and alcohol on his breath made Sky's stomach churn. She could tell he was drunk as he said, "I'm going to get what I want and fuck you until I've had enough." A crazy glint was in his eyes as her stomach churned. "And that may be a while."

"Like hell," Sky growled at the same time her skin chilled. "You'll never get close enough to me."

Gary laughed. "I could drag your pants down and do it right now in front of these shitheads who can watch me fuck you unconscious."

Sky narrowed her eyes. Her legs hadn't been bound, so she could kick the crap out of him. She was going to make him wish he hadn't shown up tonight.

"Load the bitch up and let's get the hell out of here." A man guided his horse closer to where Gary was with Sky. "You can have your fun when we get this shipment to Albuquerque."

"You're a sneaky bastard, aren't you?" Sky glared at Gary. "I bet you've been making sure the sheriff's department was always following some false lead you'd planted while you've been laughing your ass off."

The man on the horse scowled and cut in, "Yeah, but if Woods here hadn't screwed up, we'd have some of your prime stock. Damn that Rider. Kept us from scoring that pricey bull."

She found it hard to talk with her jaw clenched as she narrowed her gaze at Gary. "You were the one who trashed my office and destroyed over a hundred years' worth of records."

"And I poisoned your stupid dog—unfortunately he didn't eat enough to die." Gary gave a loud snort. "Some payback for blowing me off."

Rage filled her. "You. Poisoned. Blue." Her entire body burned and the additional heat rising up within her actually made her sweat. "I'm going to kill you."

Gary snorted.

Sky's mind was still so overcome with fury over Blue that she could barely speak. "Why are you doing all of this?"

Gary shrugged. "Business is business. I've got bills, and working for the county doesn't pay for shit."

"Ah, this ain't nuthin'." The man on the horse slicked his hair back with one hand while his gaze raked over Sky. "This has just been a cover for the real money."

"Shut up, asshole." Gary's expression darkened as he looked at the man.

"Were you the one who beat up Hector?" Sky said as she glared at Gary.

"Fucker should have died." Gary's mood seemed to turn blacker as he glanced at the other men. "Let's get the hell out of here."

The man turned his horse toward the other two men who were standing at the back of the truck, men Sky hadn't recognized.

The men were all out of sight when Gary said, "Yeah, this is going to be fun." He stood and leaned over to grab Sky by her upper arms.

As he started to touch her, Sky drew her knee up and shot out her foot. "No goddamned way." At the same time, she screamed with the force of her fury and slammed her foot into Gary's kneecap with all the power she possessed. "That was for Blue," she shouted.

A sickening pop traveled from the sole of her boot and up her leg as his knee buckled.

Gary screamed and dropped to the ground, landing flat on his ass.

At the same moment, Sky clenched the handle of the pocketknife with both bound hands and launched her body at him. "And this is for Hector."

She brought her arms down hard, driving the knife through the thick leather of his boot as she came down, and drilling the blade into his foot.

"Fuck!" he screamed again.

"You sonofabitch." She landed on her belly, her hands still around the knife hilt, her face close to the foot she'd just impaled.

"Bitch!" Gary's face was contorted with pain, a sheen of sweat glossing his forehead, glittering strangely in the moonlight.

Gary yanked a gun out of his holster, his hands trembling and sweat rolling down his face. "You're going to pay, you goddamn whore," he said before he backhanded her so hard her head snapped to the side.

Sky's vision went blurry as pain burst in her head. Dizzy, she looked at Gary.

And felt blood draining from her face as she stared down the barrel of the gun that shook from the force of his trembling— the metal a mere foot from her face.

I'm going to die.

Just as she expected to feel a bullet slam into her, a snarling blur flung itself at Gary, knocking the gun out of her face.

Blue.

The gun flew from Gary's hand and he screamed as the Border Collie sank his sharp canines into the deputy's arm.

And then it was chaos.

Zack whipped around the truck, his gun pointed right at Gary.

At the same moment, Clay Wayland shouted, "Police. You're under arrest," as he trained his weapon on one of the men while on guard for the men who weren't in sight.

"'Sonofabitch!" Gary shouted as he struggled to get the vicious border collie to let go of his arm. "Should've given you more poison."

Just hearing Gary talk about what he'd done to her dog burned fury through her veins again. With everything she had, Sky rammed her boot into Gary's balls. "And that one's for me, you bastard!"

Gary curled into a fetal position, tears actually rolling down his face.

The man on the horse wheeled his mount around and bolted into the darkness.

Zack kept his gun trained on Gary as he grabbed handcuffs from his belt. "If Sky and Blue hadn't taken you down first, you'd be unconscious right now."

Fear, relief, and fury cycled through Sky like a tornado as she watched Zack and the scene unfolding before her.

Hands still tied, Sky scrambled away from Gary, leaving the knife in his boot. She saw that Sheriff Wayland had the other two men cuffed and facedown in the dirt. " 'Bout time you made it, Rider," the sheriff said.

Squinting, Sky peered into moonlit night and saw that the man who'd been on the horse was being marched back toward them at gunpoint—and Luke Rider was the man behind the gun.

"Nice of you to join us," Zack said as he cuffed Gary, who was still rolling in pain and trying to get Blue to release his hold.

Luke offered a tight smile. "Are we missing anyone?"

"One more," Sheriff Wayland said. "You keep an eye on these bastards and I'll get the other."

"No need."

Everyone swung around and Sky caught her breath as she saw Wade Larson—with a rifle pointing at the fourth rustler's back. "This sonofabitch was one of my ranch hands. Figured out today he was one of the rustlers screwing us over."

"I'll take it from here, Larson." Clay Wayland drew out another set of handcuffs and had the fourth man down and cuffed in two seconds flat.

Sky's attention turned to Zack and Gary. The sour, acidic smell of puke made her want to gag. Gary had upchucked when she'd let him have it in the balls. Yeah, it'd take him weeks before he'd be walking straight again.

One-handed, Zack grabbed Gary by the front of his shirt and hauled him up. Gary's face was white and he was shaking, his eyes nearly rolling back in his head, and there was no way he could stand on his own.

Zack brought Gary's face close to his. Zack's eyes and expression were tight with fury—Sky had never seen him so angry. "If you ever touch my woman again, I'll kill you, you miserable bastard."

Zack shoved Gary away from him. The deputy went sprawling flat on his back, shrieking out in pain.

Zack turned and scooped Sky up from the ground, holding her so tight she could hardly breathe. She thought she felt his body tremble against hers.

"Don't you ever scare me like that again," he said before he kissed her hard, like he was reassuring himself she was okay. And like he was never going to let her go.

Sky kissed him back with such equal fervor that she thought she might cry—what if she'd never had the chance to kiss him again?

To not have Zack . . . she couldn't even begin to think about that right now. She was just thankful they were both alive.

Eric Torres, Rider's men, Tyler and Joe, Zack's brother, Cabe, and several of Wayland's deputies arrived about the same time they finished subduing the prisoners.

After Zack kissed Sky over and over again, reassuring himself that she was all right, he removed her bonds and insisted she sit with Blue off to the side with one of the deputies. She seemed a little shaken up, which was no surprise, but still the tough, confident woman Zack loved.

When he could get himself to leave her, he checked beneath the trailer's chassis. Sure enough, dried yellow mud was clumped beneath it.

Clay Wayland took Luke and Zack aside. "Fill us in on how the hell you're involved, Rider," Wayland said. "Must have something to do with smuggling drugs across the line."

"We've been after Woods for some time." Rider jerked his head in the direction of the former deputy, who was sitting and shouting out promises to hurt Sky for what she'd done to him. "He got himself involved with a Mexican drug cartel. Woods has been trying to pay off heavy gambling debts.

"From the intelligence we've gathered," Rider continued, "this whole rustling scheme was designed not only to provide Woods with more cash but to keep the focus off what's really going on. The biggest drug deal of its kind is going down around here, and soon. Real soon."

Clay Wayland narrowed his brows. "Why the hell wasn't I informed about any of this?"

Rider said, "We couldn't be positive that no one else in the sheriff's department was involved, or in any of the law enforcement branches here for that matter. That's part of my job—to sort out the good guys from the bad guys."

Rider's gaze cut to Sky, who was walking toward them. "But this stays with the three of us. You're not to tell anyone else."

Zack studied Rider. "I expect full details tonight. We may have enough evidence that we can get an affidavit signed by the assistant U.S. Attorney and the magistrate that'll get us our search warrant. Especially if we can get any of these bastards to talk. That'll take care of the way the beef is getting to Mexico."

Chapter 28

It had been a long fucking thirty-six hours.

Zack rubbed the bridge of his nose as he drove the half-hour trip along Highway 80 to Sky's ranch. It was dark as hell out.

His mind replayed the events since last night. By the time everything had gone down, Zack's massive adrenaline rush had faded. He was ready to sleep for a week, minimum.

He sure hoped Sky was expecting him, because he was going to climb into bed and hold her all night.

His mind whirled over the events since they'd met with the informant, gotten reports back from a surveillance team, run NCIC and TECS on suspects, caught the rustlers, and conducted the raid.

Thank God that Sky and Blue were fine. After the paramedics had taken a look at Sky's face, she'd insisted she didn't need to go to the hospital to be checked out any more than she'd already been. Zack had reluctantly left her home with her S&W but took off to take care of business.

The rustlers had been hauled off to the county jail and

questioned. One of the men broke almost immediately to save his own ass.

Turned out the man was one of another agent's informants. The agent considered him a reliable source even though he was as crooked as the dirt road leading up and into Horseshoe Canyon. The rustler slash informant had told them plenty, and the information he'd given them had backed up every bit of information that Marlin Jones, their other informant, had provided.

Zack yawned and turned up the radio to keep himself awake as he drove through the darkness along the lonely highway. An occasional car passed by, their headlights almost blinding to his tired eyes.

Before dawn, Zack and Eric had hustled to the office. Zack tweaked the affidavit, and by 6:00 A.M. the junior agent hauled ass on the two-hour drive to the U.S. Attorneys' satellite office in Tucson.

In the meantime Zack had e-mailed the affidavit to Paul Davidson, one of the assistant U.S. Attorneys, to give him the opportunity to review the document by the time Torres reached Tucson.

Davidson had signed off and Torres went straight to the magistrate. Torres swore out the information in the affidavit and the magistrate agreed there was probable cause to execute a search warrant and signed the document.

By 9:00 A.M., Torres had the signatures and he contacted Zack. They had their search warrant.

Zack gave a grim smile as he drove. *Like clockwork.*

Most of the area's ICE agents, including the asshole Denning, conducted the raid. The sheriff and every available deputy from the sheriff's department were in on the fun.

The raid hadn't exactly gone as smoothly as Zack would have

liked, but they'd accomplished what they'd come to do. There'd been a little gunfire and one agent had been downed with a bullet to the thigh. Two of the smugglers had died.

Zack ground his teeth as he recalled the pens holding cattle bearing Sky's Flying M brand. Cattle with Larson's Coyote Pass brand as well as cattle with brands from other ranches had also been there. The cattle were ready to be butchered and processed.

What had looked like a barn had been exactly what Zack had thought—a meat-packaging plant.

Zack grimaced. The place had stunk like shit.

Smugglers had been apprehended tossing sides of beef into a tractor trailer retrofitted to be a reefer truck to keep the meat cool, the truck bearing Mexican license plates.

Smugglers in another truck had already been headed toward Mexico and floored it when ICE raided the plant. The truck almost crossed the border, but a team of ICE agents and sheriff's deputies cut off their path. The smugglers driving the vehicle had been apprehended and dragged back to the ranch.

It was with grim satisfaction that Zack had shoved that case down Denning's throat.

When Zack reached the turnoff to the dirt road leading to Sky's place, he rubbed his tired eyes. He was so ready for the movies of the night's and the day's events to stop playing in his head.

It was over. It was finally goddamned over.

At least this case was and Sky's cattle weren't going to keep disappearing.

When Zack pulled his Silverado up to Sky's ranch house he turned off the engine and for a moment just listened to the hot engine tick.

His Adam's apple grew tight as Sky opened the door,

silhouetted by the light shining from inside. To have Sky wait-ing for him at the end of every day would be the most amazing thing that could happen in his life.

Blue tore from the house and straight for Zack's truck. He climbed out and shut the door behind him as Blue wiggled his entire body in greeting. Every muscle in Zack's body started aching as if he'd been working out the entire day.

"Hey there, boy." Zack crouched and stroked Blue's head. "I owe you big-time for what you did for Sky. Steaks for life."

"Don't go spoiling him," came Sky's soft voice. "He's on a prime, vet-approved diet, and that doesn't include steak."

Zack couldn't hold back a smile as he rose and faced Sky. A second later he had her in his arms, embracing her so hard she gave a soft gasp.

"I missed you." She leaned her cheek against his shirt as she wrapped her arms around his waist. "I thought you'd never get home."

Home.

That damned lump crowded Zack's throat so tight he almost couldn't speak. "Nothing could keep me from coming back to you, sweetheart."

Sky gave a sigh. "God, you feel so good." She tilted her head to look up at him, her nose wrinkled. "But you stink. What have you been into?"

Zack laughed softly. "You don't want to know."

"Let's throw you into the shower." She met his gaze. "And then I'm kicking your butt into bed. You look like hell."

Tempting aromas teased Zack's nose. He blinked away the light and realized he was alone in Sky's bed. By the early-morning light peeking in the window he guessed it was close to eight in the morning.

Through the open bedroom door came the delicious scents of coffee, sausage, and eggs—and, if he wasn't mistaken, maple syrup. His stomach, tired of dry cornflakes and milk every morning in his lonely apartment, growled a loud demand for the food he smelled.

Zack pushed away all thoughts of the past few days and concentrated on Sky and his eagerness to have her in his arms again. Last night he'd been too exhausted to do anything but take a quick shower and fall straight into Sky's bed.

He got up and pulled on his jeans, then walked barefoot and shirtless along the cool ceramic tile to the kitchen. The sizzle of sausages and clanking of plates met him as he rounded the corner and saw Sky.

She stood in front of the huge stainless-steel range top, using a spatula to scoop a pancake from the griddle and then flip it onto a plate.

For a moment he leaned against the doorway and just watched her as she poured more batter onto the griddle and then set the bowl down. She scooped sausages out of another pan and onto a plate, then turned the burner off beneath the frying pan.

Her long copper hair hung wild and loose down her back, and if he wasn't mistaken she was wearing his T-shirt. It came to mid-thigh on her, and her legs and feet were bare.

A lump formed in Zack's throat at the homey image Sky made as she cooked breakfast. What would it be like to wake up with her every morning? Having her beside him for conversation over pancakes and coffee. Being with her after work and sharing what had happened in each of their days. And to have her to hold in his arms every night.

Sky glanced over her shoulder and greeted him with a grin that warmed his blood and made his cock rise. " 'Bout time you got up, cowboy."

Smiling, Zack walked across the floor. When he reached her, he slid his arms around her waist and hugged her from behind, nuzzling her ear. "Mornin'."

She sighed and leaned back against him. "Hungry?"

"Starving." He nipped at her ear and moved to the curve of her neck. "Everything smells so damn good." He met her eyes. "Including you."

With a soft laugh, she replied, "This pancake is going to be burnt to a crisp if you don't stop messing with the cook."

"Small price to pay," he murmured. But he stepped back, releasing his hold on her. For now.

"Where's that hero dog?" he asked as he shoved his hands in his front pockets. "I've got to give him one of those steaks I promised."

"He's outside." Sky wrinkled her nose and gave a pretend haughty sniff. "And you're not going to ruin his diet."

Zack grinned. He'd have to sneak Blue a New York strip.

The rumble in Zack's stomach was louder and more painful this time. He leaned over the plates of pancakes, sausages, and scrambled eggs. Damn, they smelled good.

"Sounds like breakfast is none too soon." Sky flipped the last pancake onto the stack and turned the burner's heat off. "Help me carry these to the breakfast nook and you can dig in."

Zack took his hands from his pockets and picked up the plates of pancakes and sausages. "Your every desire is my command," he said as he headed to the round oak table near the bay window.

"That's what I'm counting on." Her tone was sultry and teasing, and damned if it didn't make his cock ache.

He set the food in the middle of the table, which was already set with plates, flatware, and napkins. He went back to the counter and picked up the dish of scrambled eggs and the pot of coffee.

Sky grabbed a glass carafe of orange juice from the fridge. She stopped to retrieve the saucepan of maple syrup that had been heating on the range top, and then joined him at the table.

"Oh, the cream." She jumped back up and went to the fridge. Zack watched her as she bent over to search the lower shelves, his T-shirt hiking up over her hips and exposing her bottom.

She wasn't wearing any underwear.

Zack's mouth fell open as he stared at the exposed pink folds, and he wondered what refrigerator sex would be like.

Ice-cold air blowing over their naked bodies as he bent her over in the open door of the fridge. Sky clutching the shelves that held milk and eggs, her nipples hard from the chill. Her screams of pleasure as she yelled at him to take her harder while he thrust his cock deep inside her.

"Found it." She stood and turned, holding the small container of cream, then shut the fridge door with a bump of her hip.

She returned to the table and sat in a chair with a grimace as she put the cream on the table.

He frowned. "Did you get hurt last night?"

"Could have been worse." Sky shrugged. "One of the men knocked me on my ass and my tailbone's a little sore."

With a scowl, Zack raked his gaze over her. "Are you hurt anywhere else?"

"Just a headache." Sky pushed aside her hair that had been covering the side of her face that was bruising near her eye. "And nothing any worse than you've already seen."

He nearly vibrated with renewed anger at Woods. Zack wanted to knock the shit out of the sonofabitch. Between Sky's and Blue's assaults on Woods, the former deputy was in a world of hurt.

"That night doesn't seem real, does it," she stated.

Zack heaved an angry sigh. "Glad that's over in more ways than one."

Sky nodded, then looked at his plate. "Aren't you hungry? You haven't touched a thing."

His thoughts turned to the image of Sky bent over with her pussy showing. He cleared his throat. "Ah, just waiting for you."

She gave him a smile and poured two cups of coffee. "So, my cowboy prince is a gentleman, too."

"I wouldn't say that," he muttered as he added a touch of cream to his coffee. He piled pancakes on his plate and had just slathered them with butter and warm maple syrup when he glanced at Sky.

The way she was looking at him made him wonder how he managed to keep himself from wiping the tabletop clean with one swipe of his hand and taking her on top of it.

When they finished, he captured her around the waist and lifted her onto the polished granite surface of the kitchen island.

She laughed, her eyes sparkling, and moistened her lips with the tip of her tongue. "What do you think you're doing?"

"I'm having brunch." Zack brushed his lips over Sky's and her nipples went ice hard. "And this is just the right height."

Sky shivered. "I never knew granite could feel so cool and delicious against my skin."

Trailing his thumb over her bottom lip, Zack said, "Especially when you're not wearing any underwear?"

She cradled his jaw with one hand, stroking his stubble with her thumb. "How did you know that?"

"Lucky guess?"

She pulled him toward her and kissed him hard. His groin tightened as her fingertips skated over his chest and worked on down to the button of his jeans.

Her orange blossom scent flowed over him, his cock already hard from the feel of her soft body pressed to his. As she drew back, Sky's mouth was red from his kiss, her nipples pebbled under his T-shirt.

His gaze dropped to the open neck of the T-shirt and he saw a familiar chain and his throat grew tight. He reached up and grasped the heart pendant he'd given her their first Christmas together. Their only Christmas together. He'd chosen the stone because it matched the color of her eyes and it was her birthstone. And he had chosen the shape because she had captured his heart.

He grasped the pendant in his palm. As his gaze met hers, he shook his head in wonder. "I thought you might have thrown it out in the pasture."

Lips curving into a grin, she gave a throaty laugh. "I gave that some serious consideration."

"I'll bet you did." Zack released the heart and kissed her softly.

How could he be so blessed with such an incredible woman?

The truth was loud and clear as he slowly and softly moved his mouth over hers. This was the most special woman in the world and she was his.

* * *

Sky's entire body went on alert as Zack slid his hands onto her bare ass. He pushed the T-shirt up and over her head before he tossed it onto the kitchen floor, leaving her naked.

Thoughts of last night and the pain in her head vanished, replaced by thoughts of Zack.

Tingling thrills went through her body as he pressed his jean-clad cock against her folds. She wiggled her hips and worked on the button and zipper that kept his cock out of her hands. And not inside her.

She moaned as the button finally came undone and she fumbled for the zipper's tab. "Don't play around, baby. I can't wait."

Zack pushed her hands away from his zipper, then palmed her breasts and squeezed her nipples. "Not yet. Your nipples are in the perfect place for me to taste."

Whimpers and more moans rose from her throat as he nuzzled and licked and sucked her breasts. She tilted her head back while holding on to his shoulders, bracing herself as she squirmed from the feel of his tongue on her.

He thrust one of his fingers inside her while rubbing her clit with his thumb. She gasped and cried out, and dug her fingers into his shoulders.

When she couldn't take his erotic teasing another moment, she almost sobbed as she clenched her fingers in his hair and begged him, "Please, Zack."

She let his hair slip through her fingers as he unzipped his jeans and her mouth watered as she saw his huge erection. She was vaguely aware of being relieved that he had a condom in his jeans pocket.

Thank God he didn't wait, as he lifted her hips and positioned his cock at her center. Her cry of pleasure echoed through the kitchen as he thrust himself inside so deep she felt it nearly to her belly button.

Sky grasped Zack's shoulders, digging her nails even more into his muscles and taking him deep as his lips, teeth, and tongue found one of her nipples again. She wrapped her legs around his hips and bucked at a frenzied pace and Zack clenched her to him.

As Sky arched her back, her hair slid against her naked shoulders, an erotic combination with Zack's warm mouth on her breasts as he drove in and out of her.

The orgasm building inside made her head spin. He was so big, he fit inside her so perfectly and touched every sensitive spot inside her. The sensations inside her raged like nothing she'd ever felt before.

When it hit, her climax was so massive that a loud cry tore from her throat. The spinning in her head increased and her core spasmed around his cock at the same time he continued his hard thrusts.

Zack shouted as he came, and somewhere from the height of her climax Sky felt him pulsating deep within her even when he stopped moving in and out.

She collapsed against him, and they held on to each other, their sweat mingling, their breathing heavy, their hearts pounding.

Sated by their lovemaking, Sky allowed herself to enjoy the comfort of Zack's embrace. His earthy presence surrounded her. Filled her.

Zack leaned back and traced one finger over a hardened nipple. "Cold?"

"Not with you to warm me," Sky murmured in a teasing tone.

The look in his eyes was suddenly too serious and a strange fear gripped her.

Grasping a lock of her hair, he wrapped it around his hand. "I love you, Sky." He took a deep breath, an uncertain look on his handsome face. "Marry me."

For countless seconds Sky stared at Zack as he looked at her. His dark hair was mussed, his face unshaven, his masculine body large and imposing, his gray eyes stormy.

"When I left ten years ago I knew I'd made the biggest mistake of my life." Zack's gray eyes focused intently on her. "I love you. I've never stopped loving you. Say you'll marry me and I'll do whatever I can to make up for all the time we've lost."

For a long moment she couldn't say anything and her eyes burned with tears that wanted to come out of nowhere.

"You bastard." She flung her arms around his neck and buried her face against his chest. "I love you so much."

He pulled away from her and smiled that killer, devastating, elusive smile of his. "Is that a yes?"

"A most definite yes." Sky stroked the scar along his cheek. "And I'm not waiting another minute. We can fly to Vegas tomorrow. I don't want to give you a chance to change your mind."

"There's no danger of that." He kissed her long and slow, then murmured, "Why wait that long? We can catch a flight tonight."

"I'll hold you to that." She was so full of love and happiness that she thought she'd explode. "We'll start packing, just as soon as you finish making love to me again."

He smiled and slid between her thighs. "I love you, Sky MacKenna."

She gave him her most mischievous grin as she brought him inside her. "You'd better, Zack Hunter. You'd better."

Turn the page for a sneak peek at...

The First Sin

THE FIRST LEXI STEELE NOVEL

by CHEYENNE MCCRAY

**Coming Winter 2009
From St. Martin's Paperbacks**

March 28th Thursday noon

"Time to face your doom, Steele," Smithe said.

The words barely registered as my eyes blinked open and I stared at the seat in front of me.

Shit.

Oxford.

The familiar parking garage for RED's cover operation made it easy to tell where I was. I didn't want to be here right now.

In the agency, only Oxford knew I'd been an assassin. All anyone else knew was that I'd been in Special Forces in the army before joining RED as a Special Agent.

I owed her and I hated the thought of disappointing her or, even worse, putting her in a position where she might have to can me.

Damn. The thought of being forced to leave RED hit me like a punch to the gut.

I rubbed my goose bump–covered arms. If I lost my job, I'd lose my identity—everything that I'd worked for since she'd saved my ass.

Takamoto and Smithe headed out of the lower level of the garage with me trailing in their wake. My scalp itched and I knew I must look like I'd just come off of one of those survival reality TV shows—and lost. If I was a girlie-girl I might have cared. Right now I didn't.

Feeling started coming back into my limbs and my body as we took the parking garage elevator up to the first floor. My feet dragged like I was a kid being taken to the principal's office, as we reached the pseudo insurance claims processing center.

After my ASAC canned me from the Recovery Enforcement Division, would any other branch of the NSA take me on?

Ha. The NSA didn't know I existed. After all, RED didn't exist, right?

When the three of us passed the glass-walled reception area where the blinds were always kept shut, my reflection made it clear I looked even worse than I'd thought—which was pretty damned bad.

I glanced down the hallway that led to the exercise center and wished I could jump into the shower in the women's locker room before it was time to face Oxford.

Yeah, like she would wait for a little thing like a shower.

Takamoto scanned his handprint, then he, Smithe, and I entered the empty elevator and Takamoto punched the button for the fifth floor.

"This year the Yanks don't stand a chance against the Red Sox," Takamoto said, and I turned my attention to him.

Thinking about the baseball season that was going to start Monday was a lot better than thinking about what I was about to face.

Oxford's disappointment. And no doubt anger.

"The boys kicked ass in the Grapefruit League during spring training," I said.

"Zapato's looking particularly good," Smithe said. "He's one wicked pitcher."

As a city we were still pissed about last year's ninth-inning loss in the World Series to the Yanks on a home run by Jorge Dominique.

Every floor seemed to pass by too fast. With a soft stop, we reached my fifth floor doom.

I looked down at the CC and wished I was working with my team. But at this moment I was destined to stay above the CC on the corridor that skimmed past the TSS glass-walled offices.

"Oxford's," Smithe said.

I glared at him. "Oh, really? Thanks for informing me of that little fact."

When Takamoto and Smithe left me and headed toward the stairs to the CC, I practically dragged my feet as I went to my ASAC's office.

Darlene looked down her nose at me as she immediately showed me in, almost like she was shoving me through the door before she closed it.

I swallowed as I met Karen Oxford's dark eyes. Her gaze remained steady as she pressed a button on her glass and chrome desk.

Vertical black blinds hummed along their track as they covered the glass walls, giving us complete privacy.

This was so not good.

Oxford leaned forward and clasped her hands in front of her on her desk, her dark gaze shrewd and calculating. At times like this she made me feel as if she could peel me like an onion, layer by layer. She didn't invite me to sit, just stared at me for a long moment.

Oh, damn. As much as I'd cared for Gary, my career meant enough that I would have chosen my job over dating any guy. And I was about to lose it.

And Stacy. God, I couldn't leave before I took out her killers.

"You destroyed property in front of a street full of witnesses," she finally said.

"I caught my boyfriend in bed with a woman." Heat and numbness alternately gripped me.

For a moment I swore her gaze and her tone lessened their intensity. "I realize you just lost your best friend and coworker, as well as your significant other, in one day." Her tone was hard, though, as she continued and any possible softness was gone. "Regardless of the situation, Steele, you were completely out of line."

"Yes, ma'am—"

"Have you ever thought how it might compromise yourself and your family if your escapade ended up on the evening news?"

Uh . . .

She pulled a cell phone out of her desk. "You were recorded, Steele. If RED hadn't cleaned up the mess before it ended up as a little joke on the news, your face would have shown up on every television in the Boston area."

My cheeks burned. Shit. *That* was something that never occurred to me.

I fought the urge to start begging. *Don't can me, don't can me, don't can me.* "Nothing like that will ever happen again."

"It had better not." Oxford looked at me intently. "I won't have you compromise this agency."

I wanted to collapse with relief. I hadn't been released from RED. Yeah, I'd screwed up, but she wasn't going to let me go.

A buzzing sound made me jump.

"Is it Agent Donovan, Darlene?" Oxford said to the air. I wasn't really sure where the microphone was. "If it is, send him in."

Not two seconds and a pink-faced, obviously flustered Darlene showed in one of the most gorgeous men I'd ever seen. No wonder Darlene looked so flustered.

Just his vivid blue eyes were enough to make a woman's mouth water. A black shirt over a black T-shirt couldn't disguise what was obviously a fit, muscular body. Snug blue jeans only emphasized the fact.

Well, well, well.

Look at those broad shoulders, a well-defined chest beneath his T-shirt, and sculpted muscular biceps. Thank God for short-sleeved shirts because those biceps were made to be seen. He wasn't body-builder big, but it was obvious he had a kind of power no mortal could match. Bet he was Superman in bed. His tapered hips and snug Levis over muscular thighs completed the picture of a woman's wet dream.

He was rough around the edges with an unapproachable look to him, but it didn't disguise the fact that he was one hot male.

Oxford gestured toward the big hunk of a man now standing next to me. "Special Agent Nick Donovan is new to RED and has been assigned to double-team your operation. He'll work the op with you as a Team Supervisor until we complete Operation Cinderella."

I let my gaze linger, traveling over Agent Donovan in a slow perusal, trying not to be too obvious to Oxford that I was checking him out.

That was before it kicked in that she was sticking me with this guy.

Uh-uh. No way. Too dangerous in too many ways to count.

Like the fact that just looking at him made me think of hot, steamy sex in sixty-nine different positions.

When I met Oxford's eyes I tried to keep any trace of emotion out of my words. "I've put together this case from the beginning to find and bring down these sex slavers and I've worked my end alone. I don't need anyone in my way."

From the corner of my eye I saw Donovan's expression darken, but he remained silent.

My ASAC stood and braced her palms on her desk. "Steele, you will work with Agent Donovan and that is my final word on the subject."

My jogging shoes squeaked on the concrete floor of RED's almost-empty parking garage. Smells of dirty oil and antifreeze certainly didn't make the churning in my stomach any better.

Donovan and I didn't speak as we walked from RED and neared a Ford Explorer black enough to seem to absorb most of the surrounding light. I wouldn't exactly call it a comfortable silence.

Oxford had informed me that Donovan would be the agent to drop me off at my place. Like I had a choice. I glanced at my empty parking spot between my undercover vehicles. My black Cherokee was still parked in front of Gary's triple decker.

As much as I didn't want to, I climbed into Donovan's vehicle that smelled of leather and the musky, spicy scent I'd noticed in Oxford's office and when I'd walked beside Donovan to the parking garage.

Every part of me was exhausted to the point I didn't care if I dropped onto an oil slick.

The moment I relaxed against the seat, wind just whooshed right out of me and I heaved out a long breath. I had to fight my eyelids just to keep them open.

I realized Donovan wasn't heading to Southie and I looked at him. "Uh, I live in South Boston," I said as we headed toward Little Italy in the North End.

"We're not going to your home," he said, without looking at me.

"What the hell?" I came fully awake as he reached the parking garage at the corner of Congress and Sudbury Streets, across from the Haymarket T stop. "What are you pulling, Donovan?"

"I'm hungry." He guided his Explorer into a spot and parked. "And we need to talk."

"No way." I glared at him as he started to open his door. "You don't just make decisions like that when it involves me."

He looked at me with a calm expression. "I just did," he said, before he climbed out of the SUV.

Well sonofabitch. I got out of the Explorer and shut the door harder than I should have. When we met up at the back of the SUV, I narrowed my gaze at him. "So what's the deal?"

"We're going to an Italian place I just discovered on Salem." He turned away and I jogged a little to keep up.

"So you figured out Little Italy all on your own." Okay, I know my tone was sarcastic, but I was tired and irritated at this man's arrogance. He didn't have an accent that I could identify, so I knew he wasn't from Boston. He probably came from the Western side of the United States.

He looked at me. "Are you always such a pain in the ass?"

"When someone forces me to do something I don't want to, yeah, I am." I wasn't in the mood to talk anymore, so I didn't say anything else until we reached an Italian *ristorante* and bar and were seated.

Smells of Italian food about made me melt. It smelled so good that my stomach started to rumble despite the fact that I was ticked at Donovan.

As soon as the host handed us menus then walked away, I set my menu aside, folded my arms on the table, and focused on Donovan. "What the hell is going on here?"

"We need to set some things straight." His eyes had gone from vivid blue to a darker shade. Cobalt. He kept his tone neutral, but by the way the muscles in his neck corded and his jaw tensed he was obviously feeling anything but neutral.

"Let's make this clear." His gaze focused on mine and I refused to blink. "We're partners and from this point on it's *our* op. Not yours. Ours."

A busboy set glasses of ice water on the table and bread that smelled strongly of garlic, but I didn't take my gaze from Donovan's. "I built Operation Cinderella from the ground up. So you can shove that right up your ass."

The surface of the cloth-covered table was rough beneath my arms as I faced off with him. "I don't have a problem with you as a partner. But I call the shots."

"Bullshit." Donovan let out a sound that was more like a low rumble and his jaw worked as if he was grinding his teeth. "I'm not playing second fiddle in this op."

The waiter arrived and we could barely take our glares from each other long enough for Donovan to order a bottle of Chianti and grilled bruschetta for an appetizer. Right then I didn't care that he had the audacity to order for both of us. I cared more about his attitude about Operation Cinderella.

I shifted my arms, rumpling the tablecloth. "Team Supervisors don't work in pairs and I don't need your interference."

The waiter returned, presented the bottle of Chianti and poured it into our glasses when Donovan gave his approval. Without looking at the menu or the waiter, Donovan said, "We'll have the veal marsala."

Obviously the waiter sensed the fact his presence wasn't wanted. He bowed and hurried away.

"Well?" My tone was entirely hostile.

"Kristin. My sister." Donovan's voice was suddenly coarse, raw. "The bastards took her."

For Cheyenne's Readers

Be sure to go to http://cheyennemccray.com to sign up for her *private* book announcement list and get *free exclusive* Cheyenne Mc-Cray goodies. You can e-mail her at chey@cheyennemccray.com. She would love to hear from you.

The war between good and evil is about to get a whole lot hotter.

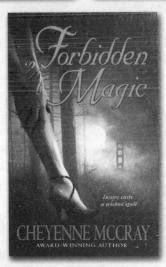

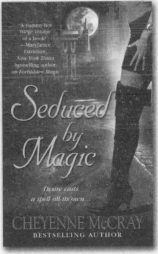

"McCray knows how to make a reader sweat."
—Romantic Times BOOKreviews

St. Martin's Paperbacks

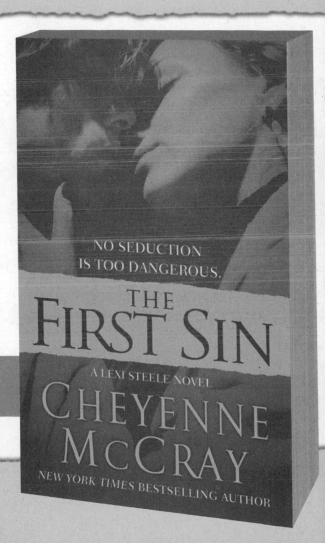